"Ye make me think I could be a[...]

"Nay, Gilchrist, never again will you be that man. And I am glad of it," Rachel whispered, leaning closer. "For this is the man I love."

"But you see with your own eyes what I am." He spread wide the fingers of his fire-ravaged hand.

"And you know in your heart what *I* am."

"Aye," he breathed against her hair. "Ye are like the spring after winter's darkness, a rare elixir, everything virtuous and good. Aye, that and more." He brushed his lips lightly across her temple. "Which is why I must go...."

Dear Reader,

In *The Bonny Bride* by award-winning author Deborah Hale, a poor young woman sets sail for Nova Scotia from England as a mail-order bride to a wealthy man, yet meets her true soul mate on board the ship. Will she choose love or money? Margaret Moore, who also writes mainstream historicals for Avon Books, returns with *A Warrior's Kiss,* a passionate marriage-of-convenience story and the next in her ongoing medieval WARRIOR series. Theresa Michaels's new Western, *Once a Hero,* is a gripping and emotion-filled story about a cowboy who rescues a female fugitive and unexpectedly falls in love with her as they go in search of a lost treasure. For readers who enjoy discovering new writers, *The Virgin Spring* by Golden Heart winner Debra Lee Brown is for you. Here, a Scottish laird finds an amnesiac woman beside a spring and must resist his desire for her, as he believes she is forbidden to him.

For the next two months we are going to be asking readers to let us know what you are looking for from Harlequin Historicals. We hope you'll participate by sending your ideas to us at:

Harlequin Historicals
300 E. 42nd St.
New York, NY 10017

Q. What do you like about Harlequin Historicals?

_____

_____

Q. What *don't* you like about Harlequin Historicals?

_____

_____

Whatever your tastes in reading, you'll be sure to find a romantic journey back to the past between the covers of a Harlequin Historicals novel. We hope you'll join us next month, too!

Sincerely,

Tracy Farrell,
Senior Editor

THE VIRGIN SPRING

DEBRA LEE BROWN

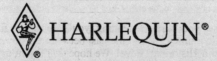

HARLEQUIN®

TORONTO • NEW YORK • LONDON
AMSTERDAM • PARIS • SYDNEY • HAMBURG
STOCKHOLM • ATHENS • TOKYO • MILAN • MADRID
PRAGUE • WARSAW • BUDAPEST • AUCKLAND

ISBN 0-373-29106-X

THE VIRGIN SPRING

Copyright © 2000 by Debra Lee Brown

This edition published by arrangement with Harlequin Books S.A.

® and TM are trademarks of the publisher. Trademarks indicated with
® are registered in the United States Patent and Trademark Office, the
Canadian Trade Marks Office and in other countries.

Visit us at www.romance.net

Printed in U.S.A.

For Jeannie

Chapter One

The Highlands of Scotland, 1208

The girl batted gold-tipped lashes in Gilchrist's direction then spurred her mount ahead into the forest.

"Harlot," he muttered under his breath.

Hugh snorted. "Christ, man! If ye willna be friendly to the lass, at the least ye can be civil."

"And why must I be civil?" Gilchrist snapped.

"Because ye are laird, and can no afford this ill temper ye bear our women."

"Hmph." He ducked to avoid a low hanging branch as his steed quickened his pace. "Aye, I am laird—so the elders say. But I am a Mackintosh—the clan will never accept me."

Hugh nudged his mount closer and cocked a tawny brow. "Ye are a Davidson, too. Your mother was born and bred on this land, and 'tis here ye were raised."

He turned in the saddle and glanced back at the Davidson warriors who rode in a tight formation behind them. A few met his gaze, but most looked away or pretended to check their weapons.

Davidson. Mackintosh. What was he now?

The pain was worse today. The rough hunting plaid, even the soft wool of his shirt, burned against his skin. He longed to tear the garments free and let the stiff breeze cool his body. But he dared not. Too many eyes were on him. He could bear their revulsion, but not their pity.

Hugh nodded to the clearing ahead. "Are ye comin'?"

Gilchrist closed his eyes and drew a breath. Rain. He could smell it in the air, cool and threatening. He almost smiled. Then a familiar, acrid scent yanked him back to reality. His eyes flew open.

There it was.

The charred remains of Braedûn Lodge, seat of Clan Davidson, the only home he remembered. 'Twas once a great house, full of laughter and hearty enterprise. How many times had he ridden up this very path, returned from hunting or a bit of wenching, to be greeted by his uncle at the door? He frowned and pushed the flood of memories from his mind.

"Well," Hugh said, "are ye comin' or no?"

It had been six months since the fire and in all that time Gilchrist hadn't returned to the spot. He'd skirted the clearing on a few occasions and once he'd even approached—but the smell, the stench of charred oak and other things he was loath to remember kept him away. Even now his gut roiled.

"Nay," he said, "I canna."

Hugh set his jaw. "'Tis just a pile o' burnt wood, nothing more." The dozen or so warriors who accompanied them rode past and into the clearing. Hugh's expression softened. "What demons remain, ye carry with ye, Gilchrist."

He met his friend's steady gaze. "Mayhap."

"Ye are laird," Hugh said. "Snap out of it, man.

There's work to be done and the clan needs a leader, no a—"

"A what?" Slowly, he drew his right hand from the folds of his plaid. "A cripple?" Clenching his teeth against the pain, he unfurled his burned fingers and willed them to grip Hugh's bare forearm. "A monster?" Hugh neither flinched nor broke his gaze, and for that Gilchrist was grateful.

"Bah! 'Tis just a burn, and it's no so bad."

"No so bad?" Gilchrist released him. "Christ, I canna hold my own sword. A laird who canna protect his clan is no leader—he's no even a man."

They sat quiet for a moment, listening to the early morning larks and the creaking of branches in the rising wind. His hair whipped at his face. Absently he brushed it back with his good hand.

"Ye can learn to fight with your left," Hugh said quietly. "There's two or three clansmen wield a sword left-handed. One of them can show you."

He shrugged, pushing the thought away.

"Ye must be fit for the spring gathering. Rumor has it the Macphearsons would join us this year. It's been months since ye've met with them."

Hugh's point could not be argued. Gilchrist had seen no one outside the clan since the fire. More importantly, no one had seen him, and that suited him fine.

"Let Alex handle it."

Hugh frowned. "Aye, I expect he'd jump at the chance to do that—and more."

He raised a brow and shot his friend a cool look.

"There's been talk," Hugh said. "Among the elders— and the clan. Alex is well liked. Some say—"

"Where *is* Alex? He didna return from his hunt last night."

Hugh shook his head. "There's no telling. Busy with affairs of the clan, I suspect. *Your* affairs."

He snorted.

"I'm lettin' ye know is all. There's been talk."

"What talk? Why d'ye harbor this ill will toward him? Alex is a trusted friend." The three of them had grown up together for God's sake.

"Mayhap," Hugh said. "But mark me—he fancies himself laird, and some say with good reason."

'Twas a serious accusation, and one that made no sense.

Gilchrist let the stallion's reins drop from his hand. He looked ahead into the clearing where a dozen warriors toiled at clearing away the burnt rubble of Braedûn Lodge. The girl, Arlys, who'd so innocently flirted with him earlier, watched them intently from her perch on a blackened log.

"Now there's your answer," Hugh said, nodding in the girl's direction.

"What answer?"

"A bride—a *Davidson* bride."

He narrowed his eyes. "What are ye talking about?"

"That's it!" A grin broke across Hugh's rugged face. "Ye shall wed and produce a son." Hugh slapped him across the back, taking care, Gilchrist noticed, to avoid his injured right side.

"You're daft."

"Think about it. Arlys is a good choice."

"She's a silly chit."

"Nay," Hugh said. "She's well liked and the right age. 'Twould cinch the clan's affection—and please the elders." Hugh nudged his mount closer and forced Gilchrist to meet his gaze. "And…'twould keep others in their place."

"Alex, ye mean." Gilchrist shook his head, again dismissing Hugh's allegation. "Nay, I willna wed."

"Och, come now. She's bonny, is she no?" Hugh nodded at her and grinned. "And she fancies you, canna ye tell?"

Arlys smiled and waved at the two of them.

Gilchrist looked away, embarrassed, and slipped his burned hand back into the folds of his plaid. "I hadna noticed."

"No so long ago ye would have had her wedded and bedded in a fortnight. Or at least bedded, and that within the week."

He ignored Hugh's well-meant, but stinging comment. Aye, he'd had a way with women—once. Before the fire. Before his betrothed left him for another man—a whole man. Gritting his teeth, he flexed his burned hand inside his plaid.

Undaunted, Hugh continued his argument for a swift marriage. After a few minutes Gilchrist began to listen, then nudged his mount forward a step and shot the girl a sideways glance. Mayhap Hugh was right. Taking Arlys to wife would solve his problem with the clan. After all, she was a Davidson.

"She'd be loyal and true," Hugh said. "No like—"

"Say her name, and crippled or nay I'll knock ye off that mare."

"Forgive me, Laird, I—"

Hoofbeats sounded on the path behind them, and their conversation was forgotten.

Instinctively, Gilchrist reached for the broadsword strapped across his back and grimaced as the familiar, brilliant pain ravaged his torso and arm.

Hugh drew his weapon. Before he could position himself on the path in front of Gilchrist, the rider appeared.

"Alex!" they cried in unison.

Gilchrist relaxed and allowed himself a rare smile as the warrior approached. His steed was near spent, and Alex himself appeared little better. His plaid was filthy and rumpled, as if he'd ridden all night.

"We expected ye last eve," Hugh said.

"Aye," Alex said. "I was…detained."

Gilchrist noticed a bit of dried blood streaked across Alex's face. "What happened?" He motioned to the faint scratch marks.

Alex brushed his cheek with a gauntleted hand. "'Tis naught. Just—" He looked ahead to the clearing and his gaze lit on the girl. "'Twas Arlys," he said and shot them a thin smile.

Arlys? "Hmph." Gilchrist leveled his gaze at Hugh. "Loyal and true, indeed."

Hugh shrugged and looked away.

Alex was clearly puzzled by their exchange. He nudged his gelding forward, even with Gilchrist's mount. "Ye should be resting, Laird," he said. "I'll take care of things here."

Hugh sprang to life, cocked a brow and set his jaw in that I-told-ye-so manner Gilchrist hated.

Aye, all right—I get the bluidy point, he replied with his eyes.

"Will ye come then, Laird?" Hugh said.

He looked again to the burnt-out clearing and wondered why the devil he had come here at all. Mayhap to see if he could bear it. He could not. "Nay, I'll leave ye both here. I'm off to the spring."

"What, the *virgin's* spring?" Alex asked.

"Aye, that's the one." He turned his mount and guided him off the path into the wood. "I find the waters soothing.'' Hugh followed but Gilchrist waved him back. ''Nay, I wish to be alone. Stay here and help Alex.''

Hugh muttered something obscene under his breath, and shot Alex a stony glance. ''As ye wish.''

Ignoring him, Alex said, ''Do ye know the story of the spring? The one the old woman used to tell when we were lads?''

''The healer?'' Gilchrist said.

''Aye, the same.''

''Go on—tell it.''

Alex drew his mount closer. ''Dinna ye remember? 'Tis said three outlanders wrecked and murdered a Scots maiden on the very spot. 'Twas brutally done, and all wept for the loss. And when the girl's father lifted her body in his arms, a spring flowed from 'neath the soft pillow of heather where rested her head.''

Gilchrist had heard the tale, but not for many a year. ''I remember this story.''

''And the rest of it?'' Hugh quipped. ''Some say the waters have the power to heal.''

Alex smirked. ''I think not. Nonetheless, for years after, women who were ill used or who'd compromised their virtue bathed in the waters as a means to restore their purity. There's many who still believe in it.''

Gilchrist snorted. ''The virgin's spring—nonsense.''

''Mayhap not,'' Hugh said, then laughed. ''Alex, 'tis said your mother frequented the place often before ye were born.''

Alex kicked his mount forward, his face contorting in rage. Hugh's hand moved like lightning to the hilt of his dirk.

''Enough!'' Gilchrist shouted. The two warriors froze. ''Get to work—the both of you. I'll return on the morrow.'' Hugh's behavior was fair testing his patience.

Alex and Hugh turned their steeds, gazes locked like two feral predators, and made their way stiffly along the path to the clearing. The girl, Arlys, scrambled down from the burnt stump and ran toward them, waving at Alex, her face alight with surprise and pleasure.

Hugh nodded at her, then called back over his shoulder, "Laird, will ye do it?"

"Do what?" Gilchrist shouted.

Hugh nodded again toward the girl. "Marry!"

Alex's eyes widened. He looked from Gilchrist to Arlys, his expression unreadable.

"I'll think on it," Gilchrist said and spurred his mount up the hill into the wood.

Thunderheads massed, full to bursting, the air chill and heavy with the scent of rain. Lightning flashed in the distance against an ominous sky. Gilchrist reined his stallion to a halt and listened. Any moment now...

Ah, there it was—the low, crackling rumble. He looked skyward and breathed deep. Winter was not yet ready to relinquish her hold, and he was glad. He favored the cool, dreary days and long nights.

The first few drops took him by surprise. Before he could react, the clouds burst and he was caught in the downpour. "Ah, well, no matter." He proceeded to strip to the waist. His movements were slow, methodical; he gritted his teeth against the inevitable pain. "Bluidy hell."

He was saved a pummeling by the thick canopy of larch and laurel that choked this part of the Highland wood. All the same, the rain stung his newly healed skin. God's truth, he welcomed it in some perverse way.

He'd grown used to the pain. 'Twas almost comforting now, in a way he couldn't fathom. Constant, true, something he could count on. It was what it was, and never deceived.

His stomach soured at the memory of the pretty, lying eyes of the woman he once thought to wed.

He spurred the stallion up a steep embankment. The horse protested, his hooves sinking deep into the mud, but Gilchrist urged him on with firm commands. They topped a ridge and turned south. 'Twasn't far now.

He looked forward to his visits to the spring. They afforded him time alone, time to think. Aye, he'd done a lot of that of late.

Hugh's words gnawed at him. He was right—the clan needed a strong laird, especially now. Gilchrist flexed the muscles in his ravaged arm and slowly opened the claw-like hand. Once, there had been no question he was that man. And now?

After the fire, when he lay near death, Alex had stepped easily into the role of leader. He was a good man, well liked by the elders and the clan. Mayhap 'twas all for the best. 'Twould be easy for Gilchrist to step down and fade neatly into the background.

As for those who loved him... What would they think of such a thing? He barely remembered his father and those early years before his death. 'Twas his uncle, Alistair Davidson, who'd raised him, God rest his soul, and his own brother, Iain. What would they expect of him now?

What did he expect of himself?

Gilchrist knew the answer. He was laird and must protect his position, do what was right for the clan. He ran his good hand through his dripping hair, pushing it off his forehead. Water streamed down his face. He tipped his chin high and closed his eyes for a moment.

Aye, he'd do it.

He'd wed and be done with it. A Davidson, a Macphearson, mayhap, it didn't matter who. Arlys *was* a good choice. He knew he could never love her, and that suited him fine. A marriage to appease the clan—but just that. Never again would he lose his heart to a woman. Never. He glanced at his burns. Besides, who could love him now...like this?

The stallion emerged from the cover of the trees as a bolt of lightning split the sky, startling and brilliant, above them. Thunder boomed in deafening response. The horse reared.

Gilchrist held fast and reined the beast into submission, soothing him with soft words. The air was thick with a sharp, metallic odor; all the hairs on his body stood on end.

"We must get to cover!"

He spurred his mount forward, toward the spring. A good-size cave where he'd spent many a night lay just beyond it. 'Twould serve to protect both him and the horse.

Halfway there lightning flashed again, this time closer. He slipped from the stallion's back and threw his shirt over the beast's head, covering his eyes. The rain whipped at him in stinging, horizontal sheets, the wind a maelstrom of some vengeful god.

Just a few more steps and—there it was! The virgin's spring, near overflowing from the torrential rains. But what's that, near the edge? A body?

He raced to the cave and tethered his stallion just inside the opening, then turned and wiped the water from his eyes. It *was* a body—a woman.

He stepped from the cave. Another flash lit up the roiling sky and he quickly stepped back again. "Well, 'tis a good thing she's already dead. She'd no last another minute out there in this.''

He studied the prone figure from the safety of the cave while the storm raged outside. She was most certainly dead, sprawled at the edge of the spring, limbs splayed, as if she'd fallen from some height—from a horse, mayhap.

Even from this distance, he could see she was soaked to the skin. Water pooled fast around her. Hmph. What if she wasn't dead? He stood for a moment, glancing from the body of the woman to the dry interior of the cave.

"Of all the bluidy nuisance—"

He waited for the next flash, then bolted toward her as a clap of thunder split the air. Reaching her in a half-dozen strides, he knelt beside her in the trampled heather.

She wore naught but a shift, thin and soaking, near translucent as it clung to her limp body. Her feet were bare. On impulse he reached out and touched one foot—cold as ice. Her hair was a raven-black mass plastered to her head. He could not see her face, and there was no time to check her for signs of life.

With his good arm he lifted her up and half dragged her, half carried her, back to the safety of the cave. In minutes he'd built a small fire—a task he loathed—and laid her carefully on the bed of dry furs he kept there for overnight stays. Gently he brushed the dripping, midnight tresses from off her face.

"Good God."

Illuminated in the firelight, she was akin to some ghostly angel. Her lips were full and slightly parted, bluish at the edges, her skin a frigid white. But her cheeks had color, the blush of spring on an otherwise lifeless landscape.

She was lovely—and she was alive.

Chapter Two

She was exactly what he didn't need.

It had been months since Gilchrist had been this close to a woman—and he didn't like it. Women were unpredictable, shallow. A faithless lot. He'd revive this one and send her on her way.

He lifted her hand in his and shook it. No response. Her fingers were stiff and icy, and the fire seemed to do little to warm her skin. In truth, he was half frozen himself, soaked as he was. He needed dry garments and so did she.

He rummaged in a corner of the cave for some extra plaids and shook one out. 'Twould have to do. He spread it over her and tucked the bottom edge under her feet. There. She'd be fine in no time. He paced the earthen floor, occasionally glancing at her still form.

''Ah, Christ.'' He ripped the plaid away again and took a deep breath. It had to be done—and he had to do it. If he didn't, she might die. Fine. It wasn't as if he'd never handled a naked woman before. He'd handled plenty—more than he cared to remember.

So why did he hesitate?

He swore under his breath and picked at the tie that

gathered her shift about her shoulders. 'Twas impossible with one hand. With no small effort he flexed the fingers of his burned hand and attacked the tie again. There, he'd done it. Now to get the bloody thing off her.

He lifted her with his good arm and tugged at the shift. His injured fingers screamed, but he gritted his teeth and continued. He managed to bare her to the waist, then laid her gently back upon the furs.

"Good God."

She was beautiful.

Gilchrist swallowed hard and let his gaze rove over her. For the barest moment he watched her pink-tipped breasts rise and fall with each shallow breath.

Then, out of the corner of his eye, he caught the hideous juxtaposition of his fire-scarred hand against her milky flesh. 'Twas revolting. Thank God she was unconscious.

He pushed the roil of emotions from his mind and finished the job. In a matter of minutes he had her wrapped in the dry plaid and hung her shift to dry on a tree root that breached the craggy wall of the cave.

As an afterthought he lifted her head and shoved a rolled-up fur under her neck for support. When he drew his hand away he saw the blood.

"What's this?" He ran his fingers gingerly over her scalp until he found the spot, swelled big as a wren's egg. She'd hit her head. He dabbed at the spot. The bleeding was slight, naught to fear. But the injury itself...

There was no telling when she would wake—if she woke at all.

Something smelled good—delectable, in fact.

She was hungry. Nay, she was starving. She took a deep breath and opened her eyes. Someone had forgotten to shade the window. She squinted and rolled toward the brilliant morning sunlight.

Then she saw him.

God's blood! She shot from the crude pallet of furs into a crouch, her heart hammering, her head throbbing. The plaid that covered her slipped to the ground. She felt gooseflesh rise on her naked skin. Quickly, she snatched up the garment and wrapped it around herself, then skidded backward away from the entrance to the—why, 'twas a cave!

What on earth had happened?

She flattened herself against the uneven rock wall and scanned the interior, eyes darting over every shadow. She was alone, except for the hare roasting on a spit over the small fire—that's what had smelled so good—and except for...

Him.

She crouched lower and crept forward, stopping just short of the blinding sunshine that lit the cave's irregular entrance. She caught a whiff of something else here— horse, though she did not see one.

Once her eyes adjusted to the intensity of the light, she could see the man clearly. He was big, well made—and had not a stitch on! Under normal circumstances she would have averted her eyes. But the circumstances, from what she could tell, were far from normal.

He was bathing, in what appeared to be a good-size spring. 'Twas a pretty place, alive with greenery and shoots of new heather and— What was she thinking? She was in danger. She must get away. She must get to—to where?

Her head pounded and a brief bout of dizziness threatened to knock her off her feet. She pushed back against the cool wall and took a few deep breaths. There, 'twas better now.

Splashing sounds drew her attention back to the spring. The man was pulling himself up onto the bank, but ever so slowly. He turned, awkwardly, in an attempt to seat himself on the bed of new grass that graced the water's edge.

Then she saw what her barely focused eyes had missed the first time—he'd been burned, and badly. Mother of God. She let her gaze trace the angry red path the flames had blazed across his body.

'Twas only on the one side, the right, that he'd been hurt, from upper thigh, across the hip and up the length of his torso. His face had been spared, but his arm and hand had seen the worst of it.

She watched him as he slowly unfurled his fingers, flexed them, then made a crude fist. He did this several times, grimacing against the pain she knew must be unbearable. 'Twas a miracle he lived at all, really. Someone had healed him—someone highly skilled.

He braced himself with his good hand, then leaned back a little and tilted his face to the sun, eyes closed. She crept forward a few steps more to study him closer.

He was handsome, almost strikingly so. His face was clean-shaven; for some reason that seemed odd to her. 'Twas strong, angular, and framed by a mass of long, fair hair. She narrowed her eyes and—aye, she was right. He had thin braids, one at each temple. Never had she seen them on a man.

She let her gaze roam over the well-muscled expanse of his chest. 'Twas lightly furred with darker hair that tapered lower. Her cheeks grew hot and her pulse quickened as she took in the rest of him.

God's blood, what am I doing? I've got to get away—

He opened his eyes.

She gasped and flattened herself against the wall of the cave. Too late—he'd seen her. Oh God, what now?

He sprang to his feet and grabbed the pile of garments lying next to him. She must flee—now! But where were her clothes? There wasn't time to find them. She pulled the plaid tighter around herself and shot from the cave. In two strides he cut her off. She whirled in the other direction then stopped short. Before her rose a sheer rock wall, impossible to scale.

She was trapped.

Eyes wide and breath coming in short gasps, she backed into the sanctuary of the cave, pulling the plaid tighter around her body. She mustn't panic. She mustn't! She must find a weapon, something with which to defend herself.

She turned and ran toward the fur-covered pallet and the small fire that blazed near it. She kicked up the bed-covers and rummaged through a pile of food and cooking gear—nothing! Something moved behind her. She whirled.

There he was, clothed now in a dark hunting plaid, coarse shirt and boots. A dirk was belted at his waist and she could see the hilt of his sword peeking up over his shoulder. He looked every bit a warrior. His expression was hard, unreadable, and whatever he intended she couldn't fathom from the cool blue eyes that now studied her.

He took a step toward her and her eyes widened. He read her fear. She could see it in his face, in the way he tilted his head and arched a brow. Another step, then another.

She scanned her immediate surroundings, looking for something, anything—there! She crouched and with the back of her hand sent the spitted hare flying from its position over the coals. She seized a brand from the fire—one that glowed red-hot at its tip—and rose to meet her assailant. She brandished it before her, her gaze locked on his.

He stopped. Dead in his tracks. He looked from her to the brand and narrowed his eyes. "Put it down."

She frowned. His voice— Something was not right. She backed up a step, and he took another toward her.

"Woman, I said put it down." His face was rigid, his jaw set, yet tiny clues belied his confidence. She watched the lump in his throat move up and down as he swallowed hard. A fine sheen of perspiration broke across his brow.

The brand. Why, he was afraid of it! The realization sparked her courage. She lurched forward and thrust the fiery end of her weapon at him. 'Twas a mistake. He grabbed her wrist and yanked her toward him.

Jesu! Her feet flew out from under her but he held fast, his hand a steel trap. She scrambled to regain her balance, then found herself looking up into his cool eyes.

"Let go," he said and proceeded to squeeze her wrist.

He hurt her, the brute. She felt the sting of tears glass her eyes, but she did not look away. Instead, she pursed her lips and shot him her most defiant expression.

A corner of his mouth turned up at the edge, ever so slightly. What, did he think this amusing? His eyes warmed then, and he loosened his grip. "I willna hurt ye, woman. Ye have my word."

His speech was strange—that's what had bothered her. She understood him but something was not right. What was it?

"Now drop your weapon." He nodded at the brand, which now seemed small and useless in light of his size and superior strength.

She let go, and it fell to the earthen floor. He kicked it neatly back into the fire. Only then did he let go her wrist. Shrinking backward, she pulled the edges of the plaid tighter around herself. Surprisingly, he turned and strode from the cave.

Where was he going? Before she had time to consider her options he was back. In his hand was a balled-up garment. Her shift! He tossed it to her and she caught it with one hand.

"Dress yourself," he said.

She swallowed hard and examined the thin, white garment. 'Twas clean and dry. She started to slip the plaid from her shoulders then stopped. Her eyes met his. Oh, no.

"Hmph," he grunted, and to her surprise he turned his back on her.

In seconds she was dressed. Well, half-dressed. A shift and a coarse, woolen plaid. Not exactly proper attire.

He turned to face her. "Now sit," he commanded and nodded to the pallet of furs.

Her eyes widened and she took a step back. He didn't move. It occurred to her if he meant to—to harm her, he wouldn't have allowed her to dress. She obeyed.

He knelt in front of her and his expression softened. He was almost handsome without that scowl. "What in God's name are ye doing here—a woman alone, and in naught but a shift?"

What *was* she doing here? The image of a high place, desolate and windswept, flashed briefly in her mind. Standing stones, in a half circle, reached toward a dark, starless sky.

Her head throbbed. She tried to speak, but couldn't make the words. She ran a hand over her scalp and drew a sharp breath when she met the source of tenderness.

"Aye, 'tis a fair-size lump, but ye seem right enough now." He reached out to touch her and she instantly drew back, her eyes riveted to his. "Hold still," he commanded.

Her pulse quickened as he moved closer and ran his huge hand across the nape of her neck then slowly upward, seeking out her injury. Her skin warmed under his touch and she fought the strange urge to let her head roll back in his hand.

He was so close she could feel his breath on her face as he traced the bump with gentle fingers. He had a clean, male scent about him she found pleasing.

She felt strange all of sudden, confused—by him and by the muddle of emotions that erupted inside her: fear, excitement, attraction. What was happening?

Abruptly, he drew back and looked away, his face contorting, as if the exploration had been distasteful. "You'll live," he said, then stood.

He strode to the far corner of the cave and stooped to retrieve the spitted hare. "Too bad about this. I expect you're hungry." He inspected it and shrugged. "'Tis still edible. Here." He tossed it to her and she caught it.

His manner had changed completely. He was stiff, cold. She felt a pang of disappointment. Was she daft? She had to get out of here. She must get to…where was she going? She could see the place in her mind, but—

"The storm has passed. I'm leaving now," he said. He gathered up the scattered plaids and cooking gear and placed them in the corner of the cave. "Ye'd best do the same. 'Tis no safe here for a woman alone." He kicked some dirt onto the fire and, before she could even get up, he was gone.

Her stomach growled. How long had it been since she'd eaten? She looked longingly at the roasted hare, then at the cave's entrance. After a moment, the warrior appeared by the spring, leading a gray horse. She'd been right about that.

Without another thought, she ripped the hare from the spit, gathered the edges of the plaid about her, and followed him outside.

What a nuisance.

Gilchrist shook his head and urged the stallion into a trot. The woman clung to his back, a slender arm wrapped around his waist. He noticed she took great care to avoid touching his right side. She'd seen him bathing. Damn her prying eyes.

Christ, what was he going to do with her? He couldn't just leave her here, now could he? And what was wrong with her? She had yet to utter a single word.

"Hmph." None of this mattered as he'd be rid of her as soon as was practical. He tried to ignore her and focus on his own problems, but she made it damned difficult holding him as tightly as she did.

He guided his mount into the forest and the gray settled in at a casual pace. Sunlight streamed through the emerald canopy of larch, laurel and a few scattered pines. Everything was green, fresh, the damp ground and a few downed tree limbs the only evidence of yesterday's storm.

Casting his head back, he inhaled deeply. There it was after all, the unmistakable scent of spring. He swore silently under his breath.

They reached the forest path in no time and he quickly reined the stallion south, away from the burnt-out clearing and toward the clan's new demesne. The woman let go of him for a moment. She looked back, he was certain, at the charred rubble.

He issued one subtle command and the stallion lurched

forward. The woman gasped and her arms flew around him. Served her right. The edges of his mouth turned up in a smile.

They rode like that for some time, the warmth of the sun and the stallion's easy pace lulling him into a rare state of relaxation. The woman rested her head against his back, and with each footfall of the stallion he could feel the soft weight of her breasts moving against him.

For the first time in—how long?—he felt good.

He focused on the path in front of him and tried to think of something else: the clan, Alex's almost too casual helpfulness, and Hugh's words of advice.

A bride—a Davidson bride.

Moments later the sound of bells and the dull clanking of metal on metal snapped him to attention. He narrowed his eyes, quickly scanning the forest in all directions. The clamor originated in front of them. He urged his mount into the cover of the trees.

The woman squirmed and fidgeted behind him. Damn her! He grabbed one of her hands and squeezed it. "Be still!" She tensed, then quieted. Fixing his gaze on the path, he waited.

After a moment, a swaybacked draft horse came into view. The beast pulled a crude cart, laden with what looked to be household wares. Two men sat atop it, dressed in little better than rags.

Tinkers.

Gilchrist relaxed. He realized he was still holding the woman's hand. He frowned and let it go, then guided the stallion out onto the path before them. The men saw him and their hands flew to their weapons.

"I mean ye no harm," he called out to them.

The two men exchanged glances, then narrowed their eyes at him. One of them, a big, dirty-looking lout with stringy hair and bad teeth, rose from his seat. "Who are ye?" he shouted. "And what's that ye got sittin' behind ye?" The man tilted his head and eyed the woman.

Gilchrist nudged his mount closer, his left hand moving to the hilt of his dirk. "Who am I? I am Gilchrist of Clan Davidson and this is my land. Who are ye and what is your business here?"

The smaller man's gaze fixed on Gilchrist's disfigured hand. He tucked it quickly back into the folds of his plaid. "I have heard of ye," the man said. "Ye are *The* Davidson, are ye no?"

"I am."

"We are tinkers," he said, "on our way north to Inverness."

The big man continued to eye the woman. "And that one...who is she?"

"I dinna know," he said. "She doesna speak." He urged the stallion closer to the cart so the two men could get a better look at her. "Do ye know her? Have ye seen her before?"

The woman clung to him tighter as the two tinkers looked her over.

The big, dirty one grinned. "Nay, but I'd like to see more o' her."

The woman tensed.

The smaller man elbowed his sidekick in the ribs, then turned his attention to Gilchrist. "We'd gladly take her off yer hands. Perhaps ye'd like to trade?" He nodded to the cart full of goods.

The woman's grasp was like steel now. If she squeezed him much harder he wouldn't be able to breathe. He sighed. He had more important matters to tend to than the fate of a mute, half-clothed woman. He should unload her now and be done with it. He drew his mount alongside the cart.

"Go on then," he said to the big man, "take her."

The man grinned, showing a mouthful of rotten teeth. He reached out and grabbed the woman around the waist and tried to pull her from the saddle. She screamed, startling them all, and held fast to Gilchrist's waist, struggling against the tinker's grip.

"Oh, so ye can talk, can ye?" the man said and grinned wider.

Gilchrist could smell him now—he stank of wine and sweat. No matter. His decision was made. He swore and ripped the woman's hands from his waist.

The tinker pulled her awkwardly onto his lap. Something about the way he looked at her made Gilchrist bristle. She fought wildly, but the tinker gripped her around the waist and clamped his other hand roughly over her mouth.

Gilchrist turned his mount abruptly and looked away. What difference did it make what happened to her? She was nothing to him. He nudged the stallion forward, down the path, but could still hear her struggles and the tinker's low laughter. His gut roiled as he fought the ridiculous wave of emotion that threatened to overcome his better judgment.

"Ah, now here's a pretty piece." 'Twas the small man's voice. "She won't be needin' this."

Gilchrist turned in his saddle in time to see the man rip the plaid from the woman's body. He swore silently to himself and spurred the stallion back to the cart. "You there, stop it!" he commanded. "Give it back to her— now." He nodded at the plaid.

The big man smirked and tightened his grip on the woman's mouth. Gilchrist willed himself not to look at her. "Me friend is right," the tinker said. "She willna need it." He moved his hand from her waist, slowly upward over the thin fabric of her shift, and cupped her breast.

Gilchrist came unglued.

Before he knew what he was doing, his broadsword was in his hand—his left hand—and pointed at the tinker's throat. "I've changed my mind," he said through gritted teeth. "I want her back."

The tinker's eyes widened. His friend reached for his dirk and Gilchrist shot him a feral look. "Dinna even think it." He was almost sorry when the small man backed off and the tinker released his grip. The woman scrambled from the cart then backed toward the cover of the trees.

Gilchrist weighed the sword in his hand. It felt surprisingly good. He itched to kill them both, the swine. Instead, he nodded at the path. "Off with you. And dinna come back this way again."

Without a word, the small man snapped the reins, and the draft horse lurched forward down the path. Gilchrist watched them until they were out of sight, then sheathed his sword, somewhat awkwardly, as he'd never done it left-handed before.

The confrontation buoyed his spirits. Mayhap Hugh was right. He might just learn to wield a sword again. 'Twould take a bit of practice to get it right, though.

Turning his mount, he scanned the stand of larch and laurel. The woman was backed up to a tree, eyes wide. Poor lass. He approached her slowly and, for the first time, studied her eyes. They were fair strange—gray flecked with green. He'd never seen eyes like that. They held fear—and something else.

Anger.

He dismounted and retrieved the plaid that lay at her feet. "Here," he said quietly.

For a moment she didn't move, then she snatched the garment from him and wrapped it around her shoulders.

He felt like the lowest of dogs. "Come on, lass. Come home with me." He offered her his hand. "I'll no let anyone harm ye—ye have my word on it."

Her steely gaze burned into him. As she slowly reached out to take his hand, he had the nagging feeling he'd just made the biggest mistake of his life.

Chapter Three

Gilchrist—a lofty name for so vile a man.

She leaned forward in the saddle and he abruptly pulled her back against his chest, his good arm wrapped around her like a steel trap.

To think he would have given her to those pigs! She wiped her mouth with the edge of the plaid, recalling the tinker's filthy hands. A small shudder escaped her.

"Are ye all right?" Gilchrist asked and leaned down to look at her. "You're safe now. Do ye understand?"

She meant to glare at him, but the concern in his expression disarmed her. She merely nodded.

"Well then, we'll be home soon. 'Tis just ahead." He pointed to the top of a broad ridge. She narrowed her eyes but failed to see any kind of structure.

His arm returned to her waist and they settled in for the brief ascent. The gray stallion picked his way carefully up the slope along what looked to be a well-worn path. She reached out a hand and stroked the gray's sleek neck. It reminded her of something...

Her horse!

She'd had a horse; at least she thought she had. Her head pounded again as she tried to recall what had happened to it. She tried to concentrate, to think, but the warrior—Gilchrist—kept distracting her. He had pulled her so tightly against him she could scarce breathe. He was warm, hot in fact, and she fidgeted in the saddle in front of him.

Glancing down, she noticed his injured hand resting on his thigh. The skin was nearly healed but looked tight and painful still. His fingers were balled into a fist. She didn't know what compelled her to do it, but she moved her hand to his and, very gently, ran her fingers over the angry red surface.

"Don't!" He jerked his hand away, then let go her waist and pushed her roughly forward, putting some space between them.

Fine. She was only trying to—what? What was she doing? Everything was so confusing. Him, his strange speech, and this place—it seemed familiar, and yet…

She narrowed her eyes and focused on the widening path. The stallion quickened his pace and shot ahead, muscles straining, up the last steep hillock. Suddenly they broke from the trees onto a broad, windswept ridge. Gilchrist pulled the stallion up short.

The view was so breathtaking she gasped. One could see for miles across a landscape of stark, rolling hills peppered here and there with stretches of lush forest. A thin, silver necklace of a river snaked its way across a valley far in the distance. To the south and east the hills leveled off. The land there was verdant, flourishing.

"'Tis bonny, is it no?" Gilchrist said, his voice almost a whisper.

She dared to look up at him. He stared into the distance, blue eyes riveted to the far horizon. She was conscious of his hand around her waist again, and of his muscular thighs pressed against hers.

He looked down suddenly. Their gazes locked. Her pulse quickened as his arm tightened around her ever so slightly.

God's blood, he was going to kiss her! She could see it in his eyes.

Her cheeks flushed hot with the knowledge that she wanted him to do it. Instinctively, she wet her lips. His gaze was drawn to her mouth and, for the briefest moment, she thought she could feel him trembling.

Abruptly, he looked away and let go her waist. Her heart was racing. She took a few deep breaths and tried to calm herself. The moment passed. Without a word, he turned the stallion and spurred him up the hill.

She held tight to the pommel, and was still trying to collect her thoughts when she saw it—a citadel rising to the sky.

"Monadhliath," he said. "My home."

She stared at the rough stone structure, looming dark and silent in the distance. It didn't look at all appealing. 'Twas more of a fortress than a home.

As they approached, she realized the castle was under construction. It rested atop a craggy pinnacle and was girdled by a crude, half-finished wall. A goodly number of stone and timber cottages surrounded it.

Women and warriors, dressed in plaids much like Gilchrist's, appeared along the path. A few nodded to him as the two of them rode past. She felt self-conscious, ashamed almost, as their gazes lit on her, appraising her bare feet and appalling attire.

She grasped the edges of the plaid and pulled it close about her. There was naught she could do about her shift, which barely covered her knees as she sat astride the horse.

Gilchrist guided the stallion to the very top of the hill

and stopped before a large cottage. A few of his kinsmen
followed.

"Ho, what's this?" a young warrior called out and
jogged toward them.

Gilchrist drew himself up in the saddle. "I found her,
half-drowned, at the spring."

The young warrior looked her over, one tawny brow
cocked in appraisal. He frowned and she frowned back.
"Weel, this I didna expect."

Gilchrist dropped the stallion's reins and dismounted.
"Nor did I, Hugh." He reached for her with his good arm
and she tensed. "Come on, lass. You're safe here."

Whether she was safe or not, she had no choice but to
obey. After a moment she leaned toward him. He drew
her from the saddle and set her on her feet. A small crowd
had gathered around them, and her natural urge was to
move closer to Gilchrist.

"Who is she?" the warrior, Hugh, asked.

"I know not. She hasna spoken a word since I found
her."

Another warrior pushed his way forward. He was taller
than the first, and striking. His dark eyes widened when
they met hers. "Where did ye find her?" he asked.

"At the spring."

The dark warrior's gaze burned into her and she pulled
the plaid tighter still around her body.

"What's your name, lass?" Hugh asked.

She wanted to answer him but, try as she might, no
words would come. What on earth was wrong with her?
After a moment's effort, all she could do was stare
dumbly at them all.

Hugh cocked his head and frowned. Then a young girl
stepped out in front of him and smiled meekly at her.
'Twas the first friendly face amongst the lot. She was tall

and gangly, and blushed when Gilchrist asked her what she wanted.

"The ring," the girl said, and pointed.

For the first time she noticed the finely carved, silver band circling the third finger of her right hand.

"'Tis very fine, that," the girl said and nodded. "Mayhap 'tis engraved."

Without warning, the dark-eyed warrior lunged forward and grabbed her hand. Her heart jumped to her throat as she choked back a scream.

"Alex!" Gilchrist barked. "Let her go."

The warrior scowled at him, then immediately softened his expression. She didn't like him. He frightened her with his quick moves. "Excuse me, Laird," he said and backed away, his gaze riveted to her ring.

She took a deep breath and tried to calm herself. Her pulse was racing. Gilchrist, too, stared at her ring. She supposed it couldn't hurt for him to examine it. Tentatively she offered him her hand.

He slipped the ring from her finger and peered inside the silver circle. "Rachel," he said and leveled his gaze at her. "Is that your name, woman?"

Rachel.

She stared hard at the ring. Her hand unconsciously moved to her head, which throbbed in time to her heartbeat. Her gaze darted across the small crowd of warriors and women, then settled on Gilchrist's questioning eyes.

"I...I don't know," she said. "I can't remember."

"Good God, she's English!"

Gilchrist started at Hugh's words and immediately took a step back. "She's not."

"Just listen to her," Hugh said. 'Tis plain she's no one of us."

"I…" Rachel stammered. "And—and what are you, then?"

"We're bluidy Scots!" Hugh roared.

Rachel's soft brow furrowed. Gilchrist could see her mind working, trying to fathom Hugh's words. Realization finally dawned on her face.

"Of course," she said. "Scots. But, I am not—"

"Aye, she's English all right," a voice shouted from the crowd. "An English whore!"

This was getting out of hand. Gilchrist scanned the faces of his kinsmen. "Who said that?"

Arlys elbowed her way forward. She whipped her hair behind her then arched a thin brow, fisting her hands on her hips. "Ye found her at the spring, did ye no?"

"I did," he replied.

"The *virgin's* spring," Arlys said and shot Rachel a cool look. "Just look at her."

Rachel met Arlys's disapproving gaze and tipped her chin high. "I—I am no whore."

"Oh, nay?" Arlys said. "If ye canna remember, how do ye know?"

"That's enough," Gilchrist said. "She hit her head. 'Tis no uncommon to forget things after such an injury."

Hugh tilted his head and eyed both women. "Arlys is right, Laird. How d'ye know what she is?"

Rachel moved closer to him and he fought the ridiculous urge to put his arm around her.

"Maybe she hasna forgot at all," Hugh said. "Maybe she's lying."

Gilchrist hadn't thought of that. In fact, given the circumstances in which he'd found her, 'twould never have crossed his mind that she was anything other than a victim of foul play. The small crowd had grown to near a score of clan folk. He looked out over the tops of their heads.

Where had Alex gone? 'Twas unlike him not to offer some piece of advice. Not that Gilchrist needed it. He promised the woman he'd protect her, and he would. At least until he discovered more about her.

The low murmurs and snickers of his kinsmen grew louder. A warrior in the back shouted an obscenity, unmistakably directed at Rachel. Gilchrist shot him a murderous glare and the warrior promptly shut his mouth.

A second later, the door of the cottage in front of them creaked open and Murdoch, one of the elders, stepped out. Now there'd be trouble. The crowd parted to let him approach. Murdoch studied Rachel, his expression blank, then nodded at him. "What's all this?" Gilchrist explained how he'd found her at the spring, and the old man cocked a wiry, white brow.

"She's English," Hugh said flatly.

Murdoch frowned.

"She's a whore!" Arlys shouted. "And no fit to wear our plaid!" Before Gilchrist could stop her, Arlys reached out and ripped the dark hunting plaid from Rachel's body.

All hell broke loose.

Instead of cowering, as he expected, Rachel lunged at Arlys, and the two women crashed backward into the wall of bodies that surrounded them. The crowd went wild.

He reached for Rachel at the same time Hugh stepped toward Arlys. Too late. The two women went down—a spitting, hair-tearing, roil of limbs. He and Hugh collided with a collective grunt.

"Bluidy hell!" He pushed backward, fighting to stay on his feet.

The crowd pressed closer, cheering Arlys on. He, Hugh and Murdoch elbowed them back and formed a tight circle around the combatants, trying to shield them from further harm.

Gilchrist had had enough. He leveled his gaze at Hugh, and his friend nodded. In one swift motion the two of them reached into the tangle of arms, legs, raven and gold hair, and pulled the women apart.

Arlys and Rachel came up snarling, gazes locked.

"Whore!"

"Bitch!"

"Enough!" Gilchrist shouted. "Both of you!"

He pulled Rachel backward against his chest, his good arm tight around her rib cage. His right side screamed in pain. He could feel her heart pound and the soft heaving of her breasts with each labored breath she drew. 'Twas absurd—all of it. He had no time for such foolishness.

"Peg!" he shouted into the crowd. The girl had noticed Rachel's ring. She was smart and trustworthy.

Peg's head popped through a muddle of elbows beside him. "Aye, Laird," she said, breathless and uncommonly cheerful.

"Here," he said, nodding down at Rachel. "Take her and find her a bed." He thrust Rachel toward her, then caught the eye of a warrior he trusted. "And ye, go with them—and see to it no harm comes to her." He glared hard at the warrior. "D'ye understand?"

"Aye, Laird," the warrior said and moved to take Rachel's arm. Peg rushed to help him. The two of them guided her through the crowd, which began to disperse now the commotion was ended.

Men and women alike shot Gilchrist disapproving glances and whispered among themselves as they returned to their duties. Hugh was right. His position as laird was tenuous, at best. He ignored them and watched as Rachel was led away.

Just before the trio disappeared behind a row of cottages, Rachel turned and cast one long look back at him.

He met her gaze and his gut tightened. She smiled suddenly, and by sheer will he did not return the gesture. The warrior tugged on her arm, and she was gone.

He turned away, in time to catch Hugh lecturing Arlys, whispering something about unladylike behavior. "Silly chit," he muttered. He watched, shaking his head, as Hugh sent her off home.

'Twas then he noticed Murdoch leaning casually against the cottage doorway stroking his beard, taking it all in. The elder cast him a blank but pointed look and after a moment went inside and closed the door.

Gilchrist swore under his breath and turned to leave. Out of nowhere Alex appeared, between two of the cottages that lined the perimeter of the newly constructed curtain wall.

"Alex!" he called. "Where did ye run off to, man?"

Alex strode toward him, his expression unusually serious.

Hugh joined them. "Aye, ye missed all the excitement."

"That woman," Alex said. "What will ye do with her?"

He hesitated. "I know not." He eyed Hugh's dour expression. "I care not."

"Good," Hugh said. "Ye have more important matters to attend."

Alex narrowed his eyes. "What matters?"

"The laird will take a bride—Arlys," Hugh said, a smug expression creasing his face.

"But—"

"I didna say I would do it," Gilchrist snapped. "Only that I would think on it." He glowered at Hugh.

"But, Laird," Alex said. "Why would ye marry now?

There's plenty of time.'' Alex nodded to Gilchrist's injured arm. "Ye are no full healed yet.''

"He's fit enough," Hugh said.

Gilchrist considered all he'd seen and heard yesterday at the clearing. "Ye fancy Arlys for yourself, Alex, don't ye? I've seen how she looks at you.''

"Nay, I— 'Tis just I think ye are being hasty.'' Alex nodded to the workers on the hill who were busy moving stones. "Dinna ye think ye should first finish the castle?''

Alex had a point. Perhaps he should wait. Besides, he wasn't ready to choose a bride—not yet. Arlys had seemed a good enough choice yesterday, but today, well, he wasn't so sure.

"To hell with the castle," Hugh said and glared openly at Alex. "He should wed, and soon.''

Gilchrist had the distinct impression he was the only one here without an agenda. "I said I will think on it. Now that's enough.'' He shot them both a look that precluded response, then turned and walked away.

"Laird," Hugh called out. "If ye dinna mind me saying, ye should keep away from that English who—that woman, until we know more about her.''

Gilchrist spun on his heel. "I do mind ye saying, and who are ye to tell me what to do?''

Hugh immediately shrank back.

"Gilchrist.'' Alex took a step toward him. "Laird, on this point I agree with Hugh. Let me deal with the woman. 'Twill be better that way, seeing as how the clan disapproves of her.'' He smiled. "And truly, ye canna blame them.''

He glared at the both of them and ground his teeth. They were right, damn them. Why, then, did he have the feeling he was making a mistake? "All right," he said sharply. "Deal with her, then. I care not.''

He waved them away and turned toward the castle. His arm ached and his skin itched. His burned fingers raged as he unfurled them inside his plaid and tried to spread them wide.

He looked up at the stark battlement, gritting his teeth. 'Twas not the familiar pain that plagued him, but another—one that had naught to do with his burns.

He recalled the fire in Rachel's eyes when he'd pulled her from the brawl, the blush of her cheek, the soft weight of her breast against his forearm. If he closed his eyes he knew he could conjure the beating of her heart against his palm.

He did care.

"Well, if I'm no the bluidy fool," he muttered and strode up the hill to the keep.

Peg pushed open the door of the stone-and-timber cottage. "It's no much, but 'tis dry and warm." She crossed the threshold and beckoned her to follow.

Rachel glanced briefly at the warrior. He nodded once, then turned and stood, feet apart and arms crossed over his chest. 'Twas plain he did not intend to leave.

What could she do? She sighed and ducked under the low doorway. All at once, a bouquet of familiar scents invaded her senses. She closed her eyes for a moment and breathed deep. Rosemary, laurel, and mint—nay, something else.

Just as her eyes adjusted to the dim light, Peg pulled back the furs that covered the one window. Sunlight drenched the room. The cottage was new. Small, but well kept.

A hearth, laid with peat and twigs, commanded most of the wall opposite the entry. Peg knelt before it and rummaged through the few cooking items stacked neatly on the flagstones.

A plaid-covered pallet which served as a bed rested against the wall to Rachel's left. She looked longingly at the plump straw mattress. She was exhausted.

The center of the room was dominated by a simple wooden table, flanked by benches. An old, thick book rested upon it. How unusual. She let her hand light on the stained, frayed cover. Something else caught her eye—a deep, wooden bowl and well-used pestle. Someone had been grinding herbs and nuts. An odd feeling of familiarity washed over her.

She inhaled again. Her nose drew her to the low wall to her right, which was fitted with sturdy shelves from floor to rafters. Every inch of space was crammed with—

She whirled just as Peg rose from the hearth. "Is this your cottage, Peg? Are these your things?" Her heart beat faster as she grasped at the veiled memory.

The girl smiled thinly. "Nay, well, I suppose they are my things now." She moved to the table and ran her hand almost reverently over the battered book. "This is the cottage where the old woman worked. She's gone now. Dead nigh on two moon ago."

"Oh, I'm sorry. You were close to her?"

Peg looked up with huge, liquid eyes. Rachel realized the girl was barely grown—fifteen at most. She had pale-brown hair that fell in wisps around her face. A spray of freckles dotted her impish nose.

"Aye, she was...everything to me. Ye see, I have no kin. My own parents died when I was just a bairn. The old woman raised me in the cottage next door and taught me things."

Rachel let her gaze roam over the wall of containers.

Slowly she reached out and let her hand come to rest on the book, next to Peg's small fist. The girl met her gaze.

"She was a healer," Rachel said, overcome by the strong impression. "The old woman."

"Aye."

Her head throbbed again. She unconsciously moved her hand to the tender spot.

Peg's face immediately brightened. "Ah, your head. I'd forgotten." She pulled out one of the benches and gestured for Rachel to sit. "Here, let me look at it. Mayhap there is something I might do to ease your pain."

She smiled, still rubbing the good-size lump. "So, you are a healer, too, then?"

Peg blushed and fisted her hands at her sides. "Well, sort of. The old woman had just begun to teach me in earnest when...when she passed." She drew herself up and squared her shoulders. "But I'm all the clan has now. So, aye, I'm the healer."

Apparently, 'twas important to the girl to be so viewed. She suppressed another smile and sat down on the bench. "Well then, healer, do something about this blasted throbbing." She caught Peg's expression of delight as she bent her head forward for examination.

Peg tentatively moved her hands over her scalp. She poked and prodded for a minute then stepped back, brow furrowed, and proceeded to chew on her lower lip. "Hmmm, I—I'm no so sure."

Rachel looked at her through the midnight fall of her hair, then straightened up. "I've heard it said that a leaf or two of feverfew infused in boiling water does much to ease a headache."

Peg's eyes lit up. "You're right!" She turned and quickly scanned the apothecary against the wall.

"If you haven't any," she said, "valerian and skullcap, infused together, would work as well."

Peg stood on tiptoe and reached for a clay jar on the top shelf. "Nay, the old woman kept feverfew—here, here it is." She removed the lid and handed the open container to her. "This is it, is it no?"

She quickly inspected the contents. Peg stood stock-still, eyes wide, looking at her with all the expectation of an apprentice who'd just completed her first assignment. Rachel smiled. "Aye, this is it." She drew a small handful of the dried leaves from the jar and placed them in the wooden mortar. "If you'll draw some water, I'll start the fire."

Peg grinned from ear to ear. "I'll be back straight-away!" She bolted from the cottage, leaving the door wide-open.

Rachel glanced out at the warrior whom Gilchrist had assigned to protect her. He spared her not a look. She rose and shut the door, then leaned back against the rough timbers.

A healer.

She was a healer.

That much she remembered. But where was her horse, and where had she been going when Gilchrist found her, half-clothed and unconscious? On the walk to the cottage, Peg had recounted the tale of the virgin's spring. Rachel shuddered.

What if Arlys was right?

Chapter Four

Arlys was wrong.

Gilchrist felt the truth of it in a way he couldn't explain. He sat atop the newly constructed battlement of Monadh-liath Castle and gazed down into the bailey at Rachel and Alex.

She blushed as Alex unexpectedly took her arm and guided her through the maze of hewn stone and sweating workmen. Gilchrist's stomach tightened.

"Let it go," Hugh said. "Ye've other matters to attend to."

"What d'ye mean?"

"The Englishwoman. Rachel."

He snapped to attention and leveled his gaze at Hugh. "What about her?"

Hugh smirked and raised both tawny brows.

"Well, what about her?" He was losing patience. Hugh had been acting strangely the past day, ever since he'd returned from the spring with the woman.

"It's just that…" Hugh paused and nodded below into the bailey. "At first I didna like it, ye being so smitten with her and all. But then—"

"What?" He leapt to his feet. "I'm no smitten. What are ye think—"

"Och, man, 'tis plain as the nose on yer face." Hugh pointed a finger at his chest. "But she's English. Ye must no forget that."

"Are ye daft? I told ye, I'm no—"

"'Tis a miracle, really," Hugh said, "the way she's rallied yer spirit." He nodded appreciatively in Rachel's direction.

"But—"

"Just dinna think on her too seriously. Ye've other—"

Gilchrist reached out and gripped Hugh's shoulder, stopping him in midsentence. "That's enough."

Hugh's eyes widened. "I...excuse me, Laird." He quickly lowered his gaze and Gilchrist released him.

"Ye've been my friend long years, Hugh, but dinna think to tell me my business."

He fisted his hands at his sides. Hugh nodded once in compliance, then strode to the steps leading below. Gilchrist almost called him back, then changed his mind, swearing silently under his breath.

He turned toward the battlement and peered over the edge, looking for Rachel. Ah, there she was, inspecting the masonry of the steps leading to the keep.

Peg had loaned her a gown. 'Twas no much—a thin garment of pale-green wool. He noticed how it gently skimmed her body and pulled slightly at her breasts and hips as she moved. She wore her dark hair loose—a midnight tumble of silk that reached nearly to her waist.

All at once, he recalled her scent and the feel of her in his arms as they rode astride his mount. He pushed the thoughts from his mind, but continued to watch her.

The workers paid her no mind and the few women in the bailey turned from her and pulled their children away when Alex led her toward them. No one would speak to her, save Peg and Alex. It had been like that since she'd arrived.

Rachel tipped her chin high and fisted her hands at her sides, not breaking her stride. Her cheeks flushed a pretty shade of pink, but she did not avert her eyes from the small knot of clan folk who whispered as she walked past, nor did she respond to the occasional insult tossed in her direction.

Gilchrist knew the feeling well.

"Brave lass," he whispered, and absently flexed the muscles in his burned arm.

He watched her. Every move.

She could feel Gilchrist's eyes upon her as Alex led her down the path and away from the castle. Gilchrist had not come near her since he'd sent her away with Peg, and yet everywhere she looked he was there, watching her from a distance.

On impulse she looked back. There he was, leaning against the battlement, his gaze fixed on her. A small thrill coursed through her. He fascinated her—there was no other word for it. He looked almost made of stone, him-self—a citadel within the citadel, alone by design.

"Did ye no hear me?" Alex said.

Rachel shook off the strange emotion and turned her attention back to Alex. "I—I'm sorry, what did you say?"

The warrior smiled, his dark eyes studying her face. "I said, can ye no remember anything more?"

Alex had prodded her with the same questions, over and over, for the last hour. "Nay, I've told you," she said, trying to conceal her irritation. "I remember naught before I awoke in the cave. Neither name, nor family, nor what led me to the spring."

She met his inquisitive gaze and pursed her lips. Alex's rigid posture relaxed and a warm smile broke across his face. Finally, he believed her.

"Well, 'tis a shame, but dinna worry. We shall take care of you." Alex took her hand in his and gently moved his thumb over her palm.

She resisted the urge to pull away. Her pulse quickened as she met his gaze. He'd been overfriendly and protective of her all morning. She supposed she should be grateful, but something about him unsettled her.

He was fair handsome, his brown eyes penetrating, his voice rich and soothing. Still, an uneasiness washed over her as he continued to so boldly caress her hand.

"*I* shall take care of you," he whispered.

She did pull away then, her thoughts racing. There was something about his voice…his words. What was it? Rachel stopped and massaged her brow for a moment.

"Are you unwell?" Alex asked.

"Nay, I—"

"She looks fit enough to me."

Rachel whirled toward the feminine voice. Arlys leaned against the doorway of one of the cottages that lined the castle's curtain wall, her arms folded across her chest, one hip thrust forward.

"Arlys," Alex said as he moved toward the woman. "D'ye no have chores to do?"

Arlys shot him a nasty look then flashed her blue eyes at Rachel. "And what chores have ye assigned *her?*"

Rachel started to speak but Alex interrupted her. "Rachel is our guest, and is still recovering from her… accident. She need no trouble herself with work."

"Ha!" Arlys said.

"But, I'd like to work," Rachel said and took a step toward her. "I'm not used to idleness."

Alex stepped between the two of them, worried, no doubt there would be a repeat of yesterday's sparring.

"Well, I'm sure Alex can find plenty to occupy yer time."

Before Rachel could respond, Arlys stepped into the cottage and began to close the door. She paused and glanced briefly at Alex. Her venomous expression softened. Rachel caught the barest hint of tears glassing her eyes before the door slammed shut.

She looked to Alex who stood motionless, eyes fixed blankly on the cottage, his smile faded. There was something in his face that surprised her.

Regret.

"I'm sorry," she said. "I've upset her."

Alex shook off his momentary melancholy and moved toward her, transforming himself in three strides into the delightful escort he'd played at all morning. "Bah, 'tis naught. She'll come 'round."

"She has every right to dislike me."

Alex took her arm and guided her down the hill and into the maze of small cottages that surrounded the castle. Arlys's accusation still nagged at her.

"Peg told me the story of the virgin's spring," she said.

"Och, dinna listen to those old wives' tales. The girl is a simpleton. She knows naught of what she speaks."

"Peg is sweet, and has been most kind to me." Rachel looked from one woman to the next, as they made their way through the tiny village. None returned her hopeful smile. "In truth, she's the only one who's offered to call me friend."

Alex stopped before a small structure at the end of the last row of cottages. "Come now, Rachel, have I not been a friend to ye?" He raised his brows in question and the corners of his mouth turned up in a handsome smile.

"You have," she said and felt grateful for it.

"Well, then, come—there is someone who'd like to meet you."

Alex led her to the door of the small cottage. "This is my mother's house." He tripped the latch and bade her cross the threshold.

Rachel entered and let her eyes adjust to the dim light. The cottage was tiny and ill kept. A table stood in the center of the room. An old woman sat on a crude stool near the hearth, rocking herself back and forth, seemingly oblivious to their arrival.

"Mother," Alex called to her. "I have brought ye a visitor."

The woman looked up and, as she met the eyes of her son, a dazzling smile broke across her wrinkled face. "Alex," she said and rose from the stool.

"Mother, this is Rachel, the woman of whom I have spoken."

Rachel took a step forward and smiled as the woman turned her attention to her.

"Ahh, Rachel." The old woman's eyes lit up as she studied her with surprising alacrity.

"I am pleased to meet you."

Alex hung back as his mother greeted her. "You may call me Moira," the old woman said.

"Moira," Rachel repeated. "'Tis a lovely name."

The woman chuckled. "'Tis ye who are lovely, lass. My son never spoke of your beauty." She glanced briefly at Alex, whose face colored at his mother's words. "Only that ye canna recall a thing about yourself before your fall in the wood."

"'Tis true," she said. "Except for one thing."

"What?" Alex said and moved quickly to her side. "Tell me."

Rachel hesitated for a moment. She did not like the overzealous look in his eyes. "I—I'm a healer," she said finally.

Moira's eyes widened.

"How d'ye know that, if ye canna remember?" Alex said.

"I just know," she said. "And there are other things— not so much things I remember, but things I see in my mind, like a picture."

"What things?" Alex asked, his voice a bit unsteady. He took her hand and bade her sit on the bench that flanked the table. Both of them hovered over her, waiting for her response. 'Twas odd, their interest in her.

"Well, when I close my eyes," Rachel began, "I see a place—a high place."

"A high place," Alex repeated.

"Aye, bleak and windswept, with a half circle of stones at its crest."

Moira leaned closer. "Standing stones."

"Aye, standing stones."

Alex squeezed her hand tighter. She tried to pull away but he held her fast. "This place," he said, "d'ye know it?"

The both of them leaned closer still. Rachel felt warm all of a sudden, and uncomfortable under their scrutiny. "I...not so much know it, as feel drawn to it. It calls to me, in a way I can't explain." For a moment she thought the two of them would devour her, so near did they hover.

Then a smile graced Alex's face; he abruptly let go her hand and stood tall, hands on hips. "'Tis nonsense," he said. "Ye must put such thoughts out of your mind, lass. Your recovery depends upon it."

Moira moved a wrinkled hand toward Rachel's face and

let her thin fingers come to rest in her hair. The old woman smiled. "My son is right. Forget this vision."

Rachel felt oddly comforted by their response. She would like to forget about the high place. The image disturbed her, frightened her almost.

Moira ran her hand through Rachel's hair. Her touch was cool, soothing. Rachel closed her eyes for a moment and felt the old woman fist a handful of hair at the nape of her neck.

"Lean forward, lass," Moira whispered.

Not questioning why, Rachel complied. She felt Moira's fingers rake her thick tresses. The dark fall of hair spilled forward onto her lap.

"Ahh, you were right, son," Moira said. "You were right." The door latch clunked heavily, as if someone who'd been holding it had just let it fall. Rachel looked up as Moira's hand fell away. The old woman stifled a gasp.

Murdoch, one of the clan's elders, stood in the doorway to the cottage, his eyes fixed on Moira's startled face. Rachel wondered how long he'd stood there, unnoticed. Alex shot his mother a meaningful look, the significance of which Rachel had not a clue.

"Right about what?" Rachel asked, remembering Moira's words. No one looked at her. "Right about what?"

"Alex," Murdoch said, not sparing the warrior a glance. His gaze burned into Moira. "The laird wishes to see ye."

Alex didn't move, his eyes darting from Murdoch's face to his mother's. They all knew something she didn't, but what?

Moira shook off her surprise and nodded to her son. "Go," she said, "and take the lass with ye."

Rachel stood as Alex beckoned her toward the door. Murdoch turned his attention to her at last, and his expression softened. "Aye, lass," he said. "Go with Alex. Methinks Gilchrist would like to see ye, as well."

Murdoch stepped aside and let them pass. Once outside, Rachel turned to speak to him, but he had already closed the door.

Gilchrist gripped the dirk in his left hand and lunged at his opponent.

Hugh leapt sideways as a flash of steel cut the air where he'd stood. "Christ, man! Are ye practicing or d'ye mean to skewer me?"

Gilchrist relaxed and lowered the dirk, breathless from Hugh's surprise attack.

"I told ye so." Hugh nodded and leaned against the stone wall of the keep.

He felt the weight of the dagger in his hand. 'Twas strange, but not so awkward as he'd thought 'twould be. "Hmm? What did you tell me?"

"That ye could learn to use your left if needs be."

On impulse, he tossed the dirk into the air. Hugh flattened himself against the wall. Gilchrist watched as the dagger descended, end over end. At the last moment he reached in to grab it. "Damn!" The blade nicked his palm and thudded to the ground.

Hugh laughed as Gilchrist sucked at the cut. "Weel, it may take a while."

Gilchrist was suddenly aware of the workmen in the bailey. They'd stopped their labors and were looking at him. Most stared blankly, but a few shot him looks of contempt. He grimaced as he stooped to retrieve the dirk. The quick movements of the past few minutes caused his side to burn with pain.

He motioned Hugh to follow him up the steps and into the castle. "They blame me still," he muttered as the two of them strode into the newly finished hall.

"Blame ye for what?" Hugh asked.

"For their laird's death."

Hugh met his gaze. "*You* are their laird now."

"Aye." Gilchrist strode to the center of the empty hall, his footfalls echoing off the flagstones. Sunshine streamed into the room from the small, high windows, and riddled the stone floor with a tapestry of light. He tilted his face up and let the sun bathe him in its warmth. "If only I could have saved them," he whispered.

Unbidden, memories of the fire came crashing in on him. The desperate cries of his uncle and aunt, the roar of the blaze, and the heat—the stifling, hellish heat. Gilchrist raised his hand instinctively to his brow as if to block the visions that raced through his mind.

"Ye did all any man could have done," Hugh said.

"Did I?"

"Aye, ye did." Hugh's expression softened. "Ye did all but die with them. And who would that have served?"

The stony faces of his kinsmen swam before his eyes. "Mayhap everyone," he whispered.

Footsteps sounded on the threshold. Gilchrist looked up to see the elders, all save Murdoch, enter the hall. He stood tall and quickly slipped his burned hand into the folds of his plaid.

"Thomas, Donald," he said and strode toward the older men.

"Ah, there ye are," Thomas said. "We'd have a word with ye."

"Aye, we would," Donald added.

Gilchrist joined them in the doorway and Hugh moved swiftly to his side. "So, what is it ye wish to discuss?"

The elders exchanged a brief look, then turned to him. "The Macphearson," Thomas said.

"Aye, The Macphearson," Donald repeated.

Gilchrist knit his brows. "What about him?"

"Alex thinks we should no trust him," Thomas said. "That we should move against him afore he moves against us."

"Aye," Donald said. "Afore he moves against us."

"Alex said this?" Gilchrist caught Hugh's I-told-ye-so look out of the corner of his eye and frowned.

Both men nodded.

"And do you, Thomas Davidson, think we should no trust him? And you, Donald?"

The elders exchanged another look before Thomas spoke. "Weel—"

"And why should we no trust him?" Gilchrist said, his patience wearing thin. "What has The Macphearson done to us that we should make war on his clan?"

"But Alex said—"

"Does The Macphearson no wish to join us at the gathering this summer?" He turned to Hugh. "Did ye no tell me this less than a sennight ago?"

Hugh nodded. "I did. Our scouts carried the news from the western border where they'd met up with a Macphearson hunting party."

Gilchrist leveled his gaze at Thomas. "They may wish to join the Chattan. The alliance. Did ye no think of that?"

"That's exactly what I'd thought, at first," Thomas said. "But then Alex—"

"Aye, Alex said—" Donald repeated.

Gilchrist silenced the both of them with an upraised hand. The elders stared at it, wide-eyed. He realized then, he'd raised his burned hand. To hell with the both of them. He was sick to death of concealing it.

"Think of it," he said. "The Chattan, the four—Davidson, Mackintosh, Macgillivray, and MacBain. The alliance my father worked his whole life to see, and that my brother, Iain, at long last forged." He paused to let his words sink in. "And now Macphearson. We could be five. Five Highland clans at peace instead of war." Gilchrist nodded slowly and looked from Thomas to Donald, then let his gaze fall upon Hugh.

"Aye," Hugh said, nodding agreement. "And Alex would destroy it before it's e'er begun."

The elders were quiet. Gilchrist leaned against the stone portal of the keep and looked out across the bailey which bustled with activity.

He caught sight of Rachel, arm in arm with Alex, making their way up the hill from the village. He didn't like the way Alex was smiling at her, nor the way he occasionally patted her hand with his.

"And what about *her?*" Thomas asked, nodding in Rachel's direction.

Gilchrist gritted his teeth. "What about her?"

Hugh shot him a cautionary look, which he immediately ignored.

"What will ye do with her?" Thomas asked.

"Aye, what will ye do, Laird?" Donald repeated, much to his annoyance.

God's truth, he had not a clue. His gaze fixed on Rachel, he answered in slow, carefully chosen words. "I promised to keep her safe, and that I intend to do." He glanced briefly at all three men. "D'ye have a problem with that?"

A shout went up among the workmen.

Gilchrist shot from the doorway and stood on the top

step of the keep, scanning the bailey for the source of the commotion.

"There," Hugh said and pointed east, past the village.

A small group of Davidson warriors rode up the hill toward the keep. Nothing unusual about that. As they passed the village, one by one, they turned off toward their cottages. Only one man remained. He rode his own mount, a horse Gilchrist recognized, but led another—a white mare. 'Twas small and did not bear the Davidson livery.

"Look!" Hugh cried and pointed toward the village.

Gilchrist froze.

Rachel was trying to free herself from Alex's grasp. She wrestled in his embrace and shouted something Gilchrist could not make out.

"Bluidy hell," he breathed and started down the steps toward her.

"Wait!" Hugh said. "Look."

The warrior led the white mare past the struggling couple. He appeared only mildly interested in their quarrel.

Rachel suddenly lurched forward and shot from Alex's grip. Gilchrist's stomach tightened as Alex lunged for her, then missed. She raced up the hill, after the warrior and the strange mare. Alex followed.

Gilchrist sprang from the steps with Hugh in his wake. He snaked his way through the knot of workmen and clan folk choking the bailey, and met them at the opening in the curtain wall.

He stopped short when he saw Rachel, her gray-green gaze fixed on the white mare.

"My horse!" she cried, eyes glazed and wide. "My horse!"

Chapter Five

Amethyst waves of heather shifted in the breeze. The stones rose up, gray sentinels against a flawless, cerulean sky. 'Twas bitter cold. She pulled the edges of the plaid close about her, conserving her warmth, mustering her strength.

A great bear of a man appeared on the ridge top, in the center of the stone circle, shading his eyes, scanning the horizon. She waved to him but he did not see her. She waved again and called his name. Why didn't he see her? She must reach him—make him see.

Why didn't he see her?

Rachel's eyes flew open.

"That's it!" she cried and bolted upright. "I must go there! I must find him!" She struggled against the firm hands that pushed her back on the pallet. Her vision was blurred and she fought to clear her mind.

"Hush now, ye must rest." The girl's soothing voice was familiar...Peg. "Ye've had a shock, 'tis all."

Rachel blinked a few times, then focused her gaze on the concerned face hovering above her. "Peg," she said. "Peg!" She struggled to sit up again.

"Nay, ye mustn't—"

Rachel grabbed the girl's shoulders. "I must go there! I must find him! Don't you see?"

"Go where? Find whom?" The voice was Gilchrist's, and before Rachel could respond, he'd motioned Peg out of the way and sat gently on the pallet beside her. "Here," he said, offering her a cup. "Drink this."

Rachel met his gaze briefly, then lowered her eyes to the cup. "What is it?"

"'Tis a libation I make myself. Here." He pushed the cup into her hand. "Drink it. 'Twill soothe your nerves."

She accepted the cup and put it to her lips. Before she drank, she looked up at him. His expression was different, softer. She'd not seen him look so before.

"Drink it," he whispered.

She obeyed. The warm liquid blazed a path of fire down her throat. She felt her eyes widen and she began to cough and sputter. Gilchrist grinned. He put a hand to her back and rubbed in small circles as she caught her breath. "Better?" he asked.

She looked at him and then the cup in wonder. "Aye," she rasped. "Better."

He laughed. "'Tis my own concoction. Some like it, some dinna."

"'Tis powerful."

"Aye, 'tis."

Rachel drew a few deep breaths and began to feel better. She was suddenly aware of her surroundings and the small crowd gathered around her.

She was inside the keep in a small, starkly furnished chamber—Gilchrist's chamber, she surmised. Alex stood against the far wall, his dark gaze fixed on her, his expression blank. Murdoch and two older clansmen whom Alex had called the elders, hovered behind Gilchrist. Peg knelt beside him, her face a mask of concern.

She tried to get up but Gilchrist placed a hand firmly on her shoulder and would not allow it. "What happened?" she asked.

"Ye saw the horse—the white mare—and fainted dead away."

Her horse! She tried to sit up again, and again he pushed her back. "But, my horse—I must see her. I must—"

"Your horse is being well cared for at the stable," Gilchrist said. "Later, after ye've rested, I'll take ye there to see her."

His voice was calm, reassuring, but everything in Gilchrist's demeanor told her he would not allow her to move from the pallet until he was certain she was well.

"All right," she conceded and let her head fall back on the pillow. "But I must have my horse. I must leave soon."

Gilchrist frowned. "And where would ye go?"

"To the high place. I must find it. 'Tis most urgent." She implored him with her eyes. "Don't you see?"

"What high place, lass?" Murdoch knelt beside the pallet and furrowed his great gray brows.

Rachel closed her eyes and conjured the vision.

"The name of this place, what is it?" Gilchrist whispered.

"'Tis all too much for the lass. Ye should let her rest now." The voice was Alex's. 'Twas soothing and moved closer as he continued to speak. "She's had a shock. Let her be."

Rachel ignored them all and concentrated on the image that burned in her mind. "Craigh...Mur," she said, and opened her eyes. "That's the place. Craigh Mur."

A tiny smile tugged at the edges of Gilchrist's mouth.

The elders exchanged wide-eyed looks. Alex opened his mouth as if to speak, but said nothing.

"Craigh Mur," Murdoch repeated.

"Aye," she said.

"'Tis on Macphearson land, is it no?" Peg, who'd been quiet all this time, asked suddenly.

Gilchrist nodded his head, his gaze fixed on Rachel. "It is."

The feeling that she must go there, and quickly, overwhelmed her. But the image of the man atop the ridge continued to nag at her. Who was he? They did not question her further, and she decided not to mention it again until she better understood its meaning.

All she knew was that she must go to Craigh Mur. Whatever it was, wherever it was, the place held the key to her identity, of that she was certain.

"Will you take me there?" she asked, returning Gilchrist's steady gaze.

Hugh appeared in the doorway just as Alex began to voice a protest. Gilchrist beckoned Hugh closer, and the elders moved aside to let him pass into the small chamber.

Hugh glanced briefly at her, then nodded to Gilchrist. "'Tis an English horse, but the livery has no markings. The saddlebags carry a bit of spoiled food and a few garments, that is all."

"An English horse," Murdoch repeated.

"A lady's horse." Hugh caught Gilchrist's eye. "For certain."

Gilchrist pushed the trencher of food away, untouched, and studied the faces of the elders who shared his table for the midday meal.

Hugh sat across from him on a wooden bench, and ate in silence, while Alex fidgeted in his customary place at

Gilchrist's right. Like him, the dark warrior seemed to have lost his appetite.

"Ye've ordered me to deal with her," Alex said abruptly, "now let me do it."

Hugh looked up from his food long enough to cock a tawny brow.

"Ye are laird," Alex continued. "Surely ye have no interest in what becomes of some lying English whore." He paused. "Do ye?"

Gilchrist bristled at his friend's words. His unguarded reaction was not lost on the elders. Murdoch sat quietly, taking it all in, as was his wont. They waited for Gilchrist to respond.

Hugh suddenly put down his dirk, which had been poised to deliver a chunk of roasted venison into his still-open mouth. "Whores dinna own horses, be they English or Scots."

"The lad has a point," Thomas said, nodding at Hugh.

"Aye, he does," Donald agreed. "A point."

Out of the corner of his eye, Gilchrist watched Alex's expression darken.

"Well," Alex said, "be she whore or nay, surely ye dinna mean to deliver her to Craigh Mur?" He glanced briefly at each of the elders, then turned to Gilchrist. "At least no yourself?"

"And why shouldn't I?" Gilchrist asked.

"Ye are no fit, for one thing," Alex said and gestured to Gilchrist's uncovered right hand.

He fisted it tight on the surface of the table, betraying not a hint of the pain it caused him. Blisters had risen yet again on his skin. 'Twas a condition he knew not how to prevent, and one which had plagued him continuously since the fire.

"And besides," Alex continued, his gaze fixed on

Gilchrist's burns, "ye wouldna wish the Macphearsons to see ye so, would ye now?"

Thomas and Donald nodded their heads in agreement. Murdoch merely arched a snowy brow. Gilchrist wavered, his gaze drawn to his disfigured hand. How easily Alex's words could unman him. Mayhap he was right.

"Och, what are ye talkin' about?" Hugh said. "He's fair fit." Hugh pushed back from the table and rose. "And did ye think to take her to Craigh Mur yourself, Alex?"

"Aye," Alex said. "I did."

"And pay a no-so-friendly surprise visit to the Macphearsons, as long as ye were in the vicinity?"

Alex sprang to his feet, nearly toppling the bench and Gilchrist to the floor.

"All right!" Gilchrist slammed his good fist on the table. "That's enough, both of you." Hugh and Alex stood rigid, nodding slowly, each at the other, as if some silent challenge had again been leveled. "No one is going to Craigh Mur," Gilchrist said. He glanced at Murdoch's ever calm expression. "The woman stays here—for a time, at least."

Before any of them could respond, Gilchrist rose from the table and left the cottage, pulling the door closed behind him. He leaned against the timbers of the door frame and inhaled deeply.

Damn this all-consuming interest in her! What had come over him? He'd not felt this way about a woman since…

"Bah!" Gilchrist fisted his hands at his sides. 'Twas dangerous, this interest. He could not afford to compromise his position as laird. That was the most important thing, was it not? The reason he must stay away from her.

At least that's what he told himself. And stay away from her he would.

Hugh had been right all along. He should put away such nonsense and take a Davidson bride. Secure his place as leader. Gain his clan's respect.

Gilchrist looked up to see Arlys standing not ten paces from him, a covered basket in her hand. How long had she watched him? "What d'ye want?" he asked.

She moved closer. "Alex. He is in the cottage?"

"He is."

She smiled at him suddenly. "I have brought him some fresh honey cakes."

Gilchrist stepped aside to let her pass, when his eye caught a whip of dark hair and a pale-green gown.

Rachel.

Peg was leading her down the hill from the castle, toward the row of cottages where they stood. Arlys frowned as she followed Gilchrist's gaze, which was now fixed on the Englishwoman.

Rachel appeared full recovered from her faint. She walked briskly, without assistance. In fact, Peg had to run to keep up with her. She was heading straight for them.

"Christ," he muttered under his breath. He glanced quickly at Arlys. "Those honey cakes, ye wouldna rather share them with me?"

She tore her murderous gaze away from Rachel and let her blue eyes light on him. His words surprised her, he could tell. She recovered herself quickly and smiled. "Aye," she said.

Her voice was breathy, her demeanor suddenly flirtatious. Gilchrist willed himself to hold her gaze even as he heard Rachel's footfalls approach, then stop abruptly before them.

Aye, 'twas time he lay this dangerous interest in the Englishwoman to rest. Without another thought, he grabbed Arlys around the waist with his good arm and pulled her into an embrace. She dropped the basket as he kissed her hard on the mouth. He was vaguely aware of the broken honey cakes lying ruined at their feet.

The eager girl responded with well-practiced skill. But 'twas not her lips he tasted, nor the fragrance of her hair that permeated his senses. His all-consuming awareness was for another.

Out of slitted eyes he watched Rachel's response. Shock, and something more. Pain. He read it in her face. He felt it as much as saw it, and the knowledge caused his heart to pound, his head to spin.

Damn her! And damn himself for caring.

Rachel closed the door of the cottage and pressed her forehead against its cool timbers. She drew a deep breath and tried to get a grip on her shifting emotions.

"Are ye truly an English lady?" Peg asked. "Or, or are ye a whore, d'ye think?"

She whirled on the girl and Peg jumped backward like a startled kitten.

"I—I didna mean to offend ye." Peg's wide, doe eyes and naive concern softened Rachel's anger. "I'm just curious is all."

"I know you didn't, Peg." She gestured for the girl to sit at the table, then joined her.

"Ye truly dinna remember, do ye?"

She smiled. "Nay, I do not."

"Some of the women say ye could be both—a fine lady *and* a whore. But Moira says 'tis nonsense and we must no speak such things."

Both. Could such a thing be true?

She closed her eyes and let her mind wander. As always, the image of the high place burned bright, obliterating all other thoughts. For all she knew, she could be the queen of England.

More likely a common whore. She recalled the way her cheeks burned and her blood stirred when Gilchrist held her atop his mount that first afternoon. He'd wanted to kiss her, and she'd wanted it, too. She shook off the unsettling memory.

Her path was clear to her. She must get to Craigh Mur. She must find out who and what she was. Mayhap she was a married woman with children. Rachel moved a hand across the flat plane of her belly. That possibility hadn't crossed her mind until just this moment. Children. Nay, she was certain she had none. She would feel it if she had.

"Would ye teach me?" Peg asked abruptly, interrupting her thoughts.

"Teach you?"

The girl ran her hand over the tattered cover of the book that lay on the table, then pushed it toward her. "Aye, the healing arts. Will ye teach me?"

Rachel had not had time to examine the old woman's book. She opened it now and scanned page after page of bold script, lists of herbs and their common uses, simples and other preparations, and a log of injuries and illnesses she had treated. Gilchrist's name caught her eye, but before she had time to read what the old woman had written, Peg reached out and caught her hand.

"I canna read it, ye see. The old woman wanted to teach me, but I was no much of a student." Peg's childlike face colored.

"You can't read?"

"Nay. Few can. Only the laird and a handful of others. I knew right off that ye could, though. 'Tis a wondrous thing for a woman, is it no?"

Of course the girl couldn't read; what had she been thinking? Reading was for scholars and priests, and precious few others. But Peg was right—*she* could read. Rachel's eyes flew over the words on the page. 'Twas Latin. She could easily decipher the old woman's hand.

"I am the clan's healer now," Peg said. "They depend on me."

She met the girl's gaze and smiled. "Of course they do."

Peg grinned from ear to ear. "So will ye teach me? To read the old woman's book, and all that ye know of the art?" She gestured to the apothecary that filled the wall of shelves behind her. "Ye know much more than I, and it seems ye will be staying with us for quite some time."

Rachel frowned. She would not be staying with them for quite some time. In fact, she meant to leave as soon as possible. Peg leaned forward, her face alight, awaiting Rachel's reply. She had not the heart to dash the girl's hopes.

"For as long as I remain with you," she said, "I will teach you what I know."

Peg squealed with delight and nearly leapt across the table to hug her. She returned the embrace, then disentangled herself from the girl's arms. "Now," she said. "Will you do something for me, Peg?"

"Oh, aye—anything."

Rachel rose from the bench. "'Tis time I see my horse."

Peg followed her to the door, frowning. "Oh, I dinna think the laird will like that."

"I expect he won't," she said, and let the corners of her mouth turn up in an impish smile.

Ten minutes later they arrived at the busy stable. 'Twas another newly built structure which lay inside the curtain wall not far from the keep. Alex had pointed it out to her earlier that day.

A stable lad scurried past them toting a saddle that was almost bigger than he was. Another labored in a far corner, pitching straw into a small hayloft. Peg led her down a row of stalls, past a number of impressive mounts.

She marveled at their shiny coats and supple musculature. They were well cared for, and were like no other mounts she'd seen. She recognized Gilchrist's stallion and stopped before the magnificent beast.

"He is handsome," she said, and ran her hand lightly over the beast's flank. "Do you not think so?"

"Aye, he is that," Peg sighed. "And so very smart." Another breathy sigh escaped her lips. "But he doesna notice me."

What a strange response. She turned toward Peg and her confusion vanished. The girl stood transfixed, staring at a young man who'd just come out of one of the small cottages that lined the perimeter of the stable yard.

He was tall and fair, and wore leather breeches instead of the plaids that were the garment of choice at the Davidson stronghold. Peg's wide-eyed gaze fixed on him as he passed them by, heading toward a stall. True to the girl's words, he spared them not a glance.

"Ah," she said, suppressing a smile. "You fancy him."

Peg slowly nodded her head. "Aye."

"Who is he?"

"Jamie Davidson," she breathed. "The stable master."

"I see. Well then…" She linked arms with Peg. "We'd best go speak to him." Peg sprang to life and began to protest. "About my horse," she added.

"But—"

"He looks friendly enough. I'm sure he'll let me see

her." She dragged Peg toward the stall she'd seen the man enter. "He's young to be a stable master."

"Oh, aye," Peg said. "He was apprenticed as a lad and grew up in the stable at Braedûn Lodge. I've known him since we were bairns." She paused and a pretty blush colored her cheeks. "When the old stable master died, Jamie took over. Duncan loved him like a son. 'Twas only fitting for Jamie to take his place."

"And he has reared all these fine mounts?"

"He cares for them now, aye. But the original stock was bred by Duncan and Lady Alena."

This surprised her. "A woman?"

"Aye. She's the wife of the laird's elder brother, Iain. And a finer horsewoman ye've ne'er seen. She lived with us at Braedûn Lodge for a time, before she and Iain wed and went off to live at Findhorn Castle."

"Findhorn Castle—where is that?"

Peg pondered the question for a moment. "North, me-thinks. I have never been there. 'Tis the Mackintosh stronghold."

Now she was truly confused. "I thought Gilchrist was a Davidson."

"Oh, he is—his mam was a Davidson, the old laird's sister. But his da was a Mackintosh, *The* Mackintosh, as is his brother now."

"I see." She wondered at this arrangement.

"And Alex. What is he?"

Peg stopped. "His mother is a Davidson."

"Moira. Aye, I have met her. And his father? He is a Davidson, too?"

Peg's blush deepened. "Weel, most likely. One of them is certain to be his da." She stared at the ground and idly drew a line in the soft dirt with her foot.

"What do you mean, one of them?"

"His mam ne'er married." Peg met her gaze. "D'ye catch my meaning?"

Rachel hid her surprise. "I understand," she said simply, and drew Peg further along the row of mounts.

They slowed their pace as they approached the stall Jamie had entered. Rachel could hear him whistling. She peeked inside the timber enclosure. His back was to them; he was currying a mare's coat with huge handfuls of fresh straw.

A white mare—her mare.

"Glenna," she whispered.

The stable master stopped in midstroke and spun on his heel. His expression was all interest and mild surprise. "Glenna? Is that her name, then?"

She moved closer and began to stroke the mare's snowy coat. "Aye." Glenna nudged her hand and softly nickered in response. The simple gesture brought the sting of salt tears to Rachel's eyes. She quickly wiped them away.

"Glenna," Peg repeated. "'Tis a bonny name for a mare."

Rachel smiled and threw her arms suddenly around Glenna's neck. The mare knew her. 'Twas a small thing, but it was the only tangible evidence she had of her former life. She clung to it and it buoyed her strength.

"Her saddle, and the leather bags attached to it," she said. "Where are they?"

"In the shed yonder." Jamie nodded at a small cottage on the perimeter of the stable yard. "The clothes and things that was in 'em have already been taken away."

"Who took them?"

"Alex."

Alex. He'd shown her much kindness, yet there was something about him that unsettled her, something in his eyes. "Why would Alex take my things?"

Peg stumbled forward, blushing hotly, trying for all the world not to look at Jamie. "Perhaps to keep them safe?"

"More likely to see all that ye had," Jamie said. "I had one o' the lads follow him. He carried the garments home to that daft hag."

"You mean Moira, his mother?" she said.

Jamie snorted. "Aye, if ye could call her that."

A high-pitched, pitiful wail caused Rachel's response to die on her lips. All three of them turned toward the sound.

A group of women, Arlys among them, rushed past the stable. One of them carried a struggling child in her arms, a babe no more than three or four years old, Rachel judged.

The woman was sobbing, trying to catch her breath, her face streaked with tears. She looked up suddenly and fixed her wide-eyed gaze on Peg. "There she is!"

"Who is that?" Rachel asked.

"'Tis Agnes, the wife of one of the laird's warriors," Jamie responded. In a half-dozen strides he reached the woman and lifted the child from her arms.

Agnes ran toward Peg and nearly collapsed at her feet. They both knelt to assist her, and she gripped Peg's arms fiercely. "Ye must help him! He's dying!" She began to sob again, in great, heartrending wails.

"What's wrong with him?" Peg gently shook her. "Agnes, tell me! What's wrong with the lad?"

Jamie knelt beside them with the boy in his arms. Instinctively, Rachel grabbed one thin, flailing arm and felt for a pulse. 'Twas weak and rapid. His face was ghostly pale and sheened with perspiration. She placed a hand on his small forehead.

"Dinna touch him!" Arlys spat.

Agnes wailed again and lunged toward her son, dragging Peg with her.

Rachel met Arlys's venomous gaze. "What happened?"

"Poison." Arlys opened her hand and pushed it under Peg's nose. Two large, bloodred toadstools lay crushed in her palm.

Peg examined them, her eyes widening.

"Well, what's to be done?" Arlys snapped.

Peg shook her head, openmouthed, her eyes darting from Arlys to the boy to the mother.

"Well?" Arlys quipped. "You're the healer—do something!"

Peg looked to Rachel and shrugged her shoulders. Her doelike eyes betrayed her anxiety and her fear.

Rachel held out her hand. "The mushrooms, let me see them."

Arlys tipped her chin and arched a thin, golden brow.

"For Christ's sake, woman, let her see them!" Jamie roared.

Arlys shot him a murderous look then dumped the toadstools into Rachel's waiting hand.

She held one up and studied it closely. 'Twas large and red, with white gills and a feathery ring about the stem which ended in a saclike bulb. She squeezed the fleshy cap and the toadstool secreted a milky fluid. "Good God," she breathed.

"What?" Agnes cried. "What is it?"

"Peg," she said. "Do you know the small bag that lies on the bottom shelf of the old woman's apothecary?"

"Aye," the girl replied. "The bag of simples!"

Rachel pushed up the sleeves of her gown. "Fetch it." Without a word, Peg leapt to her feet and dashed off toward the cottage.

Rachel looked to Arlys and the other women. "I'll need milk thistle—as much as you can find—some salt and wild mustard."

"Think ye to touch him?" Arlys shrieked. "You'll kill him!"

Agnes slumped to the ground and wailed louder still. The others began to object, but before Rachel could respond, a familiar, commanding voice stilled their protests.

"Let the Englishwoman try," Gilchrist said as he came up behind her and knelt before the boy. "Methinks she knows well what to do."

His cool blue gaze met hers and her pulse quickened.

"What is it?" he whispered. "D'ye know?"

Rachel held out her closed hand. He turned his palm upward and she let the toadstools slip from her fingers.

"*Amanita virosa,*" she said. "The Destroying Angel."

Chapter Six

The woman was nothing if not tenacious.

Gilchrist leaned forward on the crude bench and watched as Rachel sponged the boy's pale face for what must have been the hundredth time.

He'd convinced Agnes to let the boy remain in Rachel's care, at the small cottage where she slept. For three days, Rachel had not left the child's side. He glanced at the untouched trays of food and at her undisturbed pallet in the corner by the hearth. He was certain she'd not slept a wink in all that time.

Rachel moved slowly, deliberately, her slender fingers tracing the boy's furrowed brow with the damp cloth. The dying embers of the hearth fire bathed her features in a soft light and transformed her hair into a midnight fire fall. God, she was beautiful. She fixed her gaze upon the sleeping child and began to hum a lullaby.

He knew it. 'Twas a Scots lullaby, one his mother used to sing to him when he was a bairn. One he always thought he'd sing to his own children someday.

A brutal tenderness welled inside him, unbidden and unforeseen. Gilchrist fisted his burned hand inside the folds of his plaid until his physical pain shattered the feeling.

That day would never be.

He watched as she comforted the sick boy, a boy she neither knew nor would have any reason to care about. But she did care—and so did he.

He rose abruptly and walked to the small window. The deerskin covering was pulled back to allow the night air into the small cottage. He closed his eyes for a moment and drew a deep, cool draught.

He told himself he needed to be there, in the cottage with her and the boy, because he was laird—because both he and she were his responsibility. He told himself he felt naught for her, only what any man in his position would feel.

"Christ," he breathed.

Suddenly he was conscious of Rachel's hand on his arm, a gentle touch that caused his breath to catch. He opened his eyes and looked down at her upturned face.

"He's out of danger," she said. A smile graced her lips, but her eyes were tired and he could see the tension in her expression. "I should go and tell his mother."

She turned toward the door and without thinking he slipped his hand from his plaid and stopped her. "Wait, I would thank ye. Ye saved his life."

"I did little. 'Twas luck really. Had he eaten more than just a bit of that toadstool, he'd be dead now."

"All the same, ye knew what to do." He gestured to the table littered with bowls and pouches, mortars of various sizes, and a strew of dried plants.

She shrugged off his comment and turned again to the sleeping child. "The boy means much to you."

"Of course he does. I am laird. Each child of the clan is important." He paused, weighing his words, then said,

"Ye took a great risk in treating him, but I expect ye know that."

Her face clouded. 'Twas clear she did not catch his meaning.

"If the boy had died..."

"But he won't," she countered. "I told you, he's out of danger."

Gilchrist marveled at her confidence. Still, he would have her know the truth of things. "But if he had, dinna ye know what my kinsmen would have done with ye?"

For the barest moment her eyes widened. "You vowed to protect me."

"I did, but—"

"Then there was naught for me to fear."

A queer satisfaction blossomed inside him. She trusted him to keep her safe. Him. A man who could scare wield a sword in his own defense.

She began to clear away the things on the table and return them to the apothecary shelf. She stopped suddenly and said, "'Twas at great risk to your own reputation you allowed me to help the child. I had not thought of it before."

He smiled at that. "God's truth, there isna much to risk. Besides, 'twas no my reputation I was thinking of, but the boy's life."

"How did you know I could save him?"

He looked into her eyes and willed her to hold his gaze. "I didn't, but Peg did. The day your mount was found, and ye collapsed, she told us what she'd learned—that ye were a healer, that your skills were great."

Her dark brows arched prettily. "Some would say Peg is a fool."

"Aye, some say as much." He thought immediately of Alex. "Do *you* think her a fool?"

"Nay, I do not."

He smiled again, pleased by her response. "My uncle used to say a man's wits canna be judged by what he chooses to show of himself."

Rachel took a step toward him and, to his surprise, reached out and tugged on his shirt. "Take it off," she said.

His eyes widened as he tried to ken her meaning.

She tugged at the coarse fabric again. "Are you afraid?"

Her audacity intrigued him. He stood silent for a moment, contemplating her question. Aye, he was afraid. Afraid to let her see what he was. Afraid that once she had seen, she'd run as others had. One other, in particular.

Gilchrist drew a breath. Slowly, holding her gaze, he unpinned the clan badge that held his plaid to his shoulder, and pushed the garment to his waist. In one awkward move he shrugged himself out of his shirt, held it in front of him for only a moment, then cast it to the floor.

Her gaze moved over his bared flesh. He lifted his arms away from his sides and turned a slow circle in front of her. Why he did that, he wasn't sure. When his gaze met hers again, he saw neither revulsion nor pity, nor even surprise on her face.

"I can help you," she said simply, and nodded to the angry red blisters that peppered his arm and blazed a trail of fire up the length of his side.

Her offer unnerved him and he felt the color rise to his face. "Nay," he breathed and looked quickly away. "'Tis...no necessary."

"I have also heard it said," she whispered, "that a man's true strength is found not in his body, but in his heart."

His gut tightened and a roil of emotions gripped him. "Who told ye that?"

"My father."

"Ye remember him?"

The light in her eyes died then, and she moved a hand to her soft brow. "Nay, just that one thing."

"Rachel," he whispered and took a step toward her.

She looked away, and he felt their moment of intimacy shatter.

"I must fetch the boy's mother," she said.

His shirt lay on the earthen floor of the cottage, and without it he felt suddenly uncomfortable. He resisted the urge to pick it up. "I will stay with him until ye both return."

She nodded and moved toward the door.

"But wait," he said. "Again, I would thank ye. Is there naught I might do for ye—something in my power to give ye that ye would like?"

She tripped the door latch and stepped outside. "There is but one thing I desire."

His heartbeat quickened. "And what is that?"

"To go to Craigh Mur, so that I might remember who I am and from whence I came."

'Twas a fool's disappointment he felt at her words. He did not answer, and she said no more. He held her gray-green gaze until she quietly shut the door and slipped off into the night.

A heady potpourri of rosemary, lemon balm, myrtle and countless other fragrant herbs burst upon her senses. Rachel knelt beside her basket in the small garden that Peg and the old woman had planted just outside Monadhliath's kitchen.

The keep was nearly finished, and men labored to com-

plete the stone and timber outbuildings that would house
farriers, brewers, bakers, fletchers and all the other crafts-
men and -women who produced goods and performed ser-
vices for the clan.

The sun was high and the day warm. A number of
women passed her carrying wineskins and covered trench-
ers to their toiling husbands. She smiled cautiously at each
one, and several smiled back. It had been like that since
she'd helped Agnes's boy.

Even a few of the men nodded to her as they passed
the garden with their food and sat, backs against the curtain wall, to take their midday meal.

She scanned the well-tended rows of herbs and spied
the plants she sought—comfrey and a bit of calendula.
Working with care, she stripped off enough leaves for her
purpose and placed them in the basket.

Laughter caught her attention and made her look up.
Alex had joined the group of men lunching against the
wall. He leaned against the rough stones, and appeared to
be telling some kind of story. She was just out of earshot
and could not make out his words. Whatever it was he
said, the men seemed to enjoy it.

Alex commanded their attention, and she could see
why. He was a striking man, fair of face and finely built,
with eyes as dark as sable. What was it about him, then,
that made her uncomfortable? Even now, she found herself crouched among the herbs, hoping he would not notice her.

'Twas silly. Why should she feel so toward him? He'd
been naught but kind to her, and overattentive. She should
welcome his friendship. God's truth, it seemed he was her
only chance of ever reaching Craigh Mur—and she must
reach it.

She must.

Alex laughed again. A short, patronizing laugh—one reserved for a fool's antics or for a child who performed some amusing feat.

He nodded to the battlement and the group of clansmen followed his gaze.

From her position in the garden, she couldn't see what it was that amused him so. She returned to her gathering. A moment later, the clash of metal on metal rang from the stone battlement above her. 'Twas the last thing she expected. Her curiosity outweighed her desire to remain undiscovered. She rose from her work and walked toward Alex and the group of men.

The warrior saw her immediately and waved her over. The men's attention was riveted to the battlement, and as she approached them, she heard the unmistakable sounds of swordplay. How strange.

Alex offered her his hand. She hesitated a moment then took it. He drew her up close to his side—too close—and she turned to look up at whatever it was that held the clansmen rapt.

"God's blood," she breathed.

'Twas Gilchrist and Hugh. They were fighting, but what on earth—ah, they were practicing, she could see that now. Gilchrist wielded his sword awkwardly as Hugh drove him backward along the length of the battlement.

Alex chuckled again. "He thinks to fight left-handed."

Of course. Gilchrist was right-handed, or had been before the fire. She watched as he redoubled his efforts and lunged at Hugh. The warrior neatly sidestepped Gilchrist's attack. He lunged again.

The day was warm, and even at this distance she could see his sweat-soaked shirt and the sheen of perspiration reflecting off his face. His hair had come loose and clung to his body in long, damp hanks. 'Twas apparent he was not giving up. She felt a strange sort of pride in him, and the edges of her mouth turned up in a smile.

"'Tis a pity, that." Alex nodded to the combatants. "He'll never be the man he was." The clansmen laughed again, and Alex with them, as Gilchrist stumbled and nearly lost his footing.

Her hackles rose. "What makes you think that?" She loosed her arm from Alex's and took a step back from him. "He seems to be holding his own quite well."

The warrior turned his attention to her, one dark brow arched in amusement.

She refused to meet his gaze. "He improves with every move," she said. "Look."

Hugh suddenly put up his sword and called a halt to the mock battle. The two warriors stood facing each other, grinning and gasping for breath. Rachel caught herself smiling, as well.

Gilchrist handed Hugh his broadsword and, to everyone's surprise, matter-of-factly stripped off his shirt.

The man had courage.

He did not look down, but she was certain he was neither blind to his clansmen's wide-eyed stares, nor deaf to their rude mutterings.

Her smile broadened as her affection for him swelled.

"Och, dinna look upon him," Alex said, his voice tinged with disgust. He tried to turn her away, but she stood fast. "Your fair eyes shoudna be so offended. Come."

Her gaze slipped from Gilchrist's disfigured form to Alex's tall, dark perfection. The striking contrast between the two men had never been more clear to her. Her smile faded and she leveled her gaze at him. "The only offense here is yours."

A few of the clansmen dared laugh at her response. Her

blood boiled. She met each one's gaze in turn, feeling the color rise hot to her cheeks. "And yours," she said to them.

She turned her back on Alex and the men, and nearly collided with Murdoch. The old man must have come up behind her. She wondered how long he'd been there.

The elder stood not an arm's length from her, his expression unreadable as ever. "I'd have a word with ye, lass," he said.

Alex gripped her arm. "Shall we all go inside?"

"Alone," Murdoch said. He offered her his hand, sparing Alex not a glance.

A few minutes later they were sitting side by side on a wooden bench outside Murdoch's cottage just below the castle. Rachel smiled politely at the elder, but found her gaze drawn to the battlement where Gilchrist worked to master his left-handed swordplay.

"Ye were right," Murdoch said. "He does improve. For months he wouldna lift a weapon, and now…"

Rachel looked at him squarely. "How did it happen? The fire."

"Ah, the fire. I wondered when ye might ask me." Murdoch's expression darkened. "Truth be told, no one knows. But I have my suspicions."

"You mean 'twas deliberate?" She could hardly believe such a thing.

"Perhaps."

"That place," she said, "in the forest, where heaps of charred wood lay about a clearing. That's where it happened?"

Murdoch nodded. "Braedûn Lodge. Home of the laird and his lady—and Gilchrist and the other lads as well."

"His brother." She recalled Peg's tale of Iain and his bride, Alena, the horsewoman.

"Aye, the both of them, Iain and Conall, the elder and the younger."

"I have heard tell of the elder," she said. "But Conall, where is he?"

"Gone. He left soon after the fire. 'Twas unfortunate. Methinks 'twould have been better for Gilchrist had the lad stayed."

She watched him on the battlement and tried to sort out her peculiar feelings. "Tell me about the fire," she said. "About Gilchrist."

Murdoch arched a brow. "Are ye certain ye wish to know?"

"Aye."

"'Twas a horror none of us will soon forget." He nodded toward Gilchrist on the battlement. "Least of all him."

"Go on," she whispered.

Murdoch settled in, elbows resting on knees, as if the tale he were about to tell her was overlong. "The screaming woke me," he began. "'Twas the dead o' night. I rarely slept at the lodge, and this eve was no different. My cottage lay down the hill—'tis still there, in fact— and by the time I reached Braedûn the upper floors were already ablaze."

"'Twas timber, all of it?"

"Aye." He nodded to the battlement. "And ye'll no see him ever build with it."

He paused and they both studied the newly wrought stone of Monadhliath Castle. 'Twas a citadel, a fortress that could neither be breached nor burned. Even the curtain wall was unusually high.

Gilchrist had sheathed his weapon and now leaned heavily against the crenulated battlement. Hugh was nowhere in sight. Gilchrist looked out at her—and she looked back.

"Alistair and Margaret were trapped in their chamber, the fire all around them," Murdoch said.

"The laird and lady, Gilchrist's uncle and aunt."

"Aye," he whispered.

"And Gilchrist? Where was he?"

Murdoch cocked his head to look at her. "He was right there in the thick of it, and wouldna leave."

She drew a deep breath and felt her belly tighten. "Tell me."

"The smoke was so thick, ye couldna see but a pace or two in front of ye. The fire blazed with the devil's own heat—and still he wouldna leave."

"Because of his uncle and aunt."

"Aye. He was hell-bent on getting them out, and I could see he'd do it—or die in the trying. The door to their chamber was barred from the inside. We could hear their screams over the roar of the blaze."

Murdoch's voice faltered, and she felt strangely compelled to take his hand. He allowed it, and closed his weathered fingers around hers.

"Gilchrist took a battle-ax to the door. But something wedged against it, and he couldna open it full. He hacked away the timber so a man might almost get through, but no quite."

She squeezed his hand tighter. "He couldn't get them out."

"Nay, he couldna." Murdoch paused and swallowed hard. "He kept throwin' his body against the timbers, trying to get through. 'Twas all ablaze by now. The smoke was choking him, and his face was black with it. Hugh was right there with him when—"

"And Alex," she interrupted. "Where was he?"

"Away. Hunting." Her question surprised him, and for a moment he seemed to lose his train of thought. "When the stairway caught fire," he said finally, "we knew we had to get him out, fast."

From atop the battlement Gilchrist watched them.

"He wouldn't leave," she whispered.

"Nay. He could see them in there and hear their cries. He wedged his body in the doorway as far as he could, and reached out to them, screaming their names."

A bright fusion of horror and awe gripped her. She drew her hand from Murdoch's and fisted it in her lap.

"In the end it took three men to drag him to safety, and him fighting them the whole way. He was in such a rage, he didna even ken how bad he was burnt."

"Mother of God."

"The whole house went up—a fireball against the night. Gilchrist stood in the stable yard and watched it burn. When Alistair and Margaret's screams finally ceased, he fell to his knees in the dirt and let out a cry of anguish that no man will e'er forget."

"Gilchrist," she breathed.

"I'd ne'er seen him cry, no even as a lad, but he wept that night."

Her own eyes glassed and she buried her face in her hands.

"In the weeks after, he was out of his head. He wanted to die, and raved on about it. I'd ne'er seen burns the likes o' his from which any man lived. I couldna fathom his pain. The old woman had to drug him to treat him, or he'd have died o' the shock of it." Murdoch paused and shook his head. "He wouldna forgive himself—he still willna. He's convinced 'twas somehow his fault."

She looked up suddenly, needing to see him there on

the battlement, wanting the assurance of his eyes upon her, but he was gone.

Murdoch rose and offered her his hand. "Och, lass, I've upset ye, now." His voice took on a warm, rough timbre. "Come, let us walk awhile. There is more I would have ye know."

Rachel quickly dried her eyes and accepted the elder's hand.

"And more I would know of ye," he said pointedly, and guided her down the worn path between the row of cottages.

He couldn't sleep.

Gilchrist walked the village in the dark. The night air breached the thin linen of his shirt, cooling his overheated body.

'Twas midnight—mayhap later. He observed the position of the stars suspended above him. Aye, much later. The moon hid behind the silver skirt of a cloud and did little to tame the blackness.

He liked the dark. In it he could move unseen, safe from his kinsmen's guarded stares, the open gawks of their children, safe from his own scrutiny—and *hers*.

He paused just outside Rachel's cottage. 'Twas quiet in the village. All were abed. A few odd crickets and the breeze whistling past Monadhliath's battlements were the only sounds.

Before he knew what he was doing he found himself at her door, his hand poised over the latch. He closed his eyes and listened harder. Was that her breathing he could hear? Her soft sighs as she stirred from sleep?

Her visage swam before him. The rich ebony fall of her hair. Her milk-white radiance. The blush of cheek and lip. Long, dexterous fingers, healing hands. Aye, she was a healer, and how he longed for her to touch him, heal him.

His hand closed over the cool metal of the latch. 'Twould be so easy. All he need do was cross the threshold, kneel beside her pallet, take her in his arms.

The moon slipped from its hiding place, laying bare his intentions, casting a silvery light upon the door, upon his hand. A monster's hand, blistered and raw, red and black and white.

Fool.

As if she, or any other woman, could want him now.

Alex had made sport of him today, as had she. Or had she? Their laughter had carried to the battlement. Even now he felt their eyes burning into him. When he'd chanced a downward glance he'd seen them there, Rachel and Alex, arm in arm, watching him.

Nay. She was with him but had not shared his amusement nor his disgust. He knew it, felt it. Days ago in the cottage she'd asked to see him, and she had seen. There had been something else in her eyes that night, something other than pity, or even compassion.

He let his fingers slide from the latch and fisted his hand in front of him. He didn't remember love. He wouldn't allow himself that bitter luxury. To have lost his heart once was folly enough…and he'd paid for that mistake.

Besides, the lass was clearly unsuitable. Christ, she was English—and who knew what else? His kinsmen's laughter that afternoon made plain his unstable position with the clan. Not all shared their disdain, but enough did to sway the council. And who was their alternative? Alex?

The man was his friend—the sport he'd made of him today notwithstanding—but he was no leader of men. Left to his own devices, Alex would have them at war with the Macphearsons in the blink of an eye. 'Twould put at risk their alliance with the other Chattan clans. Nay, he couldn't let that happen.

He must strengthen his position, and soon. Hugh's advice weighed on him. 'Twas in all their best interests that he wed. Tomorrow he'd seek out Arlys and propose the match.

Already he felt better. 'Twas the right choice. He let his gaze linger on the door latch a moment longer, then turned from the healer's cottage and started back up the hill to his makeshift chamber in the unfinished castle.

He'd walked not a half-dozen paces when a muffled scream pierced the silence. Gilchrist whirled; his hand moved instinctively to his dirk.

The scream had come from the cottage—her cottage.

"Rachel," he breathed. Panic seized him.

He was there in a flash, weapon drawn. She cried out again. Wasting no time, he kicked in the door and burst across the threshold.

Chapter Seven

The warrior towered over her, a dark silhouette against the pale moonlight. His blade flashed pearly steel as he knelt before her and slowly lowered the weapon.

"Nay!" she cried and tried to beat him away with her fists. He gripped her arms and held her fast. "Nay, do not!"

Her head pounded as she struggled against him, shaking off the fitful remnants of sleep. The last chilling images crashed across her consciousness and were gone, leaving her shaking and breathless, her heart racing.

His arms went around her and drew her in close. "Shhh, 'tis all right," he whispered against the damp tendrils of hair that clung to her cheek. "'Twas only a dream. You're safe now."

"But—"

"Shhh…"

Rachel flattened her palms against the solid wall of his chest, as if to push him away, then yielded to his gentle insistence. His hand inched its way up her spine, moving in slow circles, soothing her, and came to rest at the nape of her neck.

She recalled the day he held her close in the saddle.

His warmth, his scent, his touch—even in the dark she'd know him.

"Gilchrist," she breathed.

"Aye, lass. I'm with ye now."

He rocked her, all the while lightly rubbing her back through the thin fabric of her chemise. She realized she was bathed in a fine sheen of perspiration. The gown clung to her but she did not care.

"Tell me about it," he whispered.

"The dream?"

"Aye."

"'Twas—'twas horrible."

His arms tightened around her. "Tell me."

She wanted to tell him. She needed him to know. "'Twas night and I was in the forest." She closed her eyes and conjured the vision.

"Alone?"

"Nay. He—he was there."

Gilchrist pulled away from her, and she opened her eyes. She felt, more than saw, the alarm in his expression.

"Who was there? A man?"

She nodded. "I—I think so, but I don't remember him clearly. He was big, like you, and..." She closed her eyes again and tried to recall his face, his eyes. "'Twas so dark, I couldn't see him."

"What did he do, this man?" She felt the tension grow in Gilchrist's embrace, and heard it in his voice.

"He—he tried to hurt me, and the others." In her mind's eye she saw the flash of steel as the warrior's sword cut the darkness.

"Others?"

"Aye, my kinsmen, I think." She struggled to remember their faces, but the harder she concentrated the further from her mind the vision fled. "Blood—I could smell it—

and screams, their screams.'' A wave of horror washed
over her. She gripped the front of Gilchrist's shirt and
looked up at him in the darkness. ''He—he killed them.
And—'' she hesitated ''—he would force his will upon
me.''

''Sweet Christ,'' he whispered and held her tighter.

Safe in Gilchrist's arms, her fear subsided. Only her
emptiness and her frustration remained. ''Oh, why can't
I remember?'' She slumped against his chest. ''Why?''

''Shhh,'' he whispered and drew her closer still, cra-
dling her head in his hand, his capable fingers tangled in
her damp hair.

Her arms instinctively went around him and she relaxed
in his embrace. Who was she? *What* was she?

She needed to know. 'Twas all that mattered now.

And yet, when Gilchrist held her in his arms, that need
was lessened, somehow. The emptiness of not knowing
waned, and some new and wondrous feeling blossomed
in its stead.

She was acutely aware of his beating heart, his breath
on her cheek, the solid warmth of his chest. She inhaled
his musky scent and lost herself in his soft caresses.

''Ah, Rachel,'' he breathed. ''Sweetling.''

The moon cast a pearly finger of light across his face.
She looked up and met his gaze, his eyes dark jewels
framed by the quicksilver fall of his hair. She held her
breath as his lips descended on hers in the gentlest of
kisses.

He was tentative, almost hesitant, in the way he held
her, kissed her—but she would have none of it. She parted
her lips and boldly kissed him back. As their tongues met
and mated, a rush of heat consumed her.

'Twas right and good—she knew it, felt it.

Gilchrist groaned and deepened the kiss. All the while

his hands explored her, caressed her. Her skin came alive under his touch. Her excitement grew, and with it her recklessness.

She wanted him, needed him.

Before she knew what she was doing, Rachel drew him down on top of her on the crude pallet that served as her bed. Her breasts burned as they grazed his chest, the light fabric of their garments seemed as nothing between them.

He kissed her hard, with a kind of desperation she, too, felt. Then all at once he pushed himself away. Why? His hand rested lightly on her shoulder—his burned hand. It trembled slightly.

She reached for him, confused, and he stilled her with a look. "Nay, lass," he said. "This canna be, me with you."

His words, though softly spoken, hurt her in a way she'd not expected.

Gilchrist looked away.

"But I..."

He shook his head, and her words died on her lips.

He didn't want her. 'Twas plain.

Unconsciously, she pulled the rumpled plaid she used as a blanket up over her breasts, covering her near nakedness. The burning she'd felt now centered itself in her face. A sick feeling washed over her as she recalled Arlys's accusation.

Whore.

Gilchrist rose from the pallet and walked to the open door. He turned to look back at her, but all she could see was his dark shape looming in the doorway against the pale, moonlit backdrop.

"I canna," he whispered, and closed the door quietly behind him. The latch tripped into place.

* * *

"Christ, ye reek man!" Hugh looked him over with an expression of brotherly disgust which, in fact, reminded him much of his own brother, Iain. "How long have ye been here?"

Gilchrist ignored him and raised the ale cup to his lips.

"Since before midday," Alex said.

Gilchrist closed his eyes so he would not have to look at either of them, and leaned his head back against the cool stone wall of the alehouse.

"What are ye thinking?" Hugh asked. "I thought ye wished to play at swords today." Much to Gilchrist's annoyance, Hugh pulled the bench out and sat down next to him.

"There will be no swords today, my friend," he said and took another large swallow.

"Nay, nor any other day if ye keep on like this," Hugh said.

Gilchrist cracked an eye in time to see Alex rise. "Och, leave him alone, Hugh." Alex picked up his cup and moved to the next table. The Davidson warriors moved quickly to make a place for him on the bench. "Poor sod," Alex muttered as he took his seat.

Hugh bristled at the comment, but Gilchrist merely laughed and turned his face to the wall. The damp stones cooled the fire in his head. He closed his eyes again and tried to block out the cacophony of laughter and bawdy jokes, whispered conversations and muttered insults.

His head swam with a host of visions—charred timbers, scattered honey cakes, a midnight cascade of hair. The stench of ale faded and in its stead the memory of lavender soap invaded his senses. For all he tried to forget her, the feel of her in his arms came flooding back to him—her damp tresses and dove-soft skin, their burning kisses fueled as much by her heat and desire as his own.

"Rachel," he breathed.

Then he recalled the details of her dream. A man. 'Twas not the first time she'd mentioned him. A lover? A husband, mayhap? His gut roiled—from the drink, no doubt. He opened his eyes to Hugh's accusatory gaze. Damn him. "Go on," he said, "say it."

Silence.

"Say it," he said louder. "I know ye are thinking it."

"All right," Hugh answered finally. "I'll no mince words. Ye're stinkin' drunk. No fit to wipe the boots of the men here, let alone lead them."

"Whoa ho—" Gilchrist dissolved into laughter and let his cup slip from his hand. It clattered to the floor, soaking his plaid on the way. He rolled his eyes then tried to focus them on his friend's stony expression. "'Twasn't so long ago, Hugh, ye wouldha been drunker than me."

"Aye, mayhap. But times have changed." Hugh nodded toward the next table where Alex sat in whispered conversation with their kinsmen.

Gilchrist pushed his back against the wall and tried to sit up straight. The room spun, but only a little. Christ, he wasna so very drunk. What was all the fuss? He felt good, very good, in fact. His burnt flesh pulsed but dully, and his head was near numb. There would be no demons to haunt him tonight. He'd slain them all with ale.

Or so he'd thought.

The voices at the next table rose so that both he and Hugh were within earshot of Alex's conversation.

"What would ye have us do?" 'Twas Thomas, the elder, who asked the question. Gilchrist sat straighter and tried to clear his head enough to catch all their words.

"About Macphearson?" Alex said. "Take him out. He's old, and his clan's in a shambles. 'Twould be easily accomplished."

Thomas nodded, as did the others at the table. Hugh's gaze slid sideways and met his own. Gilchrist held it for a moment, but did not speak.

"They've been on the move, 'tis certain," a warrior said.

Alex's head shot up. "What do you mean, on the move?"

"Small parties o' Macphearsons have been seen all over the Highlands of late," the warrior said. "I seen some myself, and have heard of others."

Gilchrist feigned disinterest in their conversation, and called for more ale.

"What are they about, then?" Alex asked. "Do ye know?" He looked at each warrior in turn, but they all shook their heads.

"Perhaps ye should just ask them," Hugh said loudly. All eyes turned to him. "After all, they've hinted they wish to align with us. Did ye forget that?"

Alex narrowed his eyes.

"Aye, an alliance," one of the men said. "'Twould be good, methinks. Perhaps The Macphearson has a daughter our Alex might wed."

Alex's expression turned to stone.

"Nay," Thomas said and chuckled. "Well, mayhap. Macphearson had just the one daughter. But he's near seventy. The lass would be an old woman herself now. Besides, she's long gone from here."

"Then she'd be perfect for Alex on both counts," Hugh said.

Gilchrist watched as his two friends locked gazes. Alex's eyes were live coals, but Hugh did not back down.

"Then again, Alex Davidson," Hugh said, "who are ye to make alliances or wars on behalf of our clan? 'Tis the laird's right alone, no yours."

Alex smiled thinly. "But of course. The *laird*." He turned full around on the bench and arched a dark brow at Gilchrist. The others turned their attention on him as well.

Gilchrist swallowed hard. He wiped the ale from his mouth and thrust his burned hand inside the folds of his plaid. Something grew in his gut that he'd never felt before.

Shame.

"Ye are envious, Alex," Hugh said quickly. "Ye've always been, since we were lads and Gilchrist came to live with us."

"Hugh—" Gilchrist tried to stop him, but Hugh ignored him.

"He took your place as Alistair's favorite, and why not? Gilchrist was his blood kin, his nephew, and you— why ye're just a bastard who—"

Alex shot to his feet and sent the bench near flying. Three warriors struggled to maintain their balance.

Gilchrist gripped Hugh's arm, more to steady himself than to stop him. His head throbbed with the effects of the drink. He'd pay tomorrow, but now he needed his wits about him. One more minute and his two closest friends would kill each other. Somehow he got to his feet.

"At least Alex is one of us," one man called out.

"Aye," another said, "and he's no a coward."

Gilchrist tensed.

"What d'ye mean by that?" Hugh asked and took a step toward the man.

"'Twas The Mackintosh's fault the laird and lady perished." He nodded at Gilchrist. "Aye, he couldha saved them, but he let them burn."

The clansman's words shattered Gilchrist's ale-induced complacency. His gut twisted. Ignited by anguish and rage, he shot forward. Hugh caught him as he nearly stumbled into the table full of warriors. His head spun and his stomach lurched.

"Let me go," he muttered and pulled himself from Hugh's firm grasp. Out of the corner of his eye he caught Alex's disgusted expression.

"Laird," Hugh whispered.

"Nay, I—I need to be alone." He glanced briefly at the stony expressions of his clansmen, then turned and made his way to the door. God, what had he become?

"But, Gilchrist—" Hugh called after him.

He shook his head and waved his friend back. Once outside he stood tall, locking his knees so he wouldn't fall, and drew a deep breath. The air was chill and fresh, the night black as a raven's wing. His vision cleared and with it, his head.

"Jamie," he called out in the direction of the stable. "Ready my mount."

Rachel hung the last of the freshly cut herbs to dry on the wooden racks suspended from the roof of the cottage. "There now, that should do for a while."

In the past few days she'd made great strides in replenishing the clan's dwindling apothecary. She and Peg had worked from sunup to sundown in the castle garden and the cottage, gathering and drying a variety of young spring plants.

The work kept her mind as well as her hands busy. She'd not seen Gilchrist since the night of her dream. At first she was relieved not to have to face him, and threw herself into her work with Peg. But now, her thoughts strayed often to him.

Where had he gone, and when would he return?

Absently, she ran a finger over the rise of her lips, along

her cheek, tracing the path his mouth had burned across her skin.

"Ah, there you are."

She whirled and saw Alex in the open doorway. "Oh, it's you. Good morrow."

"Aye, 'tis a bonny spring day," he said and shot her one of his charming smiles. "I've brought my mount—and yours."

"What?" She slipped past him outside, and as he'd said, there was her mare and his gelding, saddled and ready.

"I thought to take ye for a ride. Ye've done naught but work these last days. A respite will do ye good." He led her to Glenna, then started to lift her into the saddle.

"But, wait, I—our work is not yet finished. Peg will wonder where I've gone."

Alex ignored her. "Och, the lass is so simple, she'll no even notice your absence."

His arrogance made her bristle, but she bit her tongue. God's truth, she welcomed the idea of a ride. 'Twould be good for her to get accustomed to Glenna again. The mare nickered softly as she adjusted her position in the saddle.

Alex mounted his gelding and bid her follow him down the rocky hillside toward the forest, away from Monadhliath Castle. A few warriors and clanswomen noted their departure with more than mild interest.

The day was warm and she turned her face toward the afternoon sun, which inched along on its well-worn path. Her gaze followed it west, and lit upon a green, craggy landscape far in the distance.

West!

That was it! The direction in which she'd been traveling. She urged Glenna into a trot and reined her into the sun's brilliant path.

"Ho!" Alex called. "Rachel, where are ye going?" He spurred the gelding faster and caught her up.

"I—I want to go this way, over there, toward those mountains." She pointed at the craggy hills.

Alex reached out and caught Glenna's bridle, then slowed both mounts to a walk. "Nay, no that way. Come, we shall go down into the forest to the east. There is something I wish to show you."

"But—" She gazed longingly at the distant landscape.

"We shall take that path soon," he said cryptically. "But no today."

She met his gaze and sought the meaning behind his words, but his eyes were dark pools in which she read naught. She allowed him to guide her mare eastward, and soon they were back on the rocky path leading down the slope into the forest. Just before they reached the cover of the trees, Rachel reined Glenna to a halt.

"Why are ye stopping?" Alex asked. "Are ye tired?"

A strange feeling washed over her. "Nay, I—I just wished to stop."

"Very well. 'Tis a pretty spot—we shall rest here for a moment." Alex drew his mount up close to hers.

She looked back toward Monadhliath Castle. The sun reflected off the newly hewn stones of the keep, which peeked over the ridge in the distance. They were alone here—she and Alex. He watched her closely, and she found herself avoiding his gaze. Perhaps 'twas not the smartest idea to ride out with him after all.

"What are ye thinking?" he asked.

"Oh, nothing." She shook off her discomfort and quickly smiled.

"Ah, but ye were. Ye seemed far away just then." He trailed a finger across Glenna's coat and the mare stirred. "Ye were thinking of him, weren't ye?"

Rachel met his questioning eyes. "Thinking of whom?"

"Of Gilchrist—the laird."

His intuition unnerved her. "Why—why no. I was not."

Alex's lips curled at the edges. "I am glad to hear it. Ye would do best to avoid him. 'Twould no be smart for him to be seen with ye, especially now."

She frowned.

Alex's expression hardened. "Never forget, lass, ye are English, an outsider, found at the spring with bare a stitch on. While I, myself, dinna believe the tale, there's many who still do. And by your own admission, ye dinna know who or what ye are."

She bristled at his words and the calm chill of his voice. Her face grew hot but she held his gaze, all the while twisting Glenna's reins in her hands.

"And what do *you* think I am, Alex Davidson?"

He smiled unexpectedly. "Ye are like me, ye dinna fit."

She recalled Peg's words. *His mam ne'er married. D'ye ken my meaning?* She wondered at the pain this must have caused him as a child. He was a Davidson warrior, one of Gilchrist's closest friends, and while the elders respected him, she'd heard others speak of both Alex and his mother with less favor.

"We are a match, you and I," he said and took her hand in his. "Methinks we should make it known soon, before the fanfare the laird's wedding is sure to cause."

She pulled her hand away. "What do you mean, the laird's wedding?"

"Why, Gilchrist and Arlys, of course. He plans to wed her." His expression remained unchanged as he read the shock in hers. "Did ye not know?"

She did not know, but was she truly surprised? Days ago, before her very eyes, Gilchrist had kissed the girl. Her stomach tightened as she recalled his hands circling Arlys's trim waist, his mouth on hers.

And yet, 'twas another kiss which haunted her, tenderly bestowed in the moonlight, and ardently returned. God's truth, 'twas all she'd thought of these past few days.

"Fool," she breathed.

"Eh?"

Gilchrist had pushed her away. She was not suitable. Alex was right—she did not fit.

Alex took her hand again in his. "Come, let us ride into the wood."

She must get a grip on her emotions. Alex saw things as they were. She should trust him, and yet... "Nay, I don't want to ride anymore. Let us return."

She tried to draw her hand away, but Alex held it fast. "There is more I would say to ye. Please."

"Alex, I—"

"Hear me out."

His eyes warmed then, to a deep, almost comforting chestnut-brown. She relented.

"Rachel, ye are a woman alone, with neither family nor money. Ye need the protection of a man, a warrior, someone who can take care of you." He tightened his grip on her. "A husband."

She tensed but did not try to draw away. He was right. Everything he said made sense. And yet, something inside her sparked caution, compelled her not to be so easily swayed by his confidence.

"I—I don't know."

"We are a match, you and I. Admit it."

Aye, they were a match for certain—a Scots bastard

and an English whore. 'Twas madness, and yet… "Craigh Mur," she said suddenly. "Will you take me there?"

He raised her hand to his lips and gently kissed it. "Of course I will—after we are wed."

A feeling of dread and revulsion washed over her. She looked away suddenly, toward Monadhliath Castle.

"Sweet God," she breathed.

Gilchrist sat atop his mount, high on the ridge overlooking them, his gaze riveted to her. She was barely conscious of Alex brushing his lips across her open palm. Before she could react, Gilchrist turned his mount and spurred him up the hill toward the castle.

"Nay, I…" Rachel yanked her hand from Alex's grasp and reined Glenna back in the direction they'd come.

Alex grabbed the bridle. "Wait. I told you, there is something I wish to show ye in the wood." She met his gaze and he released his hold. "Come, it's just a bit further." He pointed to a copse just below the tree line. "Over here."

The hairs on her nape prickled; the barest chill fingered its way up her spine. She looked from his dark eyes to his outstretched arm.

Come, it's just a bit further—over here.

"Nay," she breathed and slowly shook her head. Before Alex could stop her, she kicked Glenna into action and raced away up the hill.

Chapter Eight

He'd been idle long enough.

For months Gilchrist had wallowed in a dark misery born of the fire. His crippling burns, his bride's betrayal, the loss of his beloved uncle and aunt. He'd let the weight of his torment crush the life from him.

No more.

He was The Davidson, the chosen. His clan needed a leader, and he was that man—not Alex. Strangely enough, seeing Alex with Rachel that morning on the hillside only strengthened the other decision he'd made at the spring.

He must forget her.

Gilchrist wrapped his burned hand with the long strip of cloth he'd cut from his plaid, then turned to Hugh. "Tie it," he said.

Hugh raised a brow. "What d'ye mean to do?"

"I mean to work. Now tie it." He thrust his bandaged hand toward the warrior.

Hugh tied off the ends of the plaid, then shot him a sanguine look. "'Tis about time."

Gilchrist held his friend's gaze. "Aye."

Ten minutes later he had the bailey in an uproar. Warriors turned stonemasons labored under his orders; boys hauled water and buckets of clay; women scurried from the cottages to the keep bearing food and housewares for the kitchen.

Gilchrist stood in their midst and nodded in satisfaction. "We shall finish the castle—before the week's out."

One of the warriors looked up from his work. "But Alex said 'twould take at least a month—mayhap longer—to finish the job proper, and that we should no rush."

"Aye," another called out. "Alex said—"

"Is Alex laird here?" Gilchrist roared.

Those who heard him stopped their work and gawked in surprise. He fisted his hands at his sides and stifled the urge to knock some heads together. After all, he had no one to blame but himself for Alex usurping his authority.

"Why, nay," a young stable lad said, his arms shaking from the weight of the water buckets he bore. "Ye are laird here. The Davidson."

Slowly, one after another, his clansmen nodded in agreement. Some did so begrudgingly—he could see it in their faces. What more could he expect? 'Twas a start.

Gilchrist swallowed his anger. He rushed to help the boy, lifting the heavy buckets from his grasp. "Off with ye, now," he whispered. "See if Jamie needs your help. We can manage here."

The boy grinned brightly, took a few steps back, then turned and ran toward the stable yard.

"All right then," he called out to his clansmen, "back to work."

'Twas then he noticed Murdoch leaning casually against the arched entrance to the keep. The elder stared hard at him. Gilchrist returned his gaze, then strode to the pit where two clansmen were preparing mortar, and set the buckets down. Murdoch nodded.

The small sign of approval buoyed Gilchrist's confidence. He threw himself into the work at hand, ignoring the persistent chafing of his clothes against his right side. Blisters had risen again on his arm and torso.

The three days he'd spent at the virgin's spring had done some good, for his head if not his body. He winced at the memory of the two-day hangover. What bloody foolery. 'Twas a wonder he'd reached the spring at all, given his state when he left the alehouse.

"Laird!"

He looked up from his work to see Alex jogging toward him, out of breath, his expression grave. Christ, what now?

"Gilchrist, Laird." Alex placed a hand on his shoulder. "What are ye doing?"

"What does it look like? I'm working."

Alex took in the activity in the bailey, the progress made in barely an hour, and Gilchrist's sweat-soaked shirt. "But, 'tis too strenuous for ye. Your burns, ye might—"

He gripped Alex's wrist and removed the warrior's hand from his shoulder. "I might just finish the bluidy construction."

"But…I only meant…och, ye should leave this to me. You should be resting. Besides, the men work well under my direction."

He leveled his gaze at Alex. "Aye, it appears they do. And methinks 'tis more than castle building ye have a mind to command."

There. He'd said it.

The words hung like rank meat in the air between them.

Alex's face fell, as if he were suddenly stricken. "How can ye say such a thing? Have I not always been your friend since we were lads?"

'Twas true. They'd been thick as thieves as boys, the merry pranksters of Braedûn Lodge. As youths they drank and wenched together, fought and triumphed in the dark days when his brother Iain forged the alliance of the Chattan clans. Mackintosh and Davidson—there had always been a bond. He and Alex were brothers as surely as if they'd been born to it.

Yet Hugh's accusations continued to gnaw at him. Gilchrist shrugged. "'Tis no that, it's just…"

Alex nodded slowly, the corners of his mouth turned up in a thin smile. "Och, no matter. 'Tis forgotten."

But he could see from Alex's expression 'twould not be forgotten. Ah, Christ. Mayhap he'd judged him too harshly. After all, *he* was the one at fault all these months, not Alex. 'Twas only natural for the man to step in and aid him.

"Tell me how can I help ye, Laird?" The deference in Alex's voice was genuine, his eyes bright and warm.

Mayhap he should put this business behind them. Dropping the hammer, he wiped his brow and considered Alex's request. Aye, there was one thing he might do. "Ye can ride to Findhorn Castle and invite my brother to a celebration."

"What kind of celebration?" Alex's gaze lit on Arlys who worked with the women cutting straw. "Ye are not thinking of…surely not so soon?"

Gilchrist smiled, but felt no joy. "Nay, it's no that. It's this." He swept his arm in a wide circle, taking in the whole of the construction. "Monadhliath Castle—seat of the Davidson clan. 'Twill be finished soon, and I mean to celebrate our new beginning, our strength—" he stared into Alex's dark eyes "—our brotherhood."

"But, Laird, Gilchrist—I would not be away from our

demesne just now. There are matters, things, that need my attention.''

Gilchrist was not listening to him. Rachel walked up the path from the village toward the keep, toting a large basket overflowing with plants and wildflowers. The sun lit up her face and lent a reddish cast to her raven's-wing tumble of hair. She paused along the way to speak with some of the women. Only Arlys scowled and would not bid her welcome.

What would he do about Arlys? Wed her and forget her? As wife of the laird she'd lead a life of privilege and responsibility. He suspected 'twas the privilege she was after, and not the other. No matter. She was acceptable to the clan, and she served his purpose. 'Twas a good match, or so he was determined to convince himself.

A small child peeked out from behind his mother's skirts and handed Rachel a flower. From this distance Gilchrist could not tell its variety, but imagined it to be lavender—his favorite. He drew a breath and tried to recall the scent of it on her hair, the feel of her in his arms.

''What say you?'' Alex asked, wresting him from his thoughts. ''Can ye no send Hugh?''

''Hugh?'' The image of Alex kissing Rachel's open palm flashed suddenly in his mind. ''Nay, I wish ye to go. Today, in fact. Take a half-dozen men, your choice, and see ye are returned within the week.''

''But—''

''Do it,'' he said and reached for his hammer, tired of their conversation and eager to resume his work.

Rachel closed the old woman's book. ''That's enough for today, Peg.''

''But we was just getting to the truly interesting bits—

about the laird's burns and the old woman's treatments. Och, ye shouldha seen him then. His skin was all—''

"That's enough, I said!" Peg flinched and Rachel was immediately sorry for her sharp tongue. She reached her hand across the table and laid it atop the girl's. "I'm sorry. Truly. I did not mean to snap."

Peg smiled and squeezed her hand gently. "Och, dinna fash. I know ye fancy him. I peeked out my window one night and saw him standin' outside your door. It pains ye to read of his injuries, don't it?"

"You peeked out—" Had Peg seen them together? "I don't fancy him. What a thought." She drew her hand away and drummed it absently on the cover of the book. "My interest in your laird is purely charitable. He is injured, and I can heal him. Besides, I've read the passages before."

"So ye know about her, then? Methinks it explains his ill temper."

"Know about whom?"

Peg's eyes widened. She rose and began to clear the table of the parchment and writing implements they'd used in this evening's lesson.

Rachel grabbed her arm as she passed. "About whom? A woman?"

"Aye, but I thought ye knew, since ye read the book."

"There is no mention of a woman here." She flipped through the brittle pages until she found the passage that dealt with the fire and Gilchrist's burns. "Nay, there is nothing."

All at once, a sick feeling washed over her. She pulled Peg down on the bench beside her. "His wife. That's what you mean, isn't it? Gilchrist's wife." How stupid of her to think he had not yet wed. A man in his position—a warrior, a laird. Rachel wondered what had happened to the woman.

"Oh, nay, they was no to be wed until the winter. They was betrothed, but that was...before."

"Before the fire, you mean?"

"Aye."

Rachel stared into the hearth fire, but did not release her grip on Peg. "Sweet God, she died in the fire, didn't she?" Why hadn't Murdoch told her?

"Nay, Elizabeth Macgillivray is alive and well. She lives far from here now. 'Tis for the best, if ye take my meaning."

A knock sounded at the door.

Peg scurried to answer it. The deerskin covering was pulled tight across the window, and it wasn't possible to see who called. 'Twas late—even Peg was usually abed by now, in the small cottage next to Rachel's.

"Jamie!" Peg opened the door wide enough for the stable master to enter.

Rachel was disappointed at the interruption, but pleased for Peg. In the morning she would ask Murdoch about Elizabeth Macgillivray. She could only guess at what must have happened.

"Hello, Rachel, Peg," Jamie said. He ducked under the low door frame and entered the cottage. For a moment no one said a word. Peg stood, transfixed, her eyes round as saucers. Jamie held out a bandaged hand. "I've cut myself. Can ye tend it?"

Peg sprang forward and reached for his hand, but at the last moment drew back. The joy lighting her face was suddenly gone. She tentatively met his gaze. "Oh, ye would have Rachel tend it. 'Twas to her ye came."

Peg started to turn from him when he grasped her hand.

"Nay, 'twas you I sought, only ye wasna home. I thought to find ye here with the Englishwoman."

"Truly?" Peg breathed.

"Aye." He blushed, a handsome pink in the fire's glow.

Peg held his gaze as he unwrapped the crude bandage around his hand. Rachel stifled a giggle when she saw the cut. 'Twas little more than a scratch. She wondered if he'd done it on purpose just to have a reason to see Peg. At any rate, this seemed a good time to leave them alone.

"Um, I'll…um…just be going," she said and hurried to pack a few things in the old woman's kit.

Neither Peg nor Jamie heard her.

She threw a plaid over her shoulders to protect against the night chill, grabbed the kit, and quietly left the cottage. As she turned to pull the door closed behind her, she saw Peg tending Jamie's cut as if it were the most serious of wounds. The stable master looked on her with a kind of awe, his eyes replete with love.

Oh, what she would give for Gilchrist to look upon her so.

Ten minutes later she stood outside the keep, gazing up at the light coming from a small window overlooking the bailey. She knew without thinking, before she'd left the cottage, that this was where she was headed. She'd packed the things she would need. Now, if only he'd let her help him.

She pushed open the heavy door to the keep and swung it inward, effortlessly, on new hinges. The whole of the first floor was dark. She'd only been inside the once, the day her horse had been found. Peg told her that, after she'd swooned, Gilchrist had carried her to his chamber. She remembered waking on his pallet, his anxious face hovering above hers.

She felt her way in the dark along the wall until her hand reached out into nothingness. Ah, the staircase. She turned and nearly stumbled over the first step. It wound its way upward into the heart of the castle. She moved slowly, quietly, so as not to wake any that might be abed, though Alex had told her no one lived inside the keep, save Gilchrist. As soon as the first stones were laid, he'd begun sleeping there. She reached the second floor and stopped. Midway down the corridor she could see light peeking out from under a door.

Gilchrist's chamber.

Before she knew it, her hand was on the latch. She paused for a moment to consider just what it was she was doing.

Alex was her only hope of reaching Craigh Mur. He'd offered to take her, and for that she was grateful. As for the other things he offered… She was not interested. Though all he said was true, she would never bind herself to a man she did not love.

She would go to Craigh Mur—with Alex if need be— but first she would heal Gilchrist Mackintosh. She was determined, and would not leave Monadhliath Castle until 'twas done.

She tripped the latch and swung the door open.

He was sitting on a bench in front of the hearth fire, much as she'd seen him the very first time, without a stitch on. His plaid was draped casually over his burned thigh, as if he'd just removed it. His weapons and boots lay scattered across the floor; his bed was not yet disturbed.

"What do ye want?" he asked, neither bothering to cover himself nor to face her.

"I…um…" Her heart raced. "Your blisters—they need trouble you no longer."

He did turn then, and she was struck by the rugged beauty of his face in the fire's glow. "Oh, nay?" he said. "And what would ye know of them?"

Why was she so nervous? She was here to heal him— a skill in which she prided herself. "Only that they cause you pain and keep your skin from healing." She stepped inside the room and closed the door behind her. "There is a cure. I have seen it work with my own eyes."

He snorted. "Where? With whom?"

"I—I'm not certain. 'Twas in a sort of a castle—not like this, though. More of a... I don't know. I only recall bits and pieces, and not all of it makes sense."

"And the patient? Who was he?"

She stepped closer. "A villager. A woman burned in a kitchen fire. I don't remember any more."

"It doesna matter." He turned back toward the hearth.

She willed herself approach him, then set her kit on the rush-strewn floor. "Might I try, then? The cure." She held her breath and waited for his answer, her fear and her excitement growing with each second.

Without warning, he rose from the bench and faced her. Her eyes widened as his plaid slipped to the floor.

"As ye wish, healer."

Chapter Nine

He knew what would happen even before she touched him.

Rachel fixed her gaze on his, eyes wide, and blushed hotly. 'Twas the first time in—how long?—he felt like a man and not a monster.

He'd been thinking about her all evening—fantasizing, really. Such fantasies were dangerous. His desire for her was near overpowering. He knew what he must do.

"What's the matter, healer, have ye no seen a man unclothed before?"

Her dark brows arched prettily. "Dozens of them," she said and tilted her chin higher.

Gilchrist snorted. "It doesna surprise me." He sat back down on the bench before the hearth. "Well then, get on with it." He was deliberately cold to her, though she seemed unflustered by it.

She gripped the plaid that covered her shoulders and spun on her heel. Nay, she wasn't leaving? He felt a knot of regret and was ready to call her back. To his surprise, she retrieved a flagon of wine from the small table near his pallet and returned to his side, her expression cool.

"Move down," she said matter-of-factly, "closer to the fire, so that I might see you better."

He obeyed, pleased that he'd not driven her off, and slid farther along the bench toward the hearth. When he could feel the heat on his bare skin, he stopped.

"Closer," she said.

"Nay." He turned away from the flames and instinctively drew his burned arm across his lap. A shudder coursed through him. "'Tis close enough."

She met his gaze and her expression softened. "All right, I can see well enough." She knelt awkwardly before him, set the flagon down, and drew her kit closer.

He was determined not to look at her, and fixed his gaze on the shield mounted on the wall opposite from where he sat. A cat reared up on hind legs, teeth and claws bared at the ready, was carved into the smooth wooden surface—the symbol of the Chattan clans: Davidson, Mackintosh, Macgillivray, MacBain. Macphearson would make them five.

When he felt Rachel's hand on his thigh he tensed, and focused all his thoughts on his family, his clan, his duty.

"Turn your leg toward me," she said quietly, "just so."

He complied, allowing her to position him to her liking. She fumbled around, one-handed, in the kit she'd brought with her. Her other hand rested absently on his knee, her light touch sparking a desire he worked desperately to control.

He traced the outline of her long, slender fingers with his eyes, then stole a glance at her. She was lovely in the firelight, her brow furrowed in concentration.

The plaid draped across her shoulders slipped to the floor. She didn't notice, so caught up was she in her work.

She looked up suddenly and caught him staring. He willed her to hold his gaze but she quickly looked away.

"All right," she said, "I'm ready to begin."

He surveyed the items she'd drawn from the kit: small leather pouches—the kind the old woman used for herbs—a mortar and pestle, some white cloth and, most strange of all, a rare glass vial. "What's that?" He nodded at the vial.

"You'll see." She inspected the smattering of new blisters that rose on his arm.

"I dinna get them elsewhere—just there—but damned if I know how to stop them."

"'Twill take some time—a few weeks, mayhap. But the cure is near foolproof."

He watched her as she worked, methodically and with the same focus and determination he'd seen when she'd treated the boy. He'd never known a woman like her, except perhaps his brother's wife. He smiled at the memory of Iain and Alena's stormy courtship. She, too, had been a woman of grit and fortitude. Rachel turned for a moment toward the hearth, and the firelight danced in her gray-green eyes.

"'Twould have to be foolproof," he murmured, "for I'm fast becoming the fool."

She looked up at him. "What did you say?"

"Och, nothing." He quickly looked away, abashed, and bade her continue.

Rachel emptied the contents of the small pouches into the mortar. He could not discern what was in them. Then, to his astonishment, she drew a wren's egg from a pocket in her gown, cracked it into the mortar, and cast the empty shell onto the fire.

"An egg?"

"Aye," she said, not looking up from her work. "To help bind the ointment."

Into the strange-looking concoction she poured some of the wine from the flagon he kept in his chamber to ease him on nights he couldn't sleep. He considered that since he'd found her at the spring, those nights had become more frequent.

She pulled a small dirk from the belt at her waist and began to cut the cloth into strips. "The arm must be tightly bound. It will be painful at first, but the discomfort will wane in a few days' time."

If there was one thing he knew about, 'twas pain. He lifted his arm so she could bind it. Working quickly, she spread the cool salve over his fire-ravaged skin. He'd expected it to burn, but 'twas surprisingly cool.

"What else is in it?" he asked.

"Crocus, camphor, a mucilage of quince—and opium." She met his gaze. "For the pain."

He began to pull his arm away, but she held it fast and finished the binding.

"Opium? I have heard of it, but from where did ye get it?"

"The old woman's apothecary. It surprised me, as well." She looked at him thoughtfully for a moment, then said, "Don't worry, 'tis a tiny dose, just enough to take the edge off the pain. What little there is goes direct into the body."

He marveled at her knowledge of such things. "How do ye know?"

"I have seen it used many times—I think." She shook her head. "Strange, the things I remember. Most of it seems useless, but this—" she gestured to the bandage which she tied tightly at his shoulder "—this I am glad to have recalled."

He smiled. There was a warmth about her that stirred him. The memory of their moonlit kiss consumed him. He longed to hold her, taste her, feel her arms around him, just once more.

Christ—he'd forgotten his nakedness!

He snatched his plaid from the floor and draped it strategically across his lap. He wanted her—there was no denying it. 'Twas apparent by her startled expression the evidence of his desire had not gone unnoticed by her.

He focused his gaze on the Chattan shield and tried for all the world to get a grip on himself. This could not be— him with her. He could not allow it. "Ye can go now," he said roughly. "My thanks to ye, healer."

"But I am not yet finished." Her voice was calm, steady.

"Aye, ye are." He dared not meet her gaze. "Now go."

Rachel ignored him, picked up the strange glass vial, and removed the stopper. Her impertinence was intolerable. She poured the clear, fragrant liquid into her cupped palm then rubbed her hands together vigorously.

Roses. Damned if the liquid didn't smell of roses. 'Twas a fragrance he'd almost forgotten. His aunt used to grow them in the garden at Braedûn Lodge. He would walk there in the afternoons with Elizabeth Macgillivray, and she would pick them and cast the petals to the ground before her.

"Nay," he breathed and tried to rise from the bench.

Rachel pushed him firmly back down. "I said I was not yet finished." He tried to interrupt her but she ignored him. "Your skin…'tis tight and pains you when you move." Her hand gripped his knee, warm and slick from the scented liquid.

"Aye," he said, "how did ye know?"

"'Tis common after a burn. Did the old woman not massage the new skin?"

He nodded. "Before she passed, she'd rub me down each day with some foul-smelling concoction. 'Tis been some months now."

Rachel ran her hand lightly over his thigh, pushing the plaid away from the burned areas. Her touch evoked a whole range of sensation—pleasure, pain, excitement, anticipation. He closed his eyes and let her do it. What else could he do?

"What is it?" he whispered. "The liquid."

"Rose oil. I found it among my things in Glenna's saddlebag."

She worked her way skillfully up his thigh, gently massaging the oil into his skin. The fragrance was heady, the fire warm. He let go his racing thoughts, his fears, and focused only on her touch. 'Twas wondrous—nothing at all like when the old woman had massaged him.

"Relax," she whispered. Even the sound of her voice calmed him.

He did relax and let his head roll back. Her fingers moved over his skin in small circles, upward along the length of his thigh and across his hip. As her hands moved higher she must have leaned closer, for her hair spilled over his naked thigh—a cascade of hot silk.

He opened his eyes and watched her. She was radiant, beautiful, and completely unaware of her effect on him. Her gaze moved over his body, taking in, he noticed, more than what a mere healer would be concerned with. She wet her lips unconsciously—ripe cherries in the firelight. He felt himself grow hard under the plaid.

Her gray-green eyes met his.

"Dinna stop," he breathed. "'Tis heavenly."

She blushed but did not lower her eyes. He felt her

fingers tremble slightly against his ribs. Damn him to hell, but he could bear this exquisite torture no longer.

"Ah, Rachel." He cast the plaid aside and slipped to the floor, drawing her into his arms. "I canna help what I feel."

"Gilchrist," she whispered.

Her arms went around him as his mouth covered hers. All his noble intentions, his well-laid plans, fled at the first taste of her. She was ardent, responsive, all that he remembered from that night in her cottage, and more.

Her lips parted in submission to the gentle prodding of his tongue. He deepened the kiss and crushed her to him. She whimpered as he ground his hips against hers and moved his hands to cup her buttocks.

He wanted her.

He loved her.

Christ, 'twas madness. He'd promised himself he'd never allow these feelings again—for any woman. They were faithless—all of them—and liars. He had loved once, and where had that got him? Elizabeth Macgillivray's coquettish laugh played at the corners of his mind.

"Say it's not true," Rachel whispered against his mouth.

Her sweetness, her warmth, her strength and fearlessness, threatened to drive out his demons and slay his better judgment. He was on dangerous ground. He kissed her again, deeply, passionately, with all that he felt for her, then buried his face in the dark fall of her hair.

"Say it's not true," she whispered again, this time more urgently.

"What, sweetling?" He should push her away, put an end to this madness. What had he been thinking to allow this to happen? She looked into his eyes, and he feared to lose his soul.

"Alex says you are to wed Arlys. Is it true?"

His heart skipped a beat.

"Is it?"

"Aye," he breathed.

She gripped him harder and stifled a gasp. "Do—do you love her?"

He was close to being out of control, his feelings for her hurtling him toward certain disaster. He'd put an end to it. Now.

"Aye," he said.

She searched his face for the truth of it, and he hardened his heart lest he give himself away.

"Yet you make love to me." Her voice was but a whisper. All the light went out of her eyes.

The lie was too much for him to bear. "Rachel, I—"

"Nay, say no more." She looked away.

"Ye—ye dinna understand."

"Oh, I understand plenty." She wrested herself from his grasp and quickly gathered her things into the kit. "Alex was right—we are two of a kind, he and I. After all, you did find me at the spring." She picked up the dirk that lay on the floor next to her, and scrambled to her feet. "Is that not where whores seek absolution?"

He willed himself answer, but could not bring himself to do it.

"Is it not?" She gripped the dirk, white-knuckled, trembling, and looked down at him. Her expression was hard, her eyes a cool shade of gray, but behind the facade he read her pain. Christ, why didn't she slit his throat and be done with it?

"Aye," he whispered, hating himself for it, and lowered his eyes. "That's what they say."

A small noise escaped her throat. She thrust the dirk

into its scabbard, grabbed the kit, and fled the chamber, leaving the door wide.

"God forgive me." Turning to the hearth, he moved his good hand, one finger extended, toward the dancing flames. He stopped only when the pain was brilliant enough to drive out all other feeling.

Try to remember.

Rachel closed her eyes and concentrated on the high place. 'Twas stark yet beautiful in her mind—not a place to be feared. "Craigh Mur," she whispered to herself. "What does it mean?"

"'Tis just a hill."

The voice startled her and she snapped to attention. One of the women working in the castle garden peeked into the dark root cellar where Rachel was arranging flats of dried herbs.

"There's no much there—I've seen it myself. Just a bunch o' stones is all." The woman shrugged and moved on.

Rachel sighed and continued with her work. Mayhap she'd never remember. That thought had not occurred to her until now. She'd read about memory loss in a rare medical book she'd once seen. But where had she seen it? And who had allowed her to read it?

When she concentrated too hard and for too long, her head ached. She'd best get Peg to gather more valerian. She was determined to remember—and return to wherever it was she had come from.

Monadhliath Castle was no place for her. Oh, the clan had come to accept her well enough. She was useful to them. They needed a good healer, and Peg was not ready to shoulder the responsibility herself.

But what did they truly think of her? Some called her

witch, and others, whore. She'd seen how the Davidsons treat such women. Moira, Alex's mother, lived in near seclusion in that filthy cottage. Many thought her mad. Who wouldn't be? 'Twas not a happy life for women labeled so.

And what of Gilchrist? Did he view *her* in that same light?

Rachel set down the tray she was holding and slumped onto the stool in the corner of the dark cellar. His words would have her think so. But his kisses, the way he'd held her, his whispered endearments—they were not without feeling.

When she'd laid her hands upon him, he gave up more than his physical pain. His tight muscles unwound as she'd worked them. He'd relaxed, he'd trusted her, yet there was something else...

His breathy sighs and nearly inaudible moans had not escaped her notice. 'Twas more than the hands of a healer he had responded to, and the knowledge of his desire had fueled her own. Had he not taken her in his arms and kissed her, she might have gone mad with need for him.

That need burned still.

"What's this, sleeping at midday?"

Rachel snapped to attention and saw Arlys's form silhouetted in the cellar doorway. She jumped up and grabbed the tray of herbs she'd been arranging. "Nay, I was just—"

"Come out of there, I need your help."

Now this was strange, Arlys asking her for help. She set the tray down, ducked under the low cellar doorway, and stepped out into the garden. She squinted as her eyes adjusted to the bright sunlight.

Arlys stood facing her, hands fisted on hips. "We are stocking the kitchen and I'm to bring some marshmal-

low." She scanned the tangle of herbs and spring wildflowers that choked the garden. "Show me what it looks
like."

Rachel suppressed a smile. "You're standing on it."

"What, this?" Arlys looked down at the trampled plant
under her feet.

"Aye, but 'tis the root they'll want." She knelt and
unsheathed her dirk. "Here, let me show you."

Arlys stepped back, but did not kneel to help her.

Working quickly, Rachel dug up the root, brushed the
dirt from it, and trimmed away the rest of the plant. She
rose and handed it to the waiting Arlys. "This will do."

They locked gazes and, for a moment, she thought Arlys might actually thank her. She didn't. God knows why
but, when Arlys turned to leave, Rachel blurted out,
"Congratulations!"

Arlys stopped and narrowed her eyes. "What for?"

"Your...upcoming marriage to the laird."

Her face immediately brightened. "Ah, 'tis true then!"

She didn't know?

"I'd heard Hugh speak of it, but I wasna certain."

Rachel's brows shot up and she fought the urge to let
her mouth drop open. "But Gilchrist, the laird, did he not
speak to you—or your parents?"

Arlys snorted. "My parents are dead."

This was very strange indeed. The girl was to wed him,
yet Gilchrist had not even asked her. She remembered
their kiss in front of the cottage, a basket of broken honey
cakes scattered at their feet. She decided to probe further.
"You are pleased with the match?"

Arlys tipped her chin high and smirked. "Aye, who
wouldna be? He is laird, is he no?"

There was a commotion in the bailey, and both of them
turned their attention toward the ruckus. Gilchrist worked

alongside three other men to move a large stone into place near the castle steps. He was shirtless and sweating, the bandages from his bound arm reduced to filthy rags. She would remember to send Peg to change the dressing. One of the fingers of his good hand was wrapped in a piece of cloth. She'd noticed it the other day and wondered what had happened.

"He was fair to look upon once," Arlys said. "Now look at him." She visibly shuddered. "I expect I can tolerate his touch—if I must."

Rachel recalled Gilchrist's mouth on hers, his strong arms around her. Her pulse quickened.

"They say he's burnt near all over. Why..." Arlys turned to her, eyes wide. "Perhaps he *canna*...ye know. D'ye take my meaning?"

She knew exactly what Arlys meant, but knew for a fact Gilchrist *could*. Her cheeks flamed at the memory of his body crushed against hers. Hot steel. Aye, he could and would have, had she allowed it.

"No matter," Arlys said. "I shall take a lover." She stroked the marshmallow root suggestively. "Two, mayhap."

The woman was outrageous. Rachel was ready to end the conversation. She turned on her heel toward the cellar, but Arlys grabbed her arm.

"No so fast, *healer*. There's another thing I wish ye to know." Rachel met her gaze. "My first act as wife of the laird, and lady of Monadhliath Castle, will be to send ye back to where ye belong."

She wrenched her arm free of Arlys's grip. "You have no cause for concern on that point. I plan to be gone long before the wedding."

Gilchrist pulled the cottage door closed behind him and leaned back on the door frame. Murdoch never stirred.

The elder sat by the hearth, smoking his pipe, ostensibly lost in thought. Curling tendrils of smoke wafted lazily upward and hung in the air like a cloud above his head. Gilchrist inhaled the familiar, aromatic blend and immediately relaxed.

"So, ye've finally come," Murdoch said without looking up.

"Aye."

It had been months, in fact, since Gilchrist had paid a late-night visit to Murdoch. Before the fire, he used to come to the elder's cottage often, sharing news, seeking advice, or just to talk. They'd sit up sometimes until dawn discussing everything from clan politics to Gilchrist's latest love interest.

Murdoch pointed his pipe toward the stool opposite him. "Sit," he said. "We've much to catch up on."

Gilchrist took his customary seat. The cottage was new, and far from Braedûn Lodge, but Murdoch's calm demeanor remained unchanged and put him at ease.

"I've come to tell ye of my plan to…to wed."

Murdoch thoughtfully blew a puff of smoke into the air. "I have heard of this plan."

"I must do it, to secure my place as laird. D'ye no agree?"

"Ye are laird already," Murdoch said. "What makes ye think ye must defend your position?"

He could think of a dozen reasons, but one would suffice. "For all that I was raised here, I am still a Mackintosh. Methinks the clan would better accept me if I were to wed one of their own."

"Arlys, ye mean?"

He nodded.

"This marriage—'twas Alex's idea?"

"Nay, Hugh's. In fact, Alex is against it. Methinks he wants her for himself, and yet…'' He considered the abrupt change he'd seen in Alex since Rachel had arrived; his affection for Arlys seemed to have all but vanished.

"Have ye no considered there might be other reasons for Alex's censure?''

He met the elder's gaze. "Nay, I have not.''

Murdoch's blue eyes reflected the firelight. They sat there for a moment, not speaking. Then Murdoch said, "Would it please the clan, d'ye think, to see their laird in a loveless union, even to one o' their own?''

Gilchrist considered his aunt and uncle's thirty-odd-year marriage. Their love was near legendary in the Highlands. "Love,'' he said derisively, wresting himself from Murdoch's all-knowing gaze. "What has that to do with my decision?''

"Mayhap nothing. Mayhap everything.''

Gilchrist snorted. "Ye would have me follow my heart? Nay, I'll no be led by the nose down that path again.''

Murdoch arched a snowy brow. "Methinks ye are half-way there already, and have covered the distance of your own free will.''

"Bah! Ye are mistaken.'' He rubbed viciously at his bandaged arm until the new dressing Peg had applied came loose.

"Am I?'' Murdoch said. He nodded to the frayed bandage.

"What? The healer? Christ, she's English!'' He shot from the stool and turned away.

"So she is.''

He whirled on the elder. "Ye would have me wed an outsider? Are ye daft?''

"Your brother did.''

Murdoch was right. Alena was half French and half

Scots...a Grant, enemy of Clan Mackintosh for years. Still, Iain had wed her and made peace among the clans. They were both highly respected, by his clan and by hers.

"Well, it doesna matter. I've no interest in her. She doesna even know who she is or what she's left behind." He sat heavily on the stool and looked at Murdoch. "How is any man to judge her?"

"As do the women."

Gilchrist frowned.

"By her actions," Murdoch said, and emptied the bowl of his pipe into the fire.

Gilchrist snorted and rose. "As usual, I've come to ye with questions, and ye answer me in riddles." He moved toward the door. "'Tis time I found my bed."

Murdoch laughed. "Ye need no have asked at all, for ye already know the answers." The elder rose stiffly, joints creaking, and held the door whilst he stepped out into the night. "But I am glad ye did—an old man likes to feel needed now and then."

Gilchrist nodded and let the corners of his mouth turn up in a smile. "So, *old man,* are ye no curious as to what I'll do?"

Murdoch looked at him thoughtfully. "Methinks soon enough we shall all know your mind—and your heart."

Chapter Ten

She was lovely.

*Dark hair floated about her as if on a whispered breath,
framing her delicate features. He took her hand in his and
together they moved through the sea of lavender and evening primrose.*

*She smiled and bade him sit with her on the stone bench
in the garden. A nightjar perched in the tree above them
began his evening revelry, though the sun had not yet set.
They both paused to listen.*

*When he tried to kiss her she laughed and pulled away.
He laughed, too. Fisting a handful of her hair, he drew
her closer. His kiss was shockingly ardent, not at all what
she'd expected. He lifted the dark tresses from off her
slender neck, revealing her secret.*

A shock of snow-white hair at her nape.

The mark.

*She broke the kiss and gazed with adoration into his
eyes. He drew her hand to his lips. The last rays of the
sun blazed over the garden wall and glinted off the silver
ring gracing her third finger.*

Suddenly, everything was dark. The lovers vanished

*and she found herself at the base of a windswept ridge—
the high place. Craigh Mur.*

*She looked up and there he was. The man—dark and
looming, framed against a slate-and-midnight backdrop
of standing stones and sky. He searched for something,
for someone—*

For her.

She called to him, why couldn't he see her?

*And then she was running, branches and brambles tear-
ing at her shift. She turned and screamed as a gauntleted
hand gripped her arm and jerked her backward.*

"Rachel, wake up!"

Her eyes flew open and she bolted from the pallet. Her
heart pounded in her chest. A sheen of sweat drenched
her body.

"Are ye not well?"

Sunlight streamed through the open cottage door. She
drew a deep, shuddering breath and focused her eyes on
the tall warrior.

Alex.

"What—what do you want?" she said and quickly
pulled the plaid from the bed to cover herself.

He scanned the room as if looking for someone else,
then stepped across the threshold. "I knocked, but ye
didna answer."

"I—I was sleeping." She felt groggy and a little dis-
oriented. Alex's unexpected visit did naught to calm her.
She recalled the strange feeling she'd had about him that
day near the wood. "I thought you were away."

"I was. I have returned." He took another step toward
her and her uneasiness grew. "I would have arrived
sooner, but my horse came up lame. He's a good mount.
I didna wish to kill him, so I walked him the rest of the
way."

His compassion surprised her. She began to relax, then remembered. "Good God, what's the time?" She rushed past him to the door and squinted against the brightness as she fixed her eyes on the sun. "I'm late!"

She turned and caught his shocked expression. "I'm to meet a few of the women this morning." She sidestepped him and reached for her gown which lay neatly folded atop the small trunk at the foot of her pallet. "I must dress. Will you…wait outside."

He smiled, all charm and accommodation. "Of course. I shall accompany you."

His presumptuousness annoyed her, but she was too late to concern herself about it now. After he closed the door behind him, she cast off the plaid and quickly donned her gown. 'Twas warm and she was still perspiring from her unsettling dreams or Alex's surprise visit, she wasn't certain which.

She poured some water from the ewer on the table into a shallow bowl and washed her face and hands. She'd no time for a bath now, even a quick one. She had promised Agnes and some of the other women that she would teach them about mushrooms—which ones were safe and which were poison.

She slipped on her shoes, sturdy deerskin slippers that had been found in Glenna's saddlebag, and smoothed her gown. Alex waited outside for her. She was not in the mood to speak with him, but could see no way out of it. She didn't realize until now just how much she'd enjoyed his absence this past week.

When she stepped outside, sure enough, there he was, waiting for her. She walked quickly up the hill toward the castle. Predictably, he fell in step beside her.

"Did ye miss me?" he asked.

The question caught her off guard. "The time went by so quickly—I was so busy I hardly noticed—"

"I've brought ye a gift."

He stopped and grasped her arm, gently but with a hint of bridled force behind it that unnerved her.

"A gift?"

"'Tis just a trinket, really. But I thought ye would like it."

He reached into the badgerskin sporran belted at his waist and drew out a long silver chain. Dangling from the end of it was a small pink stone set in hammered silver. 'Twas some kind of gemstone, the like of which she'd never seen.

Or had she?

"'Tis lovely," she said, marveling at how the natural planes of the stone reflected the light.

He beamed a smile at her and began to slip the chain around her neck.

She backed up a step. "Oh, nay, I couldn't accept it."

"But, 'tis a gift—I wish ye to have it." He frowned, his disappointment so keen she felt a twinge of remorse for her hasty refusal. He reached for her hand, brushed his lips across her fingertips then placed the necklace into her open palm. "Will ye no let me give you this one thing?"

She didn't want the gift, but felt compelled to take it. There was something in his eyes that made her feel—what? Pity, she supposed it was. The feeling intensified as she placed the chain around her neck and his face lit up.

"Have ye considered my offer?" he whispered, moving closer to her.

Whatever it was she'd felt for him the moment before, vanished. She turned and strode purposefully up the hill.

A sudden movement on her right caught her attention. She glanced up just as a cottage door closed.

Arlys's cottage.

Alex moved swiftly to her side, his gaze riveted to the closed door. His expression was blank, but she perceived a tension in his demeanor that belied his attempt at nonchalance.

"Have ye?" he repeated and took her arm as she hurried up the hill.

She had considered it, a number of times, in fact, but had rejected the idea, each time with more conviction. She would not wed a man she didn't love, regardless of her situation and how much she might need his help.

Nay, if this was his price for taking her to Craigh Mur, 'twas too dear. She'd find another way to get there, someone else to take her. Hugh, perhaps. He'd warmed to her of late. Or Murdoch. The elder seemed to understand her. In truth, sometimes she was certain he could read her every thought.

She quickened her pace but Alex did not let go her arm. He was waiting for an answer. They reached the curtain wall and she stopped before the open gate. "I have given your proposal a great deal of thought, and I—"

"Ho, what's this? I didna know ye were back."

Hugh stood in the lower bailey, a sack of what had to be grain thrown over his shoulder. He eyed Alex suspiciously.

Alex released her arm and fisted his hands on his hips. "What, have ye taken to baking now? Or is it brewing?"

Hugh heaved the sack from off his shoulder and it landed on the ground with a thud. In three strides he was there. Instinctively, she moved between the two warriors.

She had never seen two men more at odds than these

two. How they both could be close to Gilchrist—and at the same time—defied imagination.

"I am glad to see you, Hugh," she said. "There is something I would speak to you about, if you've time. I was just on my way to the stable to meet Agnes, but perhaps later…"

He was not listening to her. He glared at Alex over the top of her head. Any moment the two of them would kill each other. She could feel it.

"Hugh." She reached out and gripped his forearm.

"What?"

She was about to speak when he looked down at her, his gaze traveling from her face to the valley between her breasts.

He frowned. "What have ye here?" He stared at the pink stone hanging from the silver chain around her neck.

"'Tis a gift from me." Alex stepped closer and gripped her arms possessively from behind.

She was wedged in between the two of them, and felt not unlike a bone cast to the ground between two dogs.

"Where did ye get this gift?" Hugh demanded.

"Traveling," Alex said evenly.

She'd had enough. If they wanted to kill each other, so be it. Gilchrist would be better off without them. She wrenched herself out of Alex's grasp and stepped back out of the way.

"Traveling," Hugh repeated.

"Aye."

"There's only one place has stones the like o' that." Hugh nodded to the necklace and briefly met her gaze.

"I dinna ken what ye mean." Alex said.

She closed her hand absently over the stone and squeezed. The high place flashed in her mind. She drew a breath and caught the scent of heather on the wind.

Craigh Mur.

Hugh continued to nod. "There's only one Highland clan works silver with gems."

The day she'd first remembered the name of the high place, Peg had blurted out whose land it lay upon.

Macphearson.

She looked down at her hand clutching the stone, and studied the silver ring on her third finger. Sunlight glinted off the bright metal, reminding her of something. Lovers in a garden. Her dream!

"God's blood," she breathed.

"Hold still." Peg wrestled with the filthy and tattered bandage. Gilchrist grunted and raised his arm higher to give her better access. "What have ye been doin', rollin' in the mud?"

This was a new and bolder Peg. The mouse had become quite the little lion. He did not wonder from whom she'd learnt it—'twas plain. Rachel.

"I've been working," he said. "Ye know that."

She arched a brow at him.

"Look, 'tis nearly done." He nodded to the bailey below them where clansmen and -women worked to clear the last of the construction rubble away.

"Aye, well, 'tis fine and all o' that, but look at yer arm." Peg stripped the last of the cloth away and they both inspected the scarring.

"'Tis no so bad." In fact, his arm felt good. A fortnight of pressure bandages and rose oil massage, administered by Peg under Rachel's orders, did much to improve his condition.

"The blistering's gone for good, methinks." Peg nodded, satisfied. "But the skin is no so supple as Rachel said 'twould be. We must continue the massage."

"What, out here, on the battlement?" He twisted on the stool Peg had brought with her and insisted he sit on. They were partially hidden behind a stack of unused timbers and stones that had yet to be cleared away.

"Aye. Rachel says the fresh air will do the arm good." Peg poured a stream of rose oil into her hands, rubbed them briskly together, and began to massage him.

"Does she." He closed his eyes and tried to recall Rachel's hands moving over his body. The light, almost sensuous strokes, her warm breath on his skin, her breast grazing his thigh as she leaned too close.

"Ruck up that plaid so I can do yer leg," Peg ordered, and slapped his thigh as if it were a piece of meat.

The pleasant memory vanished from his mind. He shot her an irritated glance, but did as he was told, marveling at her transformation. In addition to her newfound skills, Peg's confidence had grown tenfold. She was nearly as ornery as the old woman had been. Aye, she'd make the clan a good healer. He had Rachel to thank for that.

"Flex that hand a bit. Rachel says ye must use it, more and more, so the skin doesna draw so tight around the flesh and bone."

He opened his scarred hand and stretched the fingers as wide as he could. It hurt, but the pain was tolerable. Since he'd been working with the men, he noticed his range of motion had improved considerably. Peg vigorously rubbed the muscles of his back and shoulders. It did feel good.

"Rachel says I'm to massage the good parts as well as the burnt."

"Is that so?" He wasn't about to stop her, but he was curious as to why she'd been given that instruction.

"Aye, she says ye've been workin' like a draft horse

and will likely be sore after so much…'' Her hands paused at the tight muscles in his neck.

"So much what?''

"Weel, the word she used was…*inactivity*.''

He sat taller on the stool.

"I think what she means is ye've done nothin' for so long and—'' he tensed and knew she could feel it ''—och, I didna mean that, I only meant—''

He shrugged off her hands and began to put his shirt back on.

"But, Laird, we're no finished yet.''

"Aye, we're done for the day.''

Peg knelt before him and gathered her things into the leather kit she'd brought with her. "I—I'm sorry, I didna mean to—''

He grabbed her wrist to still her and her eyes widened in fear. "No harm done, lass.'' She reminded him of a cornered rabbit. He fought the smile forming on his lips. "Rachel's right—I've done nothing for far too long. But that's behind me now.'' He nodded once, for emphasis, then released her.

"What about yer arm? Ye havena let me bind it.''

He rotated his shoulder and stretched his arm back as far as it would go. "Ah, the freedom feels too good.'' The pain was there, but 'twas tolerable.

"But the blisters… Rachel will—''

"Aye, she'll have your head, methinks.'' Warmth grew inside him at the thought of Rachel caring whether or not he healed or felt pain.

He'd hurt her that night in his chamber, and for that he could not forgive himself. But 'twas all for the best. She'd stayed away from him, and he'd not approached her.

How many nights had he stood before her cottage in

the dark, battling the urge to fling the door wide and gather her up in his arms.

How he longed to hold her, kiss her, make her his.

"Bluidy hell," he muttered.

"What?" Peg stood before him, ready to take her leave.

"Och, nothing. I was just… Ye may come on the morrow and bind the arm."

She smiled. "'Tis only for another week. Rachel says 'twill be full healed by then."

"What else does Rachel say?"

Peg cocked her head and wrinkled her brow. "What d'ye mean?"

He rose and stretched again, then stepped to the edge of the battlement and looked out across the Davidson demesne. "I just wondered how she was getting on."

"Oh, fine, just fine. Half the mothers of the clan have been bringing their bairns to her for all manner o' treatments."

This did not surprise him. She'd won their hearts—most of them, at any rate—when she'd saved Agnes's lad. Since then, he'd seen how the clan had warmed to her. And those who scorned her still? God's blood if she didn't seek them out apurpose!

She was fearless. He loved that about her.

"Come here, hurry!"

The feminine voice wrenched him out of his momentary stupor. He looked back at Peg who stood motionless behind the pile of timber and stone, brows arched in curiosity.

The woman giggled. He recognized the sound.

"Arlys." The deep, masculine voice belonged to Alex. "Come on, there's no one here."

Peg started to move but Gilchrist closed the distance between them in two strides and pushed her flat against the inner wall. He knelt beside her and looked up, one finger to his lips, indicating he wished her to be silent. As long as Alex and Arlys did not pass directly in front of where he and Peg were hidden, they would remain unseen.

He heard Arlys laugh and a scuffle of feet on the stone battlement. "I've work to do," Alex said. "I've no time for foolishness."

"But I've hardly seen ye since ye've been back. Didna ye miss me?" Her tone was unmistakably suggestive.

Peg's eyes widened. She opened her mouth as if to speak and Gilchrist quickly clamped a hand over it.

"Ye shouldna speak so," Alex said. "'Tis no— Wait, what are ye doing?"

Arlys giggled. Gilchrist and Peg heard the sounds of rustling clothes.

"Stop it, nay dinna—" Alex groaned then, deep and guttural.

'Twas all Gilchrist could do to keep Peg from bolting from their hiding place. He pulled her down beside him and with his eyes and expression threatened bloody murder should she utter a sound.

Alex's groans grew more and more urgent. Arlys's squeaks and whimpers joined them. 'Twas over in barely a minute. Alex let out one long, shuddering moan, then all was silent.

Peg stopped holding her breath. Gilchrist could tell because the color began to return to her face. In fact, the longer he looked at her, the brighter her cheeks flamed. Poor lass. But what could he have done? He might have shown himself immediately, he supposed. He would have, had he known what was going to happen.

"There," Arlys said. "Now kiss me."

After a moment, Alex sighed. "Why did ye do that? Christ, you'll be the death of me."

"I wished to remind ye what ye've been missing. Methinks the English healer has no my skill—be she whore or no."

"That's enough. Dinna speak such things."

"Do ye care for her? I saw the two of ye together the other day. I thought mayhap ye were trying to make me jealous."

"I must go. Gilchrist will wish to see me."

Alex's heavy boots scraped across the battlement.

"Wait," Arlys said. "There is one thing I must know."

Alex's footfalls stopped. "What?"

"Will things change between us when I am the laird's wife? Oh, Alex, say they willna."

Gilchrist bristled.

"Let go of me," Alex said. "I must leave." They heard his footfalls on the stone steps, then silence.

Peg rose and, before Gilchrist could stop her, bolted in the direction of the other staircase at the opposite end of the battlement.

Gilchrist slumped back against the wall and drove his head backward purposefully against the stone. "Hell and damnation!"

"Is someone there?" The voice startled him; he'd thought everyone had gone. Before he could rise, Arlys stepped out in front of the hiding place. Her pretty mouth dropped open. "What are— Oh God, how long have ye—"

"Long enough." He sprang to his feet and brushed past her.

"But, Laird, Gilchrist, wait!"

He waved her off and made for the stairs. "Dinna come near me." A minute later he was in the bailey, dodging workmen and small children who played in sight of their mothers.

'Twas ridiculous, his anger. What did he care for Arlys Davidson? Not a whit. 'Twas why she was such a perfect bride. Alex loved her. He was certain of it. Yet Alex didn't encourage her obvious affection—not since Hugh had hatched this wedding scheme. How could he have doubted his loyalty?

As for Arlys... She was like all women—mercenary, faithless, ready to spread her legs for the highest bidder. Elizabeth Macgillivray's twisted smile flashed briefly in his mind. He muttered a string of obscenities under his breath. A few of his kinsmen looked up, brows raised, as he barreled past them down the hill.

He rounded the curtain wall and collided with a worker. "Bluidy hell, watch where ye're going!"

"Oh, I'm sorry, I—"

"Rachel." His heart skipped a beat.

The bundles of cloth she'd been carrying slipped from her grasp and landed with a soft thud on the ground. Their eyes locked. She wanted to say something, he could tell, but no words escaped her lips.

Her hair was wild about her face, as if she'd been working and had not the time to fix it. Her cheeks were flushed a delicate shade of pink and her eyes shone, gray-green in the morning light.

The memory of Arlys's squeaks and whimpers flooded his ears. A vision of Elizabeth Macgillivray, stripped of her ladylike finery and writhing under her new husband, burned on the backs of his eyelids.

They were all alike.

Love was for fools and weaklings.

He brushed past Rachel, not even bothering to help her

retrieve the bundles. As he strode down the hill toward Murdoch's cottage, she called out after him.

"I thought you'd like to know, your brother Iain is newly arrived."

He stopped, then whirled on her.

"Didn't you see him?"

He marched back up the hill to where she stood, chin tipped so she might look directly at him. God's blood, the woman was impertinent. "Where is he?" he demanded.

She arched her dark brows, clearly not intimidated by his brusqueness. "In the stable, seeing to his mount." She hoisted the bundles of cloth with a feminine grunt. "I was just going there myself. If you were a gentleman, you'd help me with these."

The little vixen! Wrenching the bundles from her grasp, he took off up the hill, acutely aware of her light footsteps behind him as she tried to keep up.

He didn't love her. He didn't. Bloody hell, he wouldn't allow it!

Chapter Eleven

He hated her. Fine.

'Twas time she took her leave—of him, Alex and the rest of Clan Davidson. Today was as good a day as any. Now she had a name to go with the place.

Macphearson.

But why had she ridden into the Highlands of Scotland in search of them? She had no idea. She remembered nothing, nor did the name spark even vague recollection. The dreams, her ring—they were clues in what seemed an impossible puzzle.

She knew in what direction Craigh Mur lay, and from the little information she'd gleaned talking to Peg and the other women these past weeks, she deduced 'twas little more than a day's ride, two at most.

'Twas settled then. She had her own mount and a clear destination. She'd simply inform Gilchrist she was leaving. If he was any kind of gentleman, he'd provide her an escort.

Bloody man! She practically had to sprint up the hill to keep up with him. The bundles bounced atop his shoulder as he hurried toward the castle.

Why, he was carrying them in his right hand! She

smiled to herself. Peg had told her of his improvement. She would have liked to study it firsthand, but not now. Not after what had happened between them.

They reached the top of the hill and the curtain wall, passed through the main gate, and headed directly for the stable. Gilchrist didn't slow his pace.

As they approached the stable she could see a dozen or so strange mounts, horses the like of Gilchrist's stallion, tall and magnificent. Not heavy like the English horses she remembered, but lean and lithe, spirited, as if they might sprout wings and take flight at any moment.

Gilchrist stopped at the entrance to the stable yard and dropped the bundles on the ground. She came up behind him, but did not speak.

"Ho, what's this? Gilchrist, laddy!" A great bear of a man jogged toward them from one of the stalls on legs thick as tree trunks. He had wild red hair framing a beefy, jovial face, and the brightest blue eyes she'd ever seen.

"Hamish, 'tis good to see ye, man." Gilchrist embraced the huge warrior who, with a grunt, nearly lifted him off his feet.

"Ah, ye look fine, lad." Hamish slapped him on the back, then matter-of-factly inspected Gilchrist's scarred hand. "Full healed by the look of it."

"Aye, nearly so."

She knelt and reached for the bundles.

"And who's this bonny lass?"

The warrior beamed a smile at her as she looked up. Before she could retrieve the bundles, Hamish swept them from the ground in one easy motion.

"'Tis good to see a pretty woman at your side again." He winked at Gilchrist, then offered her his hand.

"I'm...um, not—"

"She's a healer," Gilchrist said curtly. "And is with us but temporarily."

Temporarily. The way he said it made her blood boil.

Hamish looked from her to Gilchrist, then cocked a bushy, red brow. "I see."

"I have heard of this healer."

The deep voice startled her. She turned, scrambled to her feet, and found herself looking up into the rugged face of a warrior who could be only one man.

Iain Mackintosh.

"Brother," Gilchrist said.

Iain grinned.

She was barely able to sidestep out of the way before the brothers collided in an awkward embrace.

"Saint Sebastian be praised, just look at you!" Iain rumpled Gilchrist's hair. He tried to pull away, but Iain wrapped an arm possessively around his shoulder. The two locked eyes and Iain slowly nodded, some silent, fraternal understanding passing between them.

She backed away, feeling suddenly embarrassed and out of place, but Hamish gently grasped her arm and pulled her forward.

"So, ye are the Englishwoman," Iain said, looking her up and down.

She straightened her spine and met his penetrating gaze. "I am."

"Alex didna tell me ye were so bonny."

The two of them stood there, arm in arm, studying her, Iain's warm smile in direct contrast to Gilchrist's scowl. They were of the same height and build, with similar features—a strong chin, long straight nose, and those blue eyes. But Iain was dark, with long chestnut hair tied back in a leather thong, while Gilchrist was fair. She recalled the weight and feel of his fine hair in her hands, how she'd run her fingers through it as he'd kissed her.

Her cheeks grew hot under their scrutiny.

"Ye are the one responsible for my brother's recovery," Iain said. He released Gilchrist and took a step toward her.

She shook her head, dismissing his comment. "Nay 'twas the old healer who saved his life, not I."

Gilchrist watched her silently, intently. She would have given anything to have known what he was thinking.

Iain glanced at him and smiled. "Mayhap."

"Da, look at me!"

They all turned in the direction of the child's voice. A boy, no older than five or six, she guessed, sat atop Glenna's back. Jamie led the mare slowly around the stable yard in a wide arc.

"That canna be young Colum?" Gilchrist said. "Why, he's huge!"

Iain smiled proudly. "Aye, he's a strappin' lad. Just turned four year old."

The boy was a small version of Iain. He waved from Glenna's back as Jamie led him past.

"I hope ye dinna mind me borrowin' your mount, Rachel," Jamie called out to her. "She's the most docile of the bunch."

She smiled and bade him continue.

"What's *docile?*" the boy asked.

Gilchrist smiled at his nephew. She'd never seen him smile like that. 'Twas achingly bittersweet, and in that moment she read the depth of his pain. "It means *fierce,*" he called out.

The three warriors laughed and she with them, although her heart was not in it.

"But where is your wife, Iain? I dinna see her." Gilchrist scanned the busy stable yard.

"Och, Alena's fat as that mare," Iain said.

"What?"

"She's with child. Our third," Iain said, nodding to her. "'Tis too near her time. I wouldna allow her to make the trip."

"Ha! And her the finest horsewoman in the land. Ye think she'll abide your decision?" Gilchrist shot Hamish a sly grin.

"She'd better, or I'll... Damn, the woman is head-strong!"

Gilchrist and Hamish laughed in unison.

"I can see no much has changed, brother, since last we were all together."

Iain took a step back and turned a full circle, taking in the newly finished castle and outbuildings. "On the contrary, much has changed. What do ye call the place?"

"Monadhliath," Gilchrist said.

"After the mountains?" Iain nodded in satisfaction. "Aye, it suits it."

Soft footfalls sounded behind her. She turned.

"Hugh!" Before he could protest, Hamish lifted him off his feet in an affectionate bear hug.

"Uggh," was all Hugh could manage until Hamish set him back down. "I saw ye ride up the hill," he said. "Welcome."

Iain nodded to him. "All seems well here." 'Twas not a question exactly, but the two men locked gazes in a way that seemed to put Gilchrist on edge.

"Much has happened since last we saw you," Hugh said. "We shall have to raise a cup together. Later."

Gilchrist frowned.

Rachel wondered at their exchange, and realized it was

not the most opportune moment to inform Gilchrist of her departure. Perhaps she would speak with him later.

She turned to Hamish who still held her bundles. "I was delivering those to Jamie. They're just some rags and cloth he might use in the stable."

Hamish hefted the bundles over his shoulder as if they weighed less than nothing. "I'll take them directly. I need to have a word with him about our mounts."

"I'll go with you," she said.

Iain reached out to stop her. "Rachel, I would thank ye for all ye have done for my brother—and the rest of the clan." His warmth surprised her. She liked this brother of Gilchrist's. "Ye have a great gift, 'tis plain to see." He glanced briefly at the now scowling Gilchrist.

"Aye she does," Hugh said. "By the way, where *is* your gift? Ye're no wearing it."

Her heart stopped. All three of them caught her startled expression.

"What gift?" Gilchrist asked. "What are ye talking about?"

She started to back away, in the direction Hamish had gone.

"A necklace," Hugh said. "Alex gave it to her."

Gilchrist looked at her, his face hard as the new-cut stone of Monadhliath Castle. "Is this true?"

"Aye," she breathed, silently cursing Hugh for mentioning it.

"Yet ye dinna wear it."

No one else said a word.

Why did she feel so awkward about Alex's gift? And why was Gilchrist so agitated?

"What does it matter?" She shot him an icy look that she hoped disguised her confused emotions. "After all, I am only here *temporarily,* am I not?"

Before he could reply, she turned on her heel and hurried toward the stable.

Gilchrist pulled the gray up short at the edge of the Highland wood. The stallion snorted impatiently, beating the ground with a weathered hoof. He watched the steam rise from the gray's coat and vanish on the chill morning air.

"Why d'ye stop?" Iain called out, reining his mount to a halt beside him.

He looked back, his gaze following the ridge line and fixing on Monadhliath Castle far in the distance. "No reason, I just like it here, this one spot."

The edges of Iain's mouth curled into a thin smile. "Aye, as do I."

He studied his brother's queer expression. "Why? What is this place to you?"

Iain slipped from the saddle and knelt before a pile of broken stones. "There used to be a ruin here, the foundation of some ancient castle."

"Aye, there was. We used some of the stones as a base for Monadhliath. The others we cleared away."

Iain's smile widened. A breathy sigh escaped his lips. He picked a small, chipped shard from among the pile of stones, placed it into his sporran, and remounted his steed.

Their eyes met.

"Ah, well..." Iain's face colored slightly. "This was the exact spot where first I kissed Alena." He stared off into the distance for a moment, then laughed. "As I recall it, she tried to slap me."

"Aye, and then stole your mount and left ye to walk the whole way back."

Both of them laughed. Iain reached over and swatted

his arm. How long had it been since they'd shared a light moment? Too long, he thought; too long.

"So, brother, why do *you* fancy the spot?"

The question caught him off guard, and he looked away. He, too, recalled a first kiss. Well, not exactly a kiss—but the promise of one. The scent of Rachel's hair, the warmth of her in his arms in the saddle in front of him, the sunlight on her hair...

"Och, no reason," he said, and spurred the gray into the wood.

An hour later they reached the burnt-out clearing where Braedûn Lodge once stood. 'Twas a hellish place. Why had he allowed Iain to lead him here?

Iain slowed his mount to a walk as they made their way along the wide path. "I passed it on the journey here," he said, dismounting. "Come, walk with me a bit."

"Nay." Gilchrist quickly turned the gray. Iain grabbed the bridle and their eyes locked.

"Come, we must talk."

For a moment neither of them moved. Then, finally, knowing his brother would have his way, Gilchrist relented. "Och, all right." He slipped from the saddle, and Iain tethered the horses in a grassy spot just outside the circle of charred ground.

Something was different; Gilchrist noticed it immediately. He could...smell it. Aye, that was it. The smell of burning was nearly gone. It had been weeks since Alex and the others had cleared away the burnt rubble. He chanced a deep breath. Nothing but damp earth.

'Twas remarkable how quickly the land healed itself. The lush greenery of the forest had already begun to finger its way into the blackened clearing. He paused at the edge of the circle and marveled at the tiny green shoots that seemed to have sprung up everywhere.

Here and there he spied fingerling-size pine and larch, pushing up through the loamy earth. Droplets of moisture clung to their whisper-thin limbs and shimmered in the white light of morning.

"In time, ye willna know this place was even here," Iain said.

"I shall always know." He flexed his burned hand inside the folds of his plaid. How could he forget? He would never forget.

"'Twas no your fault."

His brother's words seared his insides. He gritted his teeth against the roil of emotions. "Mayhap not, but the clan will ne'er forgive me for no getting them out."

Iain clapped a hand on his shoulder. "Aye, they never will—no until ye forgive yourself."

He met his brother's gaze and for once didn't try to hide his pain. It glimmered there behind his eyes, stinging and visceral. 'Twas all he had left to hold on to, the one thing he could feel that made him alive, made him a man. 'Twas the only thing—

Except Rachel.

Iain squeezed his shoulder once, then let his hand fall back to his side. "Who did it? Did ye ever find out?"

"The fire? Nay." He shrugged off the churn of emotion that threatened to consume him. "I'd had my suspicions, but..." He shook his head. What he'd thought was unthinkable; he'd never mention it to Iain.

"Conall should have been here for ye, these last months. He might have helped—with the castle and other matters."

Wild young Conall. How he missed his younger brother. Iain was right, of course. Conall might have helped him, but after the fire Gilchrist had spurned the lad until he finally left. He couldn't bear Conall's pity. That's why Iain had gone as well, and Gilchrist was grateful for it.

"Where is Conall? At Findhorn?"

"Nay, abroad somewhere," Iain said. "I know not."

He grinned. "'Tis just like him, is it no? Of the three of us, he was always the adventurer."

"Aye, he was." Iain strode over to the huge felled tree that lay on the perimeter of the clearing. Gilchrist followed.

"There's something I've been meaning to ask ye all these months," Iain said.

"Aye? And what is that?"

Iain hesitated a moment, then said, "You never loved her, did ye?"

Gilchrist stopped breathing. He met his brother's gaze but didn't answer.

"Elizabeth Macgillivray—ye didna love her."

What the hell? "What are ye talking about? We were betrothed."

"But ye didna love her—ye drove her away."

"Whilst I lay there dying, she made her bed with another man." In a flash he closed the distance between them. Iain leaned casually against the felled tree, and 'twas all Gilchrist could do to keep his fists balled at his sides. "Christ, Iain, the bitch was pregnant with his child!"

"Aye, but that was before the fire."

Nay, he would never believe it. He spat on the ground, not an inch from his brother's boot. "How d'ye know that?"

"I didn't. Alena did." Iain cocked a dark brow and crossed his arms over his chest. "No much slipped past my wife where that one was concerned."

He recalled that once, years ago, the Macgillivrays had

proposed a match between Elizabeth and Iain. His older brother, in his wisdom, would have none of it.

"Well, now she's wed him, and 'tis for the best if ye ask me," Iain said.

"I didna ask ye." He paced back and forth in front of the huge tree. "Besides, ye dinna know what ye're talking about. We were betrothed. Then there was the fire, I was burned and…and she left me. That's the sum of it."

"Ye drove her away."

He stopped dead in his tracks as something dark and feral took root inside him. "Aye, I drove her away." He shrugged off the scabbard that belted his broadsword to his back, ripped his clan badge from his plaid, and flung it to the ground. "Look!" He pulled off his shirt and cast it aside. "Look at me!"

Gilchrist turned a slow circle in front of his brother. "*This* is what drove her away—turned her affection to horror, her loyalty to betrayal." He took a step toward him. "Can ye blame her?" Another step. "Can ye?" he roared.

Iain set his jaw, and Gilchrist fought the urge to smash his fist into it. "Ye didna love her," Iain said.

Gilchrist saw red.

Another second and he'd kill him. He grabbed his discarded clothes and weapon and vaulted onto his horse. A few minutes later he was racing through the wood, driving the gray to breakneck speed.

A hundred random thoughts, images, memories burned inside him, hellish as the fire that had ravaged his body. 'Twas all he could do to focus on the blur of trees, boulders, small creeks and other obstacles as he flew deeper into the Highland forest.

To his annoyance, Iain caught him up. "Gilchrist!" He didn't stop and his brother called out again.

Damn him! He let fly a litany of obscenities, then gritted his teeth and reined the gray to a brisk trot.

Iain pulled his steed up beside him and shot him a steely look. "So, now ye'll wed Arlys."

He didn't answer.

"Will ye?"

"That's the plan," he said, not sparing Iain a glance.

"'Tis a good match."

"Ha!" He met Iain's gaze.

"When's the wedding?"

Christ, he was as bad as Hugh. "Och, I dinna know." He waved him off with a hand. "Later."

"Good. When our new babe is fit to travel, Alena and I shall return for a long visit."

His anger waned and he forced himself to cast his brother a thin smile. "Aye, 'twill be good to see her and the other bairns."

They slowed their mounts to a walk and Iain nudged his roan stallion closer. "The healer—the Englishwoman—what will ye do with her?"

There was only one thing he could do. He hardened his heart. "I'll have Alex take her to Craigh Mur."

"Why there? 'Tis Macphearson land."

"'Tis the only place she remembers." He explained to Iain how he'd found her at the spring. His brother listened attentively, and asked a number of leading questions. He ignored most of them.

"I shall pass close to Craigh Mur on my journey home on the morrow. I'll take the healer with me, and save Alex the trip."

The hell he would. Gilchrist jerked the gray's reins. The stallion stopped, but threw his head back and snorted in obvious irritation. Iain stopped as well, and turned in the saddle to look back at him.

"The healer goes when I say, and with my choice of escort."

"I see." Iain arched one dark brow, a mannerism that was quickly beginning to annoy him.

"Peg's no ready yet to take on full responsibility for the clan. Rachel's taught her well, and she's a bright lass, but she's no ready yet."

"And that's why ye'd keep the Englishwoman for a bit longer?"

"Aye." He deliberately held his brother's gaze and spurred the gray forward again.

Iain goaded his stallion into step beside him. "I've one more thing to discuss with ye."

"Christ, what more? Have ye no picked my brain clean as a vulture's carrion?"

Iain laughed, but his expression sobered quickly. "'Tis about Alex. Never have I seen him so anxious to deliver his message and leave. He stayed barely an hour under my roof."

This didn't surprise Gilchrist, although he didn't want Iain to know why. 'Twas Arlys. Alex was in love with her.

"There is much to do here yet. Alex was no doubt anxious to return and help me."

"No doubt." Iain massaged the two-day growth of stubble on his chin. "D'ye remember what our father told us when we were lads, about the friends we'd made?"

"Nay, I barely remember him."

"He said, 'Ambition devours loyalty faster than the nighthawk downs his unsuspecting prey.'"

He shot his brother a stony glance. "I'll keep it in mind," he said, and spurred the gray toward home.

Rachel stuffed the small bag of oatcakes and salted meat she'd saved from her midday meal into the saddlebag, then draped a dark hunting plaid across her shoulders.

She was ready.

Everyone would be at the celebration—or so she hoped. She counted on the stable yard being deserted. In minutes she'd have Glenna saddled and away. The only question was...dare she risk the journey to Craigh Mur alone?

'Twas foolhardy, she knew. A woman alone, in country she didn't know. There were likely wild animals, or worse, lying in wait for some lone, unprotected quarry.

The image of a bloodied sword cutting the darkness flashed briefly in her mind. She shuddered and pushed the terrifying memory away. It didn't matter now. All that mattered was she get to Craigh Mur.

Damn Alex, and Hugh as well! The warrior had laughed at her that afternoon when she'd asked his help. He'd told her Gilchrist would provide her an escort if and when he had a mind to do so.

Gilchrist—insufferable man! *If and when he had a mind to do so.* She'd not spend another night within sight of him. She'd certainly not wait around to see him wed Arlys Davidson.

She heaved the saddlebag over her shoulder and took one last look around the old woman's workroom. 'Twas all for the best, her leaving this way. Aye, her mind was made up. She turned toward the door and—

"Good God!"

Hugh leaned casually against the open jamb. She hadn't even heard him trip the latch. He looked her over, one tawny brow cocked in question, taking in her traveling clothes and Glenna's neatly packed saddlebag.

Stepping into the room, he closed the door quietly behind him. "Going somewhere?"

Chapter Twelve

She had better think of something, and quick.

Rachel nonchalantly dropped the saddlebag in the corner by the hearth. "I was just tidying up a bit." The lie came easy, but 'twas impossible to tell whether or not Hugh believed her. She tipped her chin high and folded her hands together in front of her. "Why are you here?"

"The laird sent me to fetch ye."

The hunting plaid slipped from her shoulders. Hugh snapped it up before she could react, and cast it onto her pallet. "Ye willna need this. 'Tis a warm night. Come." He extended his hand to her.

She had a strange feeling about Hugh. He seemed different, in a way she couldn't explain. When she first arrived at Monadhliath he'd scorned her, along with the rest of the clan. He'd been kind to her of late—almost friendly—but now, she wasn't certain. His eyes were warm, but his expression was cool and unreadable.

"Wh-where are we going?"

"To the celebration, of course." He shot her a surprised look. "Where did ye think?" He took her arm and guided her to the door. "When ye didna show up, Gilchrist bade me come and fetch ye."

"Did he?" Now she was the one who was surprised.

"Aye, and he doesna like to be kept waiting. Come." He paused at the door and studied her, then took another look around the cottage. "Something seems amiss here, but I canna put my finger on it."

She didn't respond, and forced an innocent expression.

Hugh stared at the saddlebag in the corner for what seemed a long time. Her pulse quickened. His gaze roamed over the rest of the cottage, then lit on the silver necklace—Alex's gift—hanging from a nail over the hearth. She'd forgotten all about it. The pink gemstone glimmered in the firelight.

Hugh grinned. "Ha! I knew ye wouldna wear it."

"What do you mean?"

"Alex's gift to ye." He shot her a knowing glance. "Aye, he made ye accept it, but I knew ye'd never wear it—especially in front of the laird."

"Why on earth not?" She wrested her arm away from him.

"Och, 'tis plain why." His grin broadened. "To me, at any rate."

Ten minutes later Hugh pushed open the door to Monadhliath Castle's great hall. Rachel stood beside him, waiting to enter, the silver necklace dangling from her neck.

The keep had undergone a complete transformation in the last week. What had been a cold, dark shell was now lively and warm, save for the spartan furnishings of Gilchrist's chamber. Dozens of beeswax tapers, along with the huge hearth fire, drenched the hall in a soft light.

Clansmen and -women, attired in their finest plaids and gowns, packed the long wooden tables assembled for the celebration. The room was alive with singing and laughter, the clash of ale cups, and the occasional squeal of a girl whose lover had risked a pinch.

The walls were decorated with all manner of weaponry. There were neither tapestries nor artwork. All had been lost in the fire at Braedûn Lodge. But everywhere—on shields and clan badges, sword hilts and ladies' embroidered garments—she saw the same symbol that was carved into the shield in Gilchrist's chamber: a cat reared up on hind legs, teeth and claws bared for battle.

Davidson, aligned with the Chattan—clan of the cats.

Rachel smiled at those she knew as Hugh led her to the table where Gilchrist and his brother sat deep in some whispered conversation. Alex rose as they approached and offered her a place next to his. Out of the corner of her eye she caught Arlys's murderous glare.

What could she do? "Thank you," she said to Alex and started in his direction. Hugh yanked her back and, to her annoyance, maneuvered her toward Gilchrist.

He and Iain looked up together, two sets of identical blue eyes taking her in, fixing on the pink gemstone dangling between her breasts.

Gilchrist's expression hardened. "So, ye have decided to grace us with your presence."

"Hugh told me that you sent for me." She shrugged out of the warrior's grasp. "Is there some service I might perform, then? Some clansman or -woman in need of a physician?" She was deliberately cool.

Iain rose and offered her his place. "Come, won't ye sit here and take some supper with us?"

Before she could respond, Hugh pushed her toward them. She shot him an irritated glance over her shoulder, then settled on the bench between Iain and Gilchrist, as directed. Gilchrist immediately shifted his position so as not to have to look at her.

Fine.

Her cheeks flamed, but she was determined not to let any emotion show in either her expression or behavior.

Gilchrist treated her much as he had the day before—cool to the point of rudeness. There was a certain determined confidence about him that she wondered at. 'Twas forced, almost contrived. He tried to engage Alex in some casual conversation, but the dark-eyed warrior seemed uneasy, and faltered in his responses.

"What think ye of my brother's clan?" Iain's deep voice interrupted her thoughts.

She smiled warmly at him. He'd treated her with kindness and respect yesterday, and she would offer him the same good manners, regardless of his brother's behavior.

"They are a hardworking and forthright people," she said. "I've been treated well here, but am anxious to be on my way."

Iain studied her in that same penetrating manner as was Gilchrist's wont. "To Craigh Mur. That is your destination?"

"Aye."

"Ye have family there." 'Twas a statement, not a question.

"Nay, I—" She toyed with the silver ring on her right hand. "I know not. 'Tis the place that I remember, nothing more."

Iain's eyes strayed again to the silver necklace. "'Tis a handsome thing, that."

She was sorry she'd worn the necklace. She hadn't intended to, but Hugh's pointed comments had angered her.

Gilchrist abruptly turned toward her. "A handsome gift from a handsome warrior, aye?" He reached out with his burned hand and fingered the pink gemstone. "What say ye, healer?"

His steely eyes bore into her as he waited like a predator for her response. She was aware, too, of Alex watching, waiting.

"I—I don't—"

"How can she judge either?" Arlys asked from across the table. "She's no one of us." She drew herself up and arched both fair brows.

"Aye, she's not," Iain said, and speared a slice of roasted venison from off the trencher on the table. He raised his dirk, ready to savor the meat. "Methinks that would make her the best judge of all."

Rachel wondered at his defense of her, and suppressed a smile as Arlys scowled, ruining her pretty features. Gilchrist merely snorted, then proceeded to ignore all of them.

They ate in silence for a while, listening to the boisterous exchange between Hamish, Hugh, and the elders farther down the table. Similar celebrations played at the edges of her memory. They were different, somehow, more formal—everyone seated in some predetermined order, based on rank and privilege. Not like this at all.

"Where is your son tonight?" she asked Iain.

"Young Colum?" he said. "Och, he's worn-out from the long journey and took early to his bed."

They ate and drank, and all the while Arlys tried to catch Gilchrist's eye. He blatantly ignored her and attacked the trencher of venison with a vengeance, as if the game still needed killing.

Rachel couldn't fathom his behavior. He would wed Arlys Davidson, yet never proposed the match to her. Nor did he appear to show much interest in her, aside from their kiss outside Murdoch's cottage.

God's truth, she had no way of knowing what transpired when they were alone, but she perceived no intimacy between them, no passion, no fire. All at once, the truth hit her like a bolt of lightning, and she nearly dropped her ale cup.

Gilchrist didn't love Arlys.

He'd lied to her that night in his chamber. Why?

Her pulse quickened. She stole a glance at him, and he pretended not to notice. She thought she knew him, but what did she really know?

Alex sat beside him staring at Arlys, neither eating nor drinking. His expression was tired, drawn, as if he bore some great weight upon his conscience.

She glanced farther down the table and met Murdoch's ever watchful eyes. The elder drew his pipe from his lips and let the edges of his mouth blossom into an all-knowing smile.

The next afternoon, Gilchrist reined the gray to a halt at the unmarked juncture where the path to the virgin's spring met the north-south trail through the Highland wood. Iain, Hamish, and their party pulled their mounts up short behind him.

"So, this is where ye shall take your leave of us?" Iain said.

"Aye."

"I could do with a soak in the waters myself, but canna spare the time."

Hamish shuddered. "Och, too much bathin' is bad for the heart. All that cold water."

"Will no ye rest just one more day, brother?" Gilchrist asked.

Iain drew his mount closer and shook his head. "Nay, I would be at my wife's side when our third son is born."

Gilchrist smiled at his sleeping nephew, cradled in the saddle in Iain's arms. He was named after their father,

Colum Mackintosh, a man Gilchrist barely remembered. "How d'ye know 'twill be a boy?" he said, arching a brow.

Iain looked as if he'd been struck a blow. "I hadna considered the alternative."

Gilchrist and Hamish dissolved into laughter and, after a moment, Iain joined them. They talked easily of home and family, of Iain and Alena's children, and the sons and daughters to come.

A familiar melancholy began to grow inside him. He pushed the feeling away, for Iain's sake, and smiled through his bitterness.

"What think ye of Alex's gift?" Iain said, abruptly changing the subject.

"What gift?"

"To Rachel, the healer."

The necklace. He preferred not to think on it at all, and didn't answer.

"Did ye recognize the make of the stone and silver work?"

He met Iain's pointed gaze. "I did."

"Where d'ye think Alex got it?"

"I know not. *Traveling,* he says, according to Hugh."

Iain nudged his mount closer, so he might whisper out of earshot of Hamish and the other men. "Methinks ye should keep a tighter rein on Alex. I'd have Macphearson as an ally, no an enemy."

Gilchrist snorted. "So, you, too, would tell me my business? Christ, I have old women enough lined up to advise me." He clicked his tongue and the gray responded, charging up the steep slope to the spring. He paused midway and turned, to see Iain shaking his head and smiling up at him.

"Ye havena changed, Gilchrist, God help ye."

He tempered his anger, then forced a smile and raised a hand in silent tribute. "Fare ye well, brother."

"And you."

Iain spurred his mount forward; Hamish and the rest of his men followed in a tight formation behind him. Gilchrist watched them until they were out of sight, then reined the gray east toward the virgin's spring.

'Twas now or never.

Rachel secured the saddlebag and led Glenna out from between the cottages where she'd been tethered since late afternoon. Jamie had agreed to let the mare graze in the sweet grass that grew there, providing Rachel returned her to his care on the morrow.

The tiny village was quiet, and the moon not yet risen. If she was very careful she'd be certain to depart undetected. Even if she was seen, who would stop her from leaving? Gilchrist had gone to the spring that morning; who knew when he'd return.

She passed Peg's cottage and a half smile tugged at her mouth. She would miss the girl, more than she had expected. 'Twas a joy these past weeks to have shared in Peg's small victories—both in her art and in love. She'd make the clan a fine healer, and Jamie a fine wife.

Rachel thought to turn into the village before she drew too near to Monadhliath's main gate, and snake her way down the hill thus avoiding the main path. From there she might enter the wood unseen.

'Twas dead dark and she felt her way along the row of crofts, keeping Glenna to a slow walk. She was about to turn when she caught a whiff of some rich, spicy aroma. She stopped and strained her eyes to see what it was her nose had detected.

As she'd suspected, the reddish glow of a pipe bowl

materialized just ahead. She could barely make out the smoker's form, leaned casually against a cottage wall. 'Twas Murdoch.

"'Tis a fair evening for a ride," he said in the dark.

She tensed, but did not try to hide herself or Glenna. What good would it do now?

"Won't ye stop awhile and have a chat. Ye can tether that mare just here."

She hesitated for a moment, then walked toward him, resigned. Damn these Davidsons! First Hugh, and now Murdoch. Would she never get away?

Murdoch took the reins from her and tied Glenna to a post behind his cottage. She followed him to the low, wide door; he pushed it open and bade her enter. She'd never been inside. 'Twas a pleasant dwelling—simple, yet warm and inviting. A comfortable fire blazed in the hearth. He gestured for her to sit on one of the stools which rested before it. He took the other, and began to refill his pipe bowl.

"You wished to speak with me," she said, not all together certain of his intent. He'd seen Glenna packed and ready. 'Twas plain she had in mind a journey, and a clandestine departure at that.

"Ah, but I thought it was ye who wished to speak with me." Murdoch lit the pipe, then turned his attention full on her.

"But, I—" What could possibly have given him that idea? She frowned and shot him a questioning look.

"I've had the feeling of late, there is something ye wished to ask me—some bit of information ye had a mind to know."

He was right. There was much she would ask him. His timing could not have been worse, however. How he knew her mind was yet another mystery. But he offered her information, and she would appease her curiosity before she took her leave.

What did she have to lose?

"Aye, there is something I would know."

"Go on then, lass, ask it."

She mustered her courage. "Tell me about Elizabeth Macgillivray."

He did not react as she'd expected. In fact, he did not react at all. Neither a twitch nor a brow arched in surprise, not even a change in his expression. He merely took a long drag on his pipe and held her gaze.

Then he told her.

Elizabeth's long history with men—she'd been widowed young and was anxious to wed again. Her rocky courtship and betrothal to Gilchrist. The fire, and her swift marriage to another. Rachel listened, took it all in, questioning bits of the story and trying to understand.

"And now, he would wed Arlys," she said absently, more to herself than to Murdoch.

"So 'twould seem."

"But why?"

Murdoch finally reacted. He arched a brow, and smiled. "Dinna ye see, healer?"

She shook her head.

"For one who understands well the workings of the body, ye are surprisingly ignorant about matters of the heart."

Her cheeks warmed, but she held his gaze. "What is it you would have me know?"

He blew a smoke ring into the air above their heads. It hovered there for a moment like some ghostly halo, then disappeared. "Much. But for now, I would tell ye a story about Gilchrist's younger brother—and a dog."

"A dog? What could that possibly have to—"

He stilled her with a look. "Conall was always the most unsettled of the Mackintosh lads. Where Gilchrist and Iain always had a sense of themselves and knew what they wanted, Conall was a restless spirit adrift in the world."

She could well relate to that, given her current circumstances.

"He journeyed to Inverness one market day and came upon a man selling dogs. They were sleek, well-trained animals, the kind that would make a man a good companion. The seller offered Conall the pick o' the litter, and at a fair price."

"So he bought one?"

Murdoch chuckled to himself. "Nay, he'd have none o' the lot. His eye was drawn instead to an iron cage at the back of the seller's stall. A small crowd of men stood 'round it, laughing and poking sticks through the bars."

An image of Gilchrist, stripped to the waist on Monadhliath's battlement, flashed in her mind. She recalled the jeers of Alex's men. "What was inside the cage?"

"The most feral beast ye'd e'er laid eyes on. A mastiff, it was, near big as a man, backed into a corner and growling low in its throat."

She'd heard of dogs like that, but had never seen one. She pulled her stool closer to the fire and bade him continue.

"The dog had been chained and beaten, more than once, but he didna cower and wouldna be subdued. His fierceness had grown with the abuse. Many taunted him, but make no mistake, all were afeared. The seller, himself, would have naught to do with the animal."

A strange feeling washed over her. "But Conall took one look at him and knew he was for him."

Murdoch smiled.

"And then what happened?"

"The seller tried to talk him out of it. In fact, he wouldna take Conall's money. He said the beast was too dangerous—a killer—no fit for any man."

"He *was* dangerous," she whispered, "but not a killer."

"Aye, lass."

All at once, the truth of it struck her. She met Murdoch's gaze and held it. "The mastiff was afraid."

The elder nodded.

"What did Conall do?" She already knew the answer, but waited to hear the words.

Murdoch drew on his pipe and exhaled thoughtfully. "He reached into the cage, and called the animal's bluff."

The trail was easy to find, even in the dark. The waxing moon peaked her head out over the treetops, a ghostly beacon eager to light the way.

Murdoch had neither questioned nor detained her. After their conversation, he had simply shown her to the door and bid her a good-night. His tranquil demeanor and quiet certainty fueled her confidence, but also her confusion.

She urged Glenna into the cover of the trees, then stopped to look back along the ridgeline. Monadhliath rose up, a citadel against the sky—seemingly impenetrable, isolated by design.

Like Gilchrist.

She closed her eyes and breathed deep of the night air. Oh, if he could love her... She was mad to think it possible. What was she to him? What was she at all?

She opened her eyes and caught the moonlight reflecting off the silver band circling her third finger. The dream pressed on her mind like a weight. Lovers in a sunset garden, a man on a windswept crag searching for one who is lost...

What did it mean?

She didn't want to know; she didn't care. She was at a crossroads, and her choice was made.

She gazed west into the night toward her shadowed past—Craigh Mur. There was nothing about it now that beckoned her.

Determined, she reined Glenna east—toward her future, toward him—and disappeared into the wood, headed for the virgin's spring.

Chapter Thirteen

She was gone and he was free.

Gilchrist breathed life into the dying embers, then lay back on the fur-covered pallet and watched the firelight dance on the walls of the cave.

Before he'd left Monadhliath that morning, he'd bid Alex take Rachel to Craigh Mur and be done with it. When he returned on the morrow, she would be gone. Good riddance.

Christ, he was dead tired, but couldn't sleep. The night was cold, yet the heat from the fire made him sweat. He pulled his shirt off and cast it into the corner with his boots and weapons.

'Twas quiet—almost too much so. For months he'd come here to get away, to be alone, but now the silence was strangely discomforting.

'Twas her fault.

Everything in his life had changed since he'd found her at the spring. "Damnable woman!" He fished a small rock from the fire ring and hurled it at the mouth of the cave.

A high-pitched yelp shattered the silence.

Grabbing his broadsword, he leapt to his feet and brandished the weapon toward the sound. "Who's there? Step into the light so I can see ye!"

The cloaked figure hovered in the shadows at the cave's entrance.

"Come forward! Do it or I'll cut ye down where ye stand."

As the figure stepped into the light, the dark hunting plaid which served as a cloak slipped to the ground. His heart skipped a beat.

"Rachel! Bluidy hell."

"'Twas not the welcome I had hoped for." She rubbed her shoulder and winced.

He'd stung her with the rock. His first instinct was to rush to her and assess the injury, but he willed his feet stay put. He lowered his sword.

"Who is here with you—Alex? Did he bring ye here?" He'd have Alex's head. Why didn't he do as he'd been told?

"Nay, I've come alone." She took a tentative step toward him.

"Are ye mad?"

Her mouth blossomed in a rosebud smile. "Mayhap."

"'Tis no safe, ye traveling alone." What if something had happened? He cast his sword back onto the pile of garments in the corner.

"You do—travel alone."

The woman was impertinent. And beautiful. The ride in the night air had put a blush in her cheeks, to which a few stray wisps of hair clung. His impulse, had he stood closer to her, would have been to brush them gently away with his hand. Instead, he made fists at his sides. Damned if he didn't feel…what?…what did he feel? 'Twas folly. Madness.

"Where is Alex?" he snapped. "Did he no inform ye of your departure?"

Her smile faded. "You would have me leave?"

"Aye." He swore under his breath then paced back and forth in front of the pallet. "Nay, I—I dinna know." Damn her! "Why have ye come?"

She moved toward him and he instinctively took a step back. She seemed so sure of herself, like that night in his chamber when she'd tended his body. He had kissed her, held her in his arms, burned for her like he had for no other. He burned now.

"Why have ye come?" he repeated.

"To heal you," she said simply, and stopped an arm's length from him.

"Ah." His gut tightened. Bloody fool. What else had he expected? All at once, he was conscious of his hideous scarring, the way the firelight played over the rough texture of his newly healed skin. He looked away and sat heavily on the pallet. "Well then, do it and be gone." If she could stand this cool association between them, so could he.

She approached and knelt before him, silent, and after a few moments he was obliged to meet her gaze. What he read in her face was startling; it both thrilled and frightened him. Warmth, an almost aching desire, and a certainty he'd seen before, as if she knew something he did not.

"Where is your kit, your medicines?" His voice was barely a whisper. He was suddenly aware of his heart beating in his chest.

"I left them behind."

"Then, how d'ye intend…"

His words died on his lips as she freed the laces of her gown, her gray-green eyes riveted to his. She drew the garment slowly over her head and cast it aside. Sweet God. The hearth fire at her back outlined the lushness of her body beneath the thin, white shift and turned her hair into a midnight fire fall.

"'Tis not your body needs healing, Gilchrist."

He loved how she said his name.

"What, then, have ye come to heal?" His voice trembled, for he already knew the answer.

"Your heart."

He tore his gaze from her and shook his head.

"Love me. Make me yours." She ran her hands up the length of his plaid, sending sparks to his very core.

"Nay, Rachel, dinna."

She was so close to him now he could smell the lavender soap in her hair. His breathing grew rapid, shallow. He could not allow this to happen.

"Do you not want me?"

The pain in her voice cut him to the quick. He forced himself to meet her gaze. "Nay."

He lies.

The knowledge of it thrilled her. She could feel his longing, pure and visceral, as he turned away from her and fisted a handful of pelts as if to stop himself from reaching for her.

She willed him to look at her, and finally he did. "If I have sinned, I remember it not. If I have loved before, I feel it not. Gilchrist, I—"

"Stop it!" He grabbed her by the shoulders and shook her. "I canna!" He pushed her away. "I canna."

"But—" The heat of shame, a fool's humiliation, bloomed inside her, flushing her face. She'd been wrong. Oh, God, he meant what he said.

She stood, shaking more from his words than his physical rebuke. Her shoulders burned where his fingers had gripped her. She watched him as he grew cold and hard before her eyes.

"I disgust you," she whispered, and turned to leave.

"Nay!" He grabbed the hem of her shift and pulled her back. "Ah, Rachel."

Her heart soared. She tried to control her breathing, but 'twas coming in short gasps.

He ran his hands lightly, almost reverently, up her calves, his touch hot as a firebrand on her skin. "Ye make me dare to hope I could be again the man I was."

It took all of her strength not to cast herself into his arms. Instead, she knelt before him and placed her hands into his. "Nay, Gilchrist, never again will you be that man."

"'Tis God's truth."

His defeat, his pain, burned into her as his grip tightened.

"And I am glad of it," she whispered, leaning closer. "For this is the man I love."

His eyes glassed. She held his intense gaze and shared the battle raging within him.

"But you see with your own eyes what I am." He spread wide the fingers of his fire-ravaged hand and looked with repugnance on his own body.

"And you know in your heart what *I* am."

Her own tears welled, but before they broke he swept her into his arms.

"Aye," he breathed against her hair. "Ye are like the spring after winter's darkness, a rare elixir, everything virtuous and good."

"Nay." Oh, would that it were true.

"Aye, that and more." He brushed his lips lightly across her temple and she thought to die with the tenderness of it. "Which is why ye must go."

"Nay!" She tightened her arms around him and tilted her face upward, her lips but a breath from his. "Never shall I leave you. Never."

One by one, the carefully erected stones he'd built around his heart, fell away. She could see it in his eyes, feel it in the way he held her. He kissed her, and her world changed.

"Sweetling," he breathed against her lips. "Rachel."

He was everything, all that her senses perceived—his heat, the taste of him as his tongue plundered her mouth, his scent, the almost frightening power of his embrace, the spark of his hair grazing her skin. She was certain now. About him, about everything.

"Gilchrist, I love you."

He groaned and drew her down on top of him on the pallet of soft furs. His kisses grew more passionate, his caresses more urgent. A slow heat spread from her woman's core as he cupped her buttocks and ground his hips against her.

"I want ye," he murmured, his voice ragged with need.

Her own desire blazed as he thrust upward against her. "Oh, aye," she breathed, aware of his hardness, his heat.

He rolled her onto her back and she gasped as his powerful thighs spread hers wide. He thrust against her again.

"Can ye feel how much?"

She was desperate for him, for…what? She knew, and yet she didn't know. Her hands moved over the taut muscles of his back and shoulders while his expert tongue explored her, tasted her.

She'd been careful of his right side, but he seemed to pay it no mind. His burns were fully healed now; but the scarring would remain. She stroked him there, gently, letting her fingers barely graze his skin.

"Nay," he whispered. "Dinna."

She knew her touch caused him no physical pain, and so she ignored his plea. Suddenly, he kissed her hard and in one swift motion pinned her arms above her head.

"I said nay."

Their gazes locked. Her breath came in short gasps now, her breasts straining upward against the thin fabric of her shift. She nodded her assent, but he did not release her. Instead, he devoured her with his eyes, all the while thrusting against her in a slow, fluid motion.

"Ohhh."

"Aye, sweetling, feel my desire."

She closed her eyes as he lowered his head and began to suckle her breast through the shift. Never had she felt such bliss. Would that she could tear the fabric away and feel his hot mouth on her skin.

His hands were everywhere, and so were hers, his body an inferno, pure animal heat, thrusting, demanding. She pulled at his plaid and the wide leather belt that held it in place. Without a word, he lifted up and fumbled, one-handed, with the buckle. The next instant he was naked. He settled again between her thighs, and she reveled in the weight of him.

This was what she wanted, what she'd always wanted since first he'd found her at the spring. More than anything she wished to please him, to make him burn as she did, to drive out all thoughts, all stinging memories of those who'd come before her.

"Tell me what to do," she whispered in his ear.

He smiled—such a smile she'd never seen from him—and kissed her gently on the lips. "Just lay back, and let me love ye."

"But—"

He stilled her protest with a kiss. Then another. And another. She closed her eyes as his mouth burned a fiery path across the rise of her breasts. He pulled at the laces of her shift; the fabric skimmed her body as he slid it lower and lower, his tongue following in its wake.

"Sweet heaven!"

She tried to pull away, but he held her fast around the waist. His tongue was a firebrand, teasing, tasting, until she thought she'd go mad with the pleasure of it.

She was barely aware of her own soft moaning as she fisted handfuls of the fur covering the pallet. She was adrift in some exquisite vortex, spinning out of control toward an unknown end.

At last she reached it—wave after wave of liquid fire. The breath rushed from her all at once. Love for him welled inside her, consumed her, body and soul. Fierce warrior, gentle savior, hero, poet—he was all those things to her now. Before she could fathom what had happened, he was there, settled between her thighs, his velvet hardness pressing against her.

"Relax now," he said, and kissed her deeply. He cupped her buttocks, and she instinctively wrapped her arms and legs around him. He was shaking, she realized, and bathed in a fine sheen of perspiration. His heart beat madly against her breast.

She met his gaze and the firelight danced in his eyes—tiny bonfires on an azure field. His hard-edged coolness had gone. Only the man remained, stripped of his defenses, trusting, vulnerable.

She clung to him as he entered her, ever so slowly, her eyes widening with every inch. He filled her, possessed her, trembled in her arms. Barely leashed passion blazed in his eyes. She thrust upward against him, heedless of the pain, and he growled low in his throat like some feral beast.

"Dinna," he rasped, panting atop her.

She kissed him and thrust again, following her instincts, ignoring his plea for her to stop. Her passion flamed anew and she moved with more confidence, fueled by her power and his uncontrollable response.

Never had she thought 'twould be like this.

All at once, he became the aggressor, and thrust harder with each stroke. She felt the deep centering again, the welling of all sensation, all emotion. His kisses grew frantic, his moans more desperate.

She closed her eyes and reached for the pinnacle, panting in time to his thrusts. Just as she thought she would never reach it, his deft fingers slipped between them and sent her over the edge. She cried out his name and he hers as he spilled his seed inside her.

They clung to each other for an eternity, exchanging kisses and whispered endearments. Later, after the fire had died down, she was barely aware of him pulling his plaid over the both of them as she settled into his arms to sleep.

He slept like the dead.

'Twas the churring of a woodcock that finally woke him, and the soft, sleepy sighs of the woman in his arms.

"Rachel," he breathed. He pulled her tight against his chest and nuzzled her ear.

"Mmm, I like that."

"Do ye, now?"

"Aye." She snuggled closer and he buried his face in the dark nest of her hair.

"How do ye feel?"

He sensed her smile.

"As if I were someone entirely different," she said.

He laughed and squeezed her tighter. "Aye, as do I." God's truth, he did. "But that's no what I meant. Are ye...do ye hurt?"

"Nay, I…well…perhaps a little."

"I didna wish to hurt ye. I'm sorry. Truly." He cursed his lack of self-control. She'd been virgin—as he knew she was from the very first time he kissed her.

"You didn't," she whispered seductively, and undulated her ripe buttocks against his loins.

He was instantly aroused, but intent on not touching her again so soon. Instead, he nibbled at her ear and tickled her in the sensitive places he'd discovered last night.

"Stop!" She giggled and tried to turn in his arms.

He held her fast and assailed her neck with a gentle onslaught of kisses. Her squeals of delight enchanted him.

Then he saw it.

A shock of white hair at her nape, hidden beneath her thick dark tresses.

"What's this?" He stilled her fidgeting and fingered the fine, snowy lock.

"What are you looking at? Here, let me see." She turned in his arms.

"Ye canna see it. 'Tis a stark white lock of hair—just here." He put his thumb on her scalp so she would know it.

Her eyes widened in alarm.

"What is it? Why are ye frightened?"

She pushed him away and sat up, a wild look in her eyes. He'd seen that look before—once, when she recognized her horse, and again when she awoke from a nightmare.

"What is it, Rachel? Does it mean something? D'ye remember something?"

"Nay, I…" She shook her head vehemently. "Nay."

She was trembling. He drew her into his arms and she clung to him, trying, he knew, to control her rapid breathing. He rocked her for a few minutes until she was

calm, whispering endearments and all the comforting
words he knew.

"I—I'm fine, now." She looked up at him and smiled.
"Truly."

He reminded himself there was much about her he did
not know. God's truth, she seemed to know little more
than he did. But it mattered not. She was his. He would
keep her safe from whatever evils plagued her past and
haunted her still.

She looked on him, eyes filled with love and the promise of joys beyond his imagining. His heart soared. Many
times that night she'd declared her love, but he'd held
back. The words were there now, on his own lips, but he
did not speak them.

Why?

He couldn't. Not yet. He knew it hurt her, but he must
be certain. He wanted to trust her, to believe in her love.
What was it kept him from it?

Fear.

There was no use denying it. 'Twas time to face it and
put it behind him. He would wed her, love her—to hell
with what the clan thought. Murdoch was right. He was
laird. They'd accept him and her. English or not, she'd be
his bride, and they'd have sons, a dozen of them.

"What are you thinking?" she said suddenly.

"What?" She kissed him and he smiled. "Och, 'tis of
no import." He threw his plaid off them. "Come, let us
return to Monadhliath. There is much I would do there
today."

She rose from the pallet and stretched, naked and lovely
in the morning light. 'Twas all he could do not to pull
her back onto the furs and make love to her again.

He burned for her still.

'Twas the kind of fire he knew would never be quenched.

Outside the cave, Gilchrist had to shield his eyes from the brilliant sunlight. The sky was a flawless blue. Dewdrops graced each leaf, every flower and blade of grass. All shimmered in the breeze, a rainbow of color. The air was fresh, clean. Even the spring, which was often muddy from the rain, flowed clear.

"Our mounts seem to have passed the night well in each other's company," Rachel said, and patted Glenna's sleek neck. She shot him a mischievous glance from the saddle.

"'Tis a blessing, since from now on I would have them spend all their nights together."

He could tell she took his meaning. Her eyes warmed and she blushed ever so slightly. Oh, what a happy day this would be. This, and every day he spent with her.

As he mounted his steed he noticed Glenna's bursting saddlebags. He pulled the gray up beside her and bid Rachel stop. "What have ye got in there, the whole of the castle's larder?" He'd been pleased earlier, when she fetched the food she'd brought with her. But her provisions seemed overmuch for a two-hour journey.

She said naught, and her blush deepened. She held his gaze, though he could tell she willed herself to do so.

"Ye meant to leave then?" He could see the truth of it in her eyes, and it stung him.

"I... Gilchrist." She reached for his burned hand, and he let her take it. "Aye, I did mean to leave." She squeezed him gently. "But I did not. I could not." Her eyes implored him to believe her, and he did.

After all, had not he, himself, given an order that would

have sent her from him? 'Twas a stroke of luck, a miracle really, that Alex had not already taken her.

Had it not been for her boldness, her certainty about her feelings, and his, last night might never have happened. She'd be gone from him now. He found the thought unbearable.

"'Tis no matter," he whispered, and pulled her closer for a kiss. "We are together now, and I'll let naught divide us."

They made their way down into the wood below the spring. He kept Rachel behind him as their mounts snaked their way through the stands of larch and laurel peppering the hillside. A short distance into the wood, he smelled something unmistakable—

Smoke.

Not a live fire, but the smoldering remnants of one.

He scanned the trees for signs. Aye, there! Not ten yards from them a thin, white wisp rose up into the trees and disappeared on the morning breeze. He spurred the gray toward it, bidding Rachel stay close by him.

"What is it?" she called out. "Has someone been here?"

Aye, someone had been here, all right—all night from the trampled appearance of the ground. He dismounted and inspected the crude fire ring. Another familiar odor hung in the air about the place.

"Tobacco."

Suddenly, everything was clear.

"Whose? Who would have…" Rachel's eyes widened. "You mean…"

"Aye, Murdoch." He smiled as her expression changed from surprise to wonder.

He pulled himself into the saddle and guided the gray back to the main path. A thought struck him and his smile faded. Damn Hugh and Alex! He'd have both their heads. Two hundred warriors among them, and not one had known Rachel had left the village. Gilchrist had been too stunned by her appearance last night to realize it.

Only Murdoch, a man three times their age, had seen her and followed her, making certain she arrived safe. He was not an elder for naught. Gilchrist would remember that, next time he thought to ignore the old man's advice.

The day was warm and they enjoyed the ride, stopping here and there so that Rachel might gather some rare herb she did not have growing in the castle garden. It seemed the clan would have two healers after all. 'Twas a good thing, too, as Peg seemed to have taken an exclusive interest in the care and healing of the animals at the stable— and their master.

"You're smiling," Rachel said, interrupting his thoughts.

"Aye, I was thinking of Jamie and Peg."

"Ah, methinks she'd make a better stable mistress than healer." Her gray-green eyes flashed mirth.

"I was thinking the very same thing, my—" His words were cut short by the sound of thundering hoofbeats on the road below them.

"Rachel! Quickly, get behind me."

He positioned his steed in front of hers and drew his sword. All at once, he noticed 'twas in his right hand— his burned hand. It felt remarkably good. So be it. He had an advantage now that few others did. He could fight with either hand, or both! He drew his dirk in his left and waited, eyes riveted to the approaching riders.

As they drew closer, he recognized their garments and livery, and relaxed. Alex and Hugh. What was the world coming to? They rode together, shoulder to shoulder, as if they were the best of friends. Their faces were grim, as they should be. He'd have more than a word with the both of them.

"Laird!" Hugh called out.

Gilchrist and Rachel pulled their mounts up short, and the clansmen surrounded them.

"Thank God," Alex said. His face was lined and tired, as if he'd been up half the night. "She's with ye."

"Aye, she's with me, and ye ought to thank God." He glared hard at the both of them. "We shall speak of this later."

Rachel nudged her mount closer. "Don't punish them. 'Twas my fault. I meant for no one to know I had left."

"Are ye well, lady?" Alex studied her in a manner Gilchrist didn't at all like.

"Aye, I'm..." Rachel glanced at him briefly, then met Alex's scrutinizing gaze. She blushed hotly. "I'm fine."

"We're both fine," Gilchrist said flatly and wedged his mount in between them. There was no mistaking his point.

Hugh's eyes widened, and Gilchrist could see the beginnings of a smile curve at the edges of his mouth. One word and he'd have naught to smile about.

Alex merely stared, betraying not a hint of his true feelings. In truth, Gilchrist didn't know how Alex felt, nor how he'd take the news of their marriage. He had wooed Rachel himself, but Gilchrist suspected he'd done it simply to keep his mind off Arlys. Gilchrist bade Rachel stay close to his side and, without another word, led the party onto the forest road toward home.

Arlys was waiting in the stable yard when they arrived. She barely glanced at him or Rachel. Her eyes were only for Alex. Perhaps he'd judged the girl too harshly. 'Twas clear she loved the warrior. And why not? Alex was a good man.

It seemed there would be a happy end for all of them.

He dismounted and handed the gray's reins to the waiting Jamie. Rachel struggled with a foot caught in the stirrup. He smiled at how lovely she looked, even after a night in the rough. A night with him. One he'd not soon forget and was eager to repeat.

"Let me help ye down." Rachel slipped from Glenna's saddle into his arms. He held her there for a moment, marveling at his good fortune, before he set her on her feet.

"What, not a word for yer bride?"

He turned to see Arlys glaring up at him.

Rachel's smile faded. She led Glenna away toward her stall, but he noticed she paused to speak with Jamie, just out of earshot.

Alex looked up from the saddlebag he was unloading from his gelding.

Gilchrist sucked in his breath. 'Twas as good a time as any. "There's my bride, over there." He nodded toward Rachel.

Alex dropped an open wineskin whose contents splattered his plaid, his mount's dappled legs and Arlys's gown. "What d'ye mean? Who?" His face went a chalky white.

Perhaps Gilchrist had been mistaken about Alex's feelings, after all. Arlys stood there, glowering at both of them. 'Twas time to put things right.

"Rachel," Gilchrist said. "The healer. If she'll have me. I havena asked her yet."

"Typical," Arlys muttered.

Alex shot toward him, and Hugh moved to cut him off. Why was everything so difficult with these two? Gilchrist raised a hand, stopping them both in their tracks.

"Ye canna wed her," Alex said.

"Nay, Alex is right." Arlys tipped her chin defiantly. "Ye canna wed the whore."

"Enough!" Gilchrist was suddenly aware of Rachel behind him. He pulled her up close and wrapped a protective arm around her shoulder. "She's no a whore, and any man—or woman—who says otherwise shall answer to me."

Arlys's eyes blazed murder. "Whore or no, ye canna wed her."

"And why not?" he snapped.

"She's already promised to someone else."

What was this nonsense?

"The ring." Arlys pointed to the well-worn, silver band on the third finger of Rachel's right hand.

Rachel tensed in his arms, eyes wide. 'Twas her reaction, and not Arlys's words that jarred him.

"What about it?" he demanded.

Arlys arched one blond brow and smirked at the both of them. "'Tis a betrothal ring."

"What?" He grabbed Rachel's wrist and studied the silver band. "What are ye talking about? We have no such custom."

An eerie premonition coiled tight inside him as Moira stepped from the shadows of one of the stalls. Her dark eyes blazed. "Ye are right, Laird, but there is such a custom. In England."

Chapter Fourteen

Nothing prepared her for the magnitude of his rage.

Rachel stood, dumbfounded, staring at her ring. She willed herself to speak, to tell him it wasn't so, but no words would come.

Gilchrist's grip tightened around her wrist. "Tell me this isna so, and I will believe ye."

She met his gaze and he saw the truth of it in her eyes.

"Laird—" Hugh said.

Gilchrist pushed past them all, nearly dragging her in his wake. He pulled her into Glenna's stall and flung her toward the back. "Ye knew, the whole time. Didn't ye?"

The tone of his accusation and the wild look in his eyes frightened her. She drew a breath and shook her head.

"Ye knew!"

She had known, God help her.

An image of the lovers in the garden flashed in her mind. She was the woman, wasn't she? Who else could she possibly be? She had the mark—the white tuft of hair—and the ring. She'd seen it before, she knew it, but...oh, 'twas so confusing!

"Ye are betrothed, pledged to another. Yet ye would lie with me and speak of love?"

"Gilchrist, I—"

"Who is the man? Ye dreamed of him, spoke of him. Aye, I remember." He grabbed her by the shoulders, then just as quickly removed his hands as if she were something dirty. "Who is the man?" he roared.

Hugh cautiously entered the stall. "Laird, if ye would only—"

"Get out!" Gilchrist's eyes blazed. For one frightening moment she thought he might strike her. Sweet God, she would rather he did than continue to look upon her with such contempt.

Hugh backed away. She could see them all gathered outside the stall—Alex, Arlys and the rest, loath to come too close, yet anxious to see what their laird would do. Arlys met her gaze briefly, then looked away, her cheeks flaming.

"Women. Faithless liars, the lot o' ye!" He was raving now, and not even looking at her. "Ye gain a man's trust, his heart, then—"

"Won't you listen to me?" She started toward him but he threw up his hands.

"Dinna come near me, whore."

The ugly word cut her like a knife. Tears welled and she beat them back, mustering her own anger. "You, of all men, know that isn't true."

The passion they'd shared, the tenderness of their coupling—did it mean nothing to him? She'd pledged her love, and he'd reveled in her declaration. Yet he had not reciprocated. All at once, she realized why.

He didn't trust her.

She had given herself to him, body and soul, shared her innermost feelings, her fears, her dreams, and still, he didn't trust her.

When she looked in his eyes she had the strangest feeling it wasn't her whom he saw, but another. Something clicked in her mind and suddenly his wrath made sense to her.

She mustered her courage, and slowly shook her head. "I am not Elizabeth Macgillivray."

There. 'Twas done.

His eyes burned into her. She could see him shaking, hands fisted, white-knuckled at his sides. "Aye, that's the truth. At least she had the decency to get out o' my sight."

Her insides twisted. He turned to leave and, before she could call him back, he stormed off, the small crowd gathered outside scattering before him.

She buried her face in Glenna's soft coat and held tightly to the mare. It wasn't true—it wasn't! She was pledged to no man; she knew it in her heart. Aye, she bore the ring, but something about it was not right. The dreams, the man—different men—on the ridge, in the garden, in the wood. Who were they? Who was she?

Tears stung her eyes and she fought for control. She fisted handfuls of Glenna's mane, trying to calm herself. "Damn the man! Of all the pigheaded, stupid—"

A hand lit on her shoulder. "'Twill be all right, truly." The voice was a woman's.

"Arlys."

"I—I'm sorry." Arlys offered her a square of cloth. "I didna know."

Stunned, Rachel accepted the cloth and wiped the tears from her eyes.

"Ye love him, don't ye?" Arlys whispered.

She blew her nose and tried to get a grip on her emotions.

"Aye, 'tis plain he loves ye as well." Arlys grasped her hand and held it in both of hers. "Can ye…forgive me?"

She searched Arlys's face for some sign of trickery, but saw only compassion and remorse. "Why do you say these things to me?"

"I've been beastly to ye, I know. I was..." Arlys glanced outside where Alex stood in whispered conversation with a half-dozen men. "I was jealous."

"Arlys, I—"

"Och, I know ye have no interest in him—Alex—the bluidy numbskull. 'Tis just that he's, well...shunned me since ye came to us, and I—I—"

"You love him."

Arlys smiled and squeezed her hand. "I always have."

Rachel knew it was true, could see it in her eyes. 'Twas only natural for the girl to consider her a rival, given Alex's behavior these last weeks.

"You mustn't worry," she said. "Alex has no interest in me beyond Gilchrist's orders."

In truth, Alex had pursued her affections relentlessly, yet she knew he didn't love her. She'd seen the way he looked at Arlys when he thought no one was watching. He loved the girl. Any fool could see it.

"Perhaps he's been trying to make you jealous."

Arlys's eyes lit up. "D'ye think so? Aye, that's probably it!"

There was more to it than that, Rachel suspected, but what she could not fathom. One thing was certain: Arlys was not to blame. The girl had been vile to her, true, but now begged her forgiveness. Rachel would neither hurt nor worry her with the truth of things.

Then a thought struck her. "Arlys, about my ring..."

The girl stared at Alex, and Rachel had to shake her to get her attention. "Oh, aye, sorry. What about it?"

"How did you know 'twas a betrothal ring? Even I was

not certain.'' God's truth, she had not been certain, but had had bad feelings about it ever since the dream.

"Why, Moira told me, just this morning."

"After you knew I'd gone missing?"

Arlys nodded. "Aye. Alex was about early, searching the whole village for ye. When he didna find ye, Murdoch told him ye were with the laird."

"Murdoch was here, this morning?"

"Aye, he rode in just before dawn."

Some things were beginning to make sense to her. "So Moira told you about the ring, after everyone knew Gilchrist and I had passed the night together."

Arlys nodded, then wrinkled her brow. "Why is it important?"

Rachel hid her excitement. "Oh, 'tis not. I just wondered, is all."

It *was* important.

Moira deliberately planted the seed in Arlys's mind. But why? Alex was her son, and she'd heard talk amongst the clan of what a strong laird he would make.

If Gilchrist was to wed her, an Englishwoman with no memory of who or what she was, 'twould only make Alex seem a better choice in everyone's eyes. Why, then, would Moira try to sabotage their relationship? None of it made sense, and the harder she tried to understand, the more confused she became.

There was only one thing to do now. She must solve the mystery, find the truth. She had thought she could bury the past, deny it, but she'd been wrong.

'Twould always lie between them, Gilchrist and her. His reaction to the ring proved it. And he had called *her* faithless. It didn't matter now. She must find out for herself. Whatever she was, she would know it, and would have Gilchrist know it.

'Twas loathing she'd read in his eyes just now, but last night she'd seen love. Her mind was made up. She gripped Arlys's arm. "Would you do something for me?"

"Aye, anything."

"I'm leaving here and don't know when I'll return. I would have you keep a watchful eye on Peg whilst I'm gone. She needs someone strong, like you, to encourage her."

"Aye, I'll do it, but where are ye goin'? Back to England?"

"Nay." She couldn't go back. She had nowhere to go back to, no idea where she'd come from. There was only one place for her now. She brushed Arlys's cheek with her lips and the girl hugged her.

"Fare ye well," Arlys said.

"And you." She turned to leave and nearly jumped out of her skin. "Alex!"

He had a look of triumph about him that disgusted her.

"I would offer ye escort, protection on your journey," he said.

"My journey?" Her pulse quickened. There was something about him that frightened her. He'd grown strange in the last few days, as if he were not himself, but moved according to another's will.

He smiled thinly. "To Craigh Mur, of course. Is that no the place ye wish to go?"

She didn't answer.

"Ye canna go alone. 'Tis too dangerous." He grasped her hand and she fought the urge to pull it away. "Besides, ye dinna know where it is."

Twenty men waited in the stable yard behind him— Alex's men. Those she'd noticed stood by him always, ready to act on his command.

Alex was right. She couldn't go alone, and the journey

was too important to abandon. She would have to trust him. What choice did she have?

She drew her hand from his grasp and tipped her chin. "Very well. Give me one hour, and I shall be ready to depart."

Alex nodded. As he turned to leave, he flashed an almost imperceptible smile in the direction of one of the sheds flanking the stable yard.

A keen foreboding inched its way up Rachel's spine. She stepped into the light and narrowed her eyes against the sun's glare. Moira stood in the shed's doorway, smiling, as her son strode confidently toward the keep.

Gilchrist wrenched the battle-ax from its position on the wall and leveled his gaze at Hugh. "Come on. I've a need for some exercise."

"What, now?"

"Now." In an hour's time his wrath had not diminished. He pulled Hugh off the bench by his shirt collar, to the surprise of the other warriors lunching in the great hall.

"Whoa! At the least let me finish my meal."

His stomach turned just looking at the food. Christ, how could anyone eat? He grabbed a bannock from the trencher on the table and thrust it into Hugh's hands. "Here, bring it with ye."

Five minutes later they stood on the battlement, stripped to the waist, weapons drawn. The day proved warm, and already he felt the sweat break out on his back as he began carving slow, deliberate circles into the air with the ax.

Hugh wolfed down the last of the bannock and lowered his sword whilst he brushed a few stray crumbs from his mouth.

"Ahhh!" Gilchrist lunged and swung the blade.

"What the—" Hugh ducked as the ax cut the air with a whoosh. "Bluidy hell! Why ye swivin' bas—"

"Come on." He swung the ax again. "Ye've bested me for a month. Let's see ye do it today."

Hugh moved like lightning and wielded his broadsword in skillful defense. Gilchrist lunged and swung again, grunting with the effort. Ah, it felt good. First the right hand, then the left. Aye, he'd mastered the art—let any man try to prove otherwise.

They worked their way along the battlement—lunge, duck, attack, retreat—until both of them sweated like sows in labor.

"All right, enough," Hugh wheezed.

He swung again, this time with more force, determined to drive all thought of her from of his mind.

"I yield, ye've won!"

He spun around and, as Hugh ducked, swung the ax past the spot his friend's neck had just occupied. "Bluidy bitch!" The momentum of the heavy, two-headed blade nearly knocked him off his feet as it connected with the exterior wall, sending sparks flying from the stone.

"Christ, Gilchrist, I said I yield!"

He flung the battle-ax into a corner and collapsed against the wall. His breath came in short gasps; his heart hammered in his chest.

Why in God's name did she not tell him? She'd let him believe she was his when she was not. Oh, and he had believed, with every fiber of his being. He'd trusted her. Loved her. And for the second time in as many years he'd been played for a fool.

Hugh's broadsword clattered to the stone pavers. He gripped the battlement for support, trying to catch his breath. "What were ye thinkin', to kill me? Are ye mad?"

Aye, he was as mad as the hounds of hell, ready to rip out the throats of any who crossed him.

Hugh cocked his head and screwed his face up. "Bitch?"

He hadn't realized he'd spoken aloud. What did it matter? He'd have Hugh take her away in the morning. She'd be out of his life for good. She'd served her purpose. He was fully healed, back to his old self. He didn't need her anymore. He grimaced and ran a sweaty hand over the scarred surface of his skin.

"Aye, she's done a fine job with ye."

He grunted in response. What was Hugh, a bloody mind reader?

"So now ye're done with her."

He leaned his head back against the stones and closed his eyes. Aye, he was done with her, and all women.

"Weel, it seems she's done with ye, too."

His eyes flew open. "What d'ye mean?"

"Look." Hugh pointed to the bailey, below. "She's leaving."

"Who, Rachel?"

"Aye, the same. And Alex with her."

He leapt to his feet, still winded from their mock battle. "Bluidy—" He choked back his first reaction as he watched Alex lift her into the saddle.

Hugh cocked a tawny brow.

He forced a calming breath and reined in his wild emotions. "What of it?" he said, feigning disinterest. "I thought her gone hours ago." In truth, he hadn't expected this. Aye, he would have sent her away on the morrow, but for her to leave of her own accord…

He fought the ridiculous feelings growing inside him. He was back to himself now, in control, invincible. What did she matter to him?

She did matter.

He dug his nails into the rough stone of the battlement. Her declarations of love, his name whispered from her lips. His senses burned with the memory of their coupling. Aye, and once he'd burned for another.

I am not Elizabeth Macgillivray.

As the small party left the stable yard and snaked their way through the crowded bailey, Rachel looked up suddenly, and met his gaze. He saw neither tears nor other signs of anguish in her face, only hardened resolve.

"D'ye wish me to stop them?" Hugh asked, and began to gather up his cast-off garments and weapons.

"Nay, let them go." He forced the words out.

Hugh grabbed his arm. "Ye'll let her go? Now? After all that's—"

He jerked away and made for the staircase, his gut knotting as his decision crystallized. "Aye, let her go. She matters not." As he started down the steps into the keep, he looked back and caught Hugh's icy expression.

Rachel turned in the saddle and looked back, shading her eyes against the glare of the afternoon sun. She could still see Monadhliath, far in the distance, silhouetted against a cloudless sky.

She imagined Gilchrist on the battlement, his fair hair tousled in the breeze, stormy eyes fixed to the west. She wondered if he could see her, then reproached herself for the thought. They were miles away. Besides, he didn't care.

He'd let her go. Just like that.

She traced the outline of her lips with a gloved finger and recalled his touch, the heat of his body, every whispered endearment.

"Why d'ye stop?" Alex's voice wrested her from her

thoughts. Her cheeks warmed with a blush she knew he could see. He pulled his mount up close to hers and glanced briefly eastward, back the way they'd come. "What are ye thinking?"

"Nothing." Everything. She couldn't stop thinking about Gilchrist. She drew herself up and forced a pleasant expression. "I was just...wondering how far we've come."

"No far enough," he said and urged his mount forward. "Come on, there's plenty of daylight left."

She guided Glenna into the well-worn path behind him, and the twenty or so Davidson warriors riding escort fanned out around them.

The farther away from Monadhliath they rode, the more relaxed Alex became, and the more doubtful she grew. She had to do this, and yet...as she gazed westward, toward the craggy, windswept hills, a feeling of dread gripped her.

"Have ye given my proposal more thought?" Alex called back to her.

Her stomach did a slow roll. She did not answer him.

"Well, 'tis no matter. I'm a patient man, Rachel."

The way he said her name made her shudder. It reminded her of something—but what? She closed her eyes and tried to remember. 'Twas on the edge of her memory. She reached for it, focusing all her thought, but...nothing.

'Twas so frustrating!

"Does any of this seem familiar to ye?" Alex nodded to the stark landscape surrounding them.

She shook her head. "It does not."

They rode like that for some time, as the sun dipped lower and lower toward the horizon, bathing them in a golden light. She kept looking back, thinking perhaps, hoping...

"He willna follow us," Alex said.

The man's intuition was almost chilling. "What? Who do you mean?"

He slowed his mount and let her catch him up. "Gilchrist. He's done with ye. He willna follow."

"Oh, but that's not what I was—"

"He's like that, ye ken. With his women. He always has been." He shot her a meaningful glance. "Och, before the fire, he plowed through dozens. He's no the kind of man who'd be happy with just one."

She had heard tales in the village of Gilchrist's youth. He'd been quite the scoundrel, to hear Peg and others tell it, before his betrothal to Elizabeth Macgillivray.

"And now that he's full healed, well..." Alex arched a dark brow. "'Tis better for ye this way."

So, he would cast her off for belonging to another—which she did not—yet spill his seed in every castle and village in the Highlands? So Alex would have her think.

God's truth, she didn't know what to think.

The path continued west, down into another long valley. This one was open and green. The setting sun cast golden shafts of light across it, bathing their faces in a warm glow.

To her surprise, Alex left the path and reined his gelding north. He led them into a dense wood where no sunlight breached the thick canopy of trees looming dark above them.

"Where are we going? This is north, and Craigh Mur is that way." She pointed west, toward the valley.

Alex shrugged. "'Tis no safe for us to travel the road. 'Tis too open. We could be seen for miles."

Exactly.

That thought had comforted her. After all, she was not hiding. In her dream, the man on the ridge searched far

and wide, desperate to find her. He was someone who
would never harm her, she was certain of it.

"We shall remain in the cover of the trees for the rest
of our journey," Alex said. He quickened the gelding's
pace.

What choice did she have?

She took one long look back at Monadhliath Castle,
awash in sunset colors, a fiery citadel in the east, then
followed Alex into the dark wood.

Chapter Fifteen

Truth was the most brutal mistress of all.

Gilchrist leaned against the open door of Murdoch's cottage and waited for the elder's reply. Dying embers crackled in the hearth, the heat a welcome respite from the chill night air. Gilchrist had walked the village half the night, unable to sleep. He repeated his question. "Will ye council me, then?"

Murdoch sat up in his bed. "Ye dinna need my advice."

"You're wrong."

"Hmph."

He stepped into the room and closed the door behind him.

Murdoch eyed him with a paternal disgust. "For a man who's survived a trial by fire—in spirit as well as body—ye seem to have learnt damned little."

"Murdoch, I—"

"Och, get out. I've nothing to say to ye. Besides, ye're ruining my sleep." Murdoch hunkered down under the mountain of plaids that covered his narrow bed.

"I just—"

"Get out!"

The rebuke stung him more than he wished to admit. He stepped out into the predawn mist blanketing the ground and quietly pulled Murdoch's door closed behind him.

His thoughts raced. If only he could sleep. He wandered the village again, snaking between the rows of crofts just below the bailey, not heading in any particular direction, but always coming back to the same place.

Rachel's cottage.

"Ah, what the hell."

He tripped the latch and pushed open the door. 'Twas dark as midnight inside. He slumped onto her bed and let his eyes adjust to the dark. He could barely make out the old woman's book lying closed on the table, the neatly stacked mortars, and bundles of drying herbs hanging from the low ceiling. The hearth was dead and cold.

Iain's words gnawed at him.

Ye didna love her.

"Christ."

Perhaps he'd been envious of his brother's happiness— a loving wife, a home, fat bairns playing at their feet. It mattered not, the reasons Gilchrist had sought the match with Elizabeth Macgillivray.

Iain was right.

He'd never loved her.

He settled back onto Rachel's bed and drew his legs up under him for warmth. The pillow smelled of her. He closed his eyes and smiled in the dark, remembering the lavender scent of her hair, the silken softness of her skin.

'Twas time he saw things for what they were.

It had been far easier to blame Elizabeth than to face the truth about himself. He'd let Alistair and Margaret perish in the flames, and he was maimed for life—unfit to lead their clan on either count.

His own indifference had driven Elizabeth into the arms of another. He didn't love her, and she'd known it. The fire had been a convenient excuse; his burns, a way out. And after she'd gone, well…'twas easy to blame his downfall on her sin.

But the sins had been his.

Denial, self-pity, guilt, fear.

Rachel was right. 'Twas not his body needed healing, but his heart—and his thick head. What woman could love such a man? He didn't deserve to be loved, yet she offered hers, freely and without condition. And what had he done? He'd cast it off as if it were some worthless trinket.

"Fool."

Rachel had told him the truth at the stable yard—what she knew of it. She'd begged him to listen, but he'd have none of it. His distrust and rage were fueled by fear.

He'd called her *whore*. How could he have hurt her like that? He gripped his brow and recalled her stoic expression as she'd ridden from the bailey. That, and Alex's strange demeanor.

Still, there was the ring.

Proof she was promised to another? He didn't know if it was true or not—hell, even she didn't know. But she'd gone to find out, and whatever truths lay in wait for her, he'd not have her face them alone. He would stand with her.

Ten minutes later he knelt in the men's barracks and shook the snoring pile of furs sprawled across a narrow pallet. "Hugh, wake up!"

"Wha-what?"

He shook him again, harder. "Get up!"

Hugh bolted upright, furs flying, and scrambled for his weapons. "Christ, what is it? Are we under siege?"

"Nay. Get dressed." He plucked Hugh's shirt and plaid

from a hook on the wall and tossed them to his groggy friend. "I want ye and a score of men, handpicked, saddled and ready by dawn."

Hugh wiped the sleep from his eyes and gawked, blinking. "Aye, but where are we going?"

Gilchrist's head was clear for the first time in weeks, months maybe. He smiled in the dark. "Craigh Mur."

The dream woke her.

"Gilchrist," she breathed, and reached for him in the dark. Her hand lit on the damp ground.

Rachel's eyes flew open. She abruptly sat up, pushing the plaid coverlet away. My God, where was she? Gilchrist! This place—what had happened? Her heart raced as she tried to adjust her eyes to the dark.

A thick fog shrouded the forest floor. She could barely make out the trees surrounding her, ghostly sentinels in the dark. Water dripped from the thick canopy above. Her hair was damp, as was the plaid that had covered her.

She remembered now. She was in the forest camp with Alex and his men, on her way to Craigh Mur. He had led them deep into the wood for safety. She shivered and pulled the plaid close about her.

But where was Alex now?

She didn't remember falling asleep. They'd had no fire last night. 'Twas too dangerous, Alex had said. She wiped the sleep from her eyes and peered into the fog. Ah, she could see them now, Davidson warriors asleep all around her. A fair number of them snored.

She heard a soft whicker, and her eyes were drawn to the sound. Their horses were tethered among the trees, just beyond the limit of her visibility.

She felt better now and drew a deep breath.

Fragments of her dream hovered at the edges of her

consciousness. She'd seen him again—the man searching among the standing stones. Searching for her.

She rose quietly and wrapped the plaid she'd used as a blanket around her shoulders. 'Twas closer to dawn than she'd first suspected. She could see a little better now, well enough to tiptoe around the sleeping men without waking them.

The ground was soft and did not betray her movements as she snaked her way to the edge of the copse where their horses were tethered. Glenna snorted as she passed. ''Shhh, rest easy,'' she whispered to the mare, and continued on.

She didn't wonder where she was going. It seemed perfectly natural to her to be about in a strange wood in the gray hour just before dawn. Something drew her, compelled her to keep moving west. Nothing about her surroundings confirmed her direction, but she knew it all the same.

She was traveling west. To Craigh Mur.

Rachel didn't know how long she walked, only that she grew increasingly tired and cold. The wet forest floor soaked through her deerskin slippers, chilling her feet to the bone.

She reached the edge of the wood without warning and stopped. The sky had gone gray with the approaching dawn, though she could see little better than she'd been able to in the dark. The fog was thicker here, and swirled around her in ghostly white wisps. A queer sensation gripped her as she looked out into the nothingness which lay just beyond the cover of the trees.

Something was out there.

Something and someone.

The mist cleared for a split second, enough for her to see the lay of the land. A craggy hill rose up before her, carpeted in amethyst waves of heather, bright lichens, and rich green mosses which lent color to the otherwise dull surroundings.

She had a sudden, overpowering urge to step out into the open, away from the safety of the wood. What was this place? She lifted her skirts, now muddy and dripping from her trek, and prepared to step forward.

A hand closed over her mouth from behind.

Another gripped her waist.

Her eyes went wide as she tried to scream, struggling against her captor.

"Hush! Quiet now." The man lifted her off her feet and dragged her backward into the wood.

She clawed at his hands, trying desperately to wrest herself from his grip.

"Stop it," he hissed.

Sweet God, she must do something! She let out a grunt and kicked backward with all her might. She connected with his shin.

"God's blood!" He abruptly dropped her and she landed hard on her rump on a pile of wet twigs. "What are ye trying to—"

She twisted around and looked up at the warrior looming over her. "Alex!"

"Aye." He grimaced as he tenderly inspected his booted shin.

"Oh, thank God. I thought you were… I—I didn't know 'twas you." She took a few deep, calming breaths and sat there until her pulse returned to normal.

"What in God's name are ye doing so far from the camp? Are ye mad?" He offered her a hand and, none too gently, pulled her to her feet.

She blinked a couple of times. "I—I don't know." She glanced at the thick stands of larch and pine surrounding them. "I'm not certain. I just began walking and… suddenly here I was."

Alex frowned.

"What is this place? That hill over there." She pointed to the edge of the wood. "What is it?"

Alex gripped her arm and pulled her deeper into the wood. "Come on. 'Tis nearly dawn, we must get back."

"But—"

His angry look precluded further questions. They walked for a few minutes in silence. She wondered how Alex had found her. The weather notwithstanding, the wood was dense, and seemed to have no distinguishing landmarks.

A horse whinnied in the distance. She strained her eyes but could not see for the heaviness of the fog. Alex pulled her in the direction of the sound.

"Your mount?" she guessed.

"Aye."

She saw him now, the sorrel gelding, tethered to a tree. "But why—"

"I didna wish to call attention to myself."

That seemed obvious. But why?

Alex helped her into the saddle and quickly mounted behind her. Before she had a chance to ask him more questions, he spurred the gelding into a trot. The horse snaked through the heavy stands of timber while she held fast to the pommel, trying to avoid leaning back against Alex's chest.

After a time, he slowed the beast to a walk. The wood was thick here; the close canopy of trees blocked the light and, together with the mist, shrouded them in an unwelcome twilight.

Why had she come here? What was it compelled her? She began to regret her actions. She looked down at her dripping, mud-caked gown and ruined slippers. She was chilled to her very soul, and pulled the now soaked plaid closer about her.

She thought suddenly of Gilchrist, imagined him stretched out, naked and asleep, not in his chamber at Monadhliath, but in the cave, on the fur-covered pallet where they'd made love. A wave of emotion washed over her. She cursed him silently.

Alex's hand slipped around her waist and she snapped to attention, every muscle taut.

"He would have let ye come alone," he said.

"Wh-who?"

Alex leaned closer and whispered in her ear. "Gilchrist."

His words unnerved her—not because she believed them, but because of the way Alex seemed to know when she was thinking of Gilchrist.

"Ye have naught to fear," he said. "I shall protect ye." Alex pulled her back against his chest and she let out a small shudder. "Och, ye are cold." He inspected her soaking garments. "Ye shall catch your death. Here, allow me…" He started to pull the wet plaid from off her shoulders.

"Nay, I'm fine, truly." She grasped at the edges of the fabric.

Alex ignored her. "'Tis soaked through." He tugged it away from her and stuffed it into an empty saddlebag.

Now she was truly cold.

Alex fumbled around behind her. What on earth was he doing? To her surprise, he unpinned the clan badge securing his plaid to his shoulder, and unfurled a length of fabric that he wrapped around both himself and her. He pulled her back snugly against him and bid her hold the edges of the plaid together so they might conserve their heat. She obeyed, and had to admit she felt much warmer.

They rode awhile in silence, and she found herself relaxing, finally, in Alex's solid embrace. She wanted to trust him, to think he'd been kind to her because of his allegiance to Gilchrist. She knew it wasn't true.

"I had meant to return this to ye yesterday," Alex said abruptly.

"What?" She pulled away so she could turn and look up at him.

He smiled. "This." He dipped a hand into his sporran and drew forth the silver necklace, his forgotten gift to her. Even in the flat light of dawn the pink stone glimmered. "'Twas hanging by the hearth in your cottage. When I didna see ye wearing it, I sent one of the men back to fetch it."

She turned away, suddenly embarrassed. She hadn't forgotten it. She didn't want it, and had left it behind on purpose.

"Here, let me place it 'round your neck where 'twill be safe."

Reluctantly, she allowed him to slip the chain over her head. What else could she do? He had meant the gift as a show of affection, a kindness. She would not insult him with the truth of her feelings. Besides, she needed him to take her to where she must go.

"There, 'tis lovely. As are ye."

She felt the tiniest spark of panic as Alex reined the gelding to a halt and drew her close.

Her eyes widened as he brushed his lips against her hair. "Rachel, I told ye I was a patient man, but I find it difficult to be so close to ye and be denied your affection."

Her panic grew. She pulled away from him, pressing

herself as far forward in the saddle as she could, until the pommel dug into her belly. She scanned the trees surrounding them, but could see little for the mist. How close were they to the camp, to the other men? She had no idea.

Her thoughts raced. She must think of something to divert his attention from her. A thought struck her and she mustered her most confident voice. "What of Arlys? She loves you, you know."

She felt him stiffen in the saddle.

"'Tis only a fleeting fancy. Besides, Gilchrist will wed her for certain now."

She could not believe that, would not believe it.

"I know you love her." She turned to meet his gaze. "I've seen the way you look at her when you think no one's watching."

For a split second she saw the truth of it in his eyes, then he hardened his expression. "Ye are mistaken."

"I think not."

He pulled her close again and ran a finger along her upturned chin.

"Don't do that." She tried to turn away but he held her face in an iron grip.

"There is only one woman for me," he whispered so close to her she felt his breath on her lips.

His dark eyes closed to mere slits, a predator about to strike. She tried to pull away but he held her fast. The horse jerked beneath them.

Her heart hammered, her whole body stiffened in his grasp as Alex tilted his head and gently pressed his cold lips to hers.

Chapter Sixteen

Where in God's name were they?

Gilchrist slipped from the gray's saddle to study the jumble of hoofprints set deep in the muddy road. Why hadn't he taken Hugh along as planned? He was the best tracker among them. Gilchrist hadn't considered that, when at the last minute he'd asked Hugh to stay behind and watch over the clan in his absence.

The morning's mist had cleared and he could see a fair distance along the wide path that cut the Highland forest in two. Hoofprints snaked along the road in both directions. None of the marks were more than a day old.

Gilchrist had ridden like the devil himself that day to try and catch them up. The sun already dipped westward. Alex and Rachel would have arrived at Craigh Mur last night, had they kept to the road, but he wasn't so certain they had. His gaze fixed on a set of hoofprints smaller than the rest.

Glenna!

He was sure of it. The mare was small and carried Rachel who weighed no more than eight or nine stone. The prints were not deep-set like the others, confirming his suspicion.

One of his warriors dismounted and knelt beside him. "Did they rest here, Laird?"

"Aye, methinks they did." He rose and followed Glenna's hoofprints until they left the road and veered north into the forest. Most of the prints continued west on the path to Craigh Mur. He couldn't tell whether the mare had come back to the road or not. "The question is, which way did they go?"

The warrior shrugged his shoulders.

"Damn!"

They remounted, and his men looked to him for direction. He scanned the road ahead and the forest surrounding them. Which way? Christ, he had to find them. Why had he let her go? Idiot! He reined the gray north, then west again. Damn his bloody pride! He'd never forgive himself should some harm come to her.

He'd have to trust in Alex's judgment. The man was a keen warrior—and a friend, despite the events of the past few months. If he'd led Rachel off the path, there must have been a good reason to do so.

That reason became clear to him as an arrow whistled past his ear and buried itself with a *thunk* in the larch tree behind him.

He drew his broadsword, fixed his gaze on the road ahead, and goaded his mount sideways into the cover of the trees. His men followed suit. With his eyes he directed them to wait silently until he gave the command to action.

A moment later he saw them—a party of a dozen or so warriors, garbed not for battle but for a journey. Gilchrist and his men outnumbered them almost two to one. He would wait until they drew closer and he could glean their intent, before he decided what to do.

The warriors slowed their mounts to a walk and continued their approach. Their leader appeared over confident for what Gilchrist thought a precarious situation for them. He was a substantial-looking man who sat tall and proud in the saddle, as if he were the king of Scotland himself.

Gilchrist noticed the longbow slung over the leader's shoulder. 'Twas likely his arrow stuck in the tree behind him. Had the warrior wanted him dead, Gilchrist knew he would have already been dispatched.

"Bluidy hell," he muttered under his breath. His brother Iain would skin him alive had he seen what had just occurred. Iain was one of the finest archers in all the Highlands, and had taught him since childhood never to leave himself open to such a shot.

As they approached, Gilchrist recognized their livery and the clan badges decorating their plaids and bonnets.

Macphearson.

The leader drew his mount up twenty paces from where they were positioned inside the cover of the wood. His men fanned out beside him. "Ho!" the leader called out. "Who are ye and what d'ye want?"

The Macphearson had no lack of courage, Gilchrist would grant him that. With his eyes, Gilchrist cautioned his men to be ready. He lowered his weapon but did not sheath it, and nudged the gray out onto the open road. "Mayhap I should ask the same of ye."

The warrior arched a brow and appraised him. Gilchrist did the same. He was a striking man, squarely built, with long dark hair loose about his shoulders and eyes the color of stout ale.

His weapons, though sheathed, were impressive. Intricate silver work defined the hilts of both his sword and his dirk. The others bore weapons with similar markings.

What drew Gilchrist's attention most was a length of braided leather around the warrior's neck, at the end of which dangled a pinkish gemstone, much the same as the one Alex had given Rachel. Where the hell had Alex gotten it?

"I am Robert Macphearson," the warrior said. "And ye tread too close to our land to my liking."

Gilchrist casually sheathed his broadsword. "'Tis the forest road, and free to all who travel the Highlands."

Macphearson narrowed his eyes and nodded at Gilchrist's burned hand. "Ye are The Davidson. I recognize ye from the tales we'd heard some months past."

"Aye, Gilchrist Davidson Mackintosh."

"Well, Gilchrist Davidson Mackintosh, I would ask ye again. What are ye doing so far afield?"

The warrior's insolence wore thin on him. 'Twould be easy to put a stop to it, but Gilchrist was not of the mind to start a war. The old Macphearson laird wished to join the Chattan alliance, or so Gilchrist had been led to think by Hugh and others. He'd not compromise that opportunity for the short-lived pleasure of besting one overeager warrior.

"We're hunting," he said simply.

Both of them knew 'twas a lie, but Robert Macphearson remained silent.

Gilchrist was aware of his own men moving into formation behind him. "And ye," he said to the warrior, nodding at their bursting saddlebags. "On a journey, are ye?"

Macphearson held his gaze. "Carrying home our dead."

Gilchrist noticed earlier that two of Macphearson's men had plaid-covered bundles strapped awkwardly across the backs of their mounts. Now he saw the booted feet sticking out from one of the bundles.

"Canna ye smell them?" Macphearson asked.

He did, in fact, smell something fair wicked, but he'd thought it their natural odor. After all, 'twas just now spring, and not many bathed in the winter.

"When did it happen?"

The warrior shrugged. "Ten day ago, a fortnight mayhap. I'm no certain. We found them just today."

A fortnight ago Alex had traveled north to Findhorn Castle to invite Iain to their celebration. He would have traveled this very road, at least for part of the journey. Gilchrist stared again at the warrior's pink stone and recalled Alex's gift to Rachel.

"In fact," Macphearson said, "we were on a journey of sorts. We are searching for someone—a woman. Perhaps ye have seen her?"

Gilchrist tensed, digging his fingernails into the gray's leather reins.

"We expected her and her kinsmen nearly six week ago, but she never arrived."

His heart skipped a beat. "From where was she riding, this woman?"

Macphearson arched a brow. "From England."

Gilchrist's men were well trained and betrayed not a hint of their knowledge. He merely stared at the warrior, grinding his teeth so as not to speak, his thoughts racing.

"I dinna expect ye've seen her?" Macphearson's eyes burned into him.

He shrugged. "What does she look like?"

"I canna say, for I've ne'er seen her. But they say she has the mark, the same as our laird."

"What mark?"

"A birthmark—a shock o' white hair just here." Macphearson pointed to the nape of his neck.

An image of Rachel, naked and writhing beneath him, her raven hair swept upward to reveal the mark, flashed in Gilchrist's mind. He fought to control his emotions, lest they reveal his knowledge to the warrior. "But, she is an Englishwoman, ye say."

"Half."

Good God. "And her name?"

Macphearson glared at him for a moment, as if he were weighing how much to reveal. "Rachel," he said, finally. "Rachel Macphearson Hensley."

Gilchrist's blood ran cold. The gray fidgeted underneath him, acutely aware of his shock. No wonder she understood their speech so well.

Macphearson.

If Alex had taken her straightaway to Craigh Mur, she would be with the Macphearson laird even now. More and more, Gilchrist was certain Alex had not done so—and thank God for it. He needed time to think about his next move. What he'd do when he finally found them.

The muddle of hoofprints, some of them Glenna's, lay between them and the Macphearsons. 'Twas only a matter of time before the warrior wondered at their meaning. Gilchrist spurred his mount forward, closing the distance between them and obliterating the day-old marks. His men followed, flanking him closely.

Macphearson studied him, his gaze sliding over Gilchrist's burnt arm, exposed for all to see in the sleeveless tunic he wore tucked into his plaid.

Gilchrist leveled his gaze at the warrior and appraised him in turn. He wondered if this was the man to whom Rachel was promised. If she remembered, and if it were so, what then would she think?

He glanced briefly at his own horrible scarring, and fought the urge to hide his burnt hand in the folds of his plaid. His gaze lit on the burnished skin of Robert Mac-

phearson's well-muscled arms and capable hands. The
warrior was something he could never be.

Whole.

He told himself it didn't matter, that Rachel didn't care.
She loved him all the same. She'd said it, over and over,
and he believed her. But when she laid eyes on Robert
Macphearson, would her feelings change?

The forest had gone quiet of a sudden. No birds warbled overhead. Gilchrist was aware only of the Macphearsons' creaking livery and the occasional restless snorting
of their mounts.

By God, he'd know the truth of it, though 'twould
cleave his heart in two. "Why d'ye seek this woman?"
he asked.

Macphearson smiled thinly at him. "I have my own
reasons for finding her."

'Twas true then.

She was betrothed.

"He dared no risk a second kiss, eh?" The Davidson
warrior laughed so hard Rachel could swear he had tears
streaming down his face.

She glared at him, her cheeks flaming, then tossed Alex
a small leather pouch from her kit. "Infuse this in boiling
water and make of it a hot compress. 'Twill still the swell-
ing."

"What is it?" Alex asked.

"Comfrey and a bit of calendula."

"'Twas lucky for him we brought a healer with us!"
The warrior made a lewd gesture and the rest of Alex's
men dissolved into laughter.

Alex scowled, then immediately winced and sucked in
his breath. He dabbed gingerly at his blackened eye.

Served him right. Rachel's fist still stung from the blow.

"You'll live," she said, and started toward the edge of camp to return her kit to Glenna's saddlebag.

She ignored the bawdy comments Alex's men cast after her. She'd never been so thankful in her life as when they'd found Alex kissing her in the forest. She'd struck him in self-defense, but that had only fueled his ardor. What might he have done had his men not come upon them? She shuddered to think on it.

Alex had been acting more and more strangely since they'd left Monadhliath. Sometimes she caught him gazing at her with a faraway, almost wild look in his eyes. One minute he was himself, charming and gallant, and the next... God's truth, he frightened her.

She knelt beside Glenna and unbuckled the saddlebag lying on the ground. She had few possessions, thus the bag was half-empty. The rose oil she'd left with Peg, and bade her offer it to Gilchrist as a parting gift from her.

How she missed him.

She pushed the thought from her mind, then stowed her medicine kit inside the saddlebag and secured the straps. Glenna whinnied and stamped the ground with a hoof.

"Ah, you're restless." Rachel smiled. "Well, so am I." She rose and patted Glenna's sleek neck. "We've rested here far too long. We're both anxious to be on our way." The mare nickered softly in response.

Daylight waned. Rachel looked skyward and saw a few gray clouds peeking through the thick canopy of trees. Why had Alex kept her here at the camp all day? Craigh Mur was nearby—she could feel it. That morning at the edge of the wood, she was certain she'd been close, but Alex had dragged her away. Why?

Despite her growing dread of him, she had to stifle a laugh as he approached. His left eye was nearly swollen shut and had gone a striking blue-black, with a hint of purple at the edges. She straightened her spine and tipped her chin at him.

"Rachel," he said, and drew a breath. "I—I wish to tell ye I'm sorry."

"For what?"

He lowered his eyes. "For this morning."

"Ah."

"I was overcome, ye see, with my feelings for ye. I didna think—"

"When shall we move on?" She must be firm with him; show no fear. "I am anxious to reach Craigh Mur."

He met her gaze and the apology died on his lips.

"You promised to take me there. If you do not intend to honor your vow, I shall be on my way. Alone."

"Och, nay. Ye canna." He reached out to grasp her arm and she backed out of range. "I do plan to take ye. It's just…we must first make certain 'tis safe."

He was lying. She was sure of it.

"We are on Macphearson land and they are not of the Chattan alliance. The only thing in our favor is their small number and the goodly size of their demesne. Perhaps we shall be overlooked."

"But why must we hide? I don't understand. We do not threaten them, nor have they any reason to harm us."

"Our being here is reason enough."

Alex took a step closer and she backed up again, squarely against a tree. He reached for her hand, his good eye warming to that puppyish look he donned whilst trying to woo her. She relaxed a bit and allowed him to take it.

"I have promised to take ye there," he said, "and I shall. But my primary charge is to keep ye safe." He squeezed her hand gently. "Can ye no understand that?"

She could hardly argue with his line of reasoning. Still, there was something awry here.

Alex smiled. "I am glad to see ye have not discarded my gift again." He nodded at the silver necklace, letting his gaze drift to the pink stone dangling between her breasts.

In truth, she'd forgotten about the necklace, what with the events of the morning and all the comings and goings that afternoon. She wished now she'd had the foresight to cast it away in the wood. She fingered the pink stone and marveled at Alex's persistence on this particular issue.

A cry went up among the men.

Both of them turned to see what caused the commotion. A branch snapped to Rachel's right. Alex's hand moved like lightning to the hilt of his sword. She narrowed her eyes in the direction of the sound and what she saw made her heart stop.

"Gilchrist!" She fought the overwhelming urge to run toward him, and willed herself stay put.

Alex muttered a few unintelligible words under his breath. His men rose to greet their kinsmen, calling out words of welcome.

Gilchrist's gaze was fixed on her alone, his expression cool, but she perceived an undercurrent of relief in his demeanor and a warmth in his eyes that caused her pulse to quicken.

He reined his mount to a halt directly in front of her and slipped easily from the saddle, as if he'd only been out for an hour's ride. A clansman moved quickly to take the reins from him and led the gray away. Alex nodded to his laird, but Gilchrist seemed hardly to notice him.

"Rachel," Gilchrist said, "I have come to speak with ye."

Her hopes soared, but before she could answer, Alex

clapped a hand on Gilchrist's shoulder. "Laird, we are pleased—and surprised—to see ye here."

Gilchrist turned his attention to Alex and gently shrugged the warrior's hand from his shoulder. "Ye were right to take to the wood. I would speak with ye later about—"

The words died on his lips as he noticed Alex's prominent black eye. "Christ, what's happened?" He whirled on her and grasped her by the shoulders. "Are ye all right? Were ye ambushed? What in God's—"

"Och, 'tis naught!" Alex laughed and punched Gilchrist playfully on the arm. "I merely caught a low-hanging branch whilst riding." He shot her a nervous glance.

She gritted her teeth and let the lie stand. She would not have Gilchrist killing him over a mere kiss, and she was certain, despite Gilchrist's behavior yesterday, that he would not take Alex's advances to her lightly.

Gilchrist released her, his relief plain, and took a step back. His face colored slightly. "Oh, I—I thought mayhap..."

"Nay, nay, we are all well," Alex said. "In fact, we've no seen a soul excepting yourselves since we quit Monadhliath."

"Aye, well I am glad to hear it." Gilchrist glanced quickly at her, then studied the ground, kicking up a few muddied leaves with the toe of his boot.

"We have rested here a full night and a day," she said to him.

"Ah." He nodded. "Ye have?" His eyes flew to hers. "So ye have no been to Craigh Mur?"

She was about to tell him of her walk to the edge of the wood that morning, but Alex cut her off.

"Nay, we havena been there," he said quickly.

"And on your journey," Gilchrist asked, "did ye remember anything of—of your past?" She was surprised by the hint of trepidation in his voice.

"Nay, I did not. This morning I felt so close to some understanding, but nay, I remembered nothing."

Gilchrist nodded. "Ye shall, and when ye do, ye willna be alone."

She held his gaze and wondered what had caused him to be so changed toward her. Gone was his rage, but she could see he struggled to keep other emotions in check. She struggled, too.

"Nay, she shall not be alone," Alex said. "I shall be with her, naturally."

Gilchrist clapped a hand on Alex's shoulder. "I would thank ye for providing her escort."

"'Twas my duty," Alex said quickly. "Ye charged me with the task days ago."

"Aye, that I did. And now I would speak with Rachel alone."

At last. He'd come to his senses and would hear her. She drew a breath of relief.

Gilchrist nodded toward the group of clansmen mulling about the camp. "Will ye get the men settled, Alex? Set up a watch? 'Tis nearly sunset."

"Of course, but…"

"We'll be along shortly." Gilchrist gave him a little push toward the center of the camp.

Alex was not giving up; she could see it in his eyes. 'Twas clear he didn't want to leave them alone together. "But, Laird," he said. "Ye must eat something first. 'Twas a long day's ride." Gilchrist waved him off but he continued. "And Rachel—I know she's tired and cold. Look at her. She could use a bit of bread and salted meat."

"Oh, but I'm not hungry," she said quickly.

Gilchrist only then noticed her damp and rumpled gown, the mud caked to her slippers. He touched the coarse fabric and frowned. "Ye are wet, clear through to the skin. What happened?"

His concern for her made her heart swell. "'Tis from sleeping on the ground is all. There was a heavy mist last night."

"And the blasted sun doesna reach through the trees during the day," Alex added. "'Tis a miserable place, this."

"Aye, ye're right." Gilchrist looked at the clouds gathering in the rapidly darkening sky—what he could see of it through the treetops. "It smells of rain. We'll all be soaked by morning."

Alex shrugged.

"Come, then," Gilchrist said to her. "Alex is right. Let us have a bit of supper before 'tis dark."

She hid her disappointment and followed the two of them back to the group of warriors. Alex had a look of satisfaction on his face that made her blood boil. Perhaps she should have told Gilchrist the truth after all.

In the center of the camp, the men had laid out a cold supper of oatcakes, cheeses and meat. Gilchrist bade her and Alex sit on a downed log, but he did not join them. Instead, he called a few of his men to him and gave what appeared to be some very specific instructions. She could not make out his words, but he pointed several times to the treetops, then east, the way they'd come. After a few minutes of this, the men took off at a jog in that direction.

Gilchrist joined them on the log, their makeshift supper table, and they ate in silence for a while. There were many things she would say to him, but she dared not speak in front of Alex. A few times during the meal she caught

Gilchrist watching her. Each time he quickly averted his eyes. She knew not what to make of it, and could neither read his feelings nor his intent.

When they finished, Alex rose and offered her his hand. "Come, I shall prepare a place for ye to sleep."

To her relief, Gilchrist shot to his feet. "I have already arranged something." He, too, offered her a hand. His burned hand. He hadn't even noticed. Her love for him grew tenfold in that one moment.

Then his eyes fixed on the pink stone around her neck—Alex's gift. Would that she had the nerve to rip it off and fling it to the ground.

"Come," Gilchrist said and stepped toward her.

Ignoring Alex, she took Gilchrist's hand—ah, 'twas so warm—and let him lead her from the camp. "Where are we going?"

"Someplace dry and safe," he said.

She didn't care, as long as she was with him.

"I shall come with ye," Alex called out and moved quickly to her side. "For protection."

Gilchrist spared him not a glance. "'Tis all arranged. Ye shall stay here, Alex, with your men. We'll no be far off."

"But—"

"Do it," Gilchrist commanded. "And set the watch. I'll no be surprised in the night by Macphearsons."

Alex stopped in his tracks, but Gilchrist kept moving, pulling her along with him. She could feel Alex's eyes burning into the back of her. "Aye, Laird," he said. She heard him bark orders to his men as Gilchrist led her into a dense copse.

"Is it far?" she asked.

"Nay, just here."

The sun had set less than an hour ago, but the wood

had already grown dark. She could see a few of Gilchrist's men scattered here and there among the trees. They were the protection he'd mentioned.

"Here, here we are," Gilchrist said and stopped just inside a tight circle of laurel trees.

The ground was wet here, far wetter than the uncomfortable place she'd slept in last night.

"Here?" She kicked at a soggy branch and arched a brow in question.

Gilchrist smiled. "Aye, but no *here*," he said, nodding at the wet ground. "Up there." He pointed to the thick foliage above them.

Her eyes widened as she followed his gaze higher and higher. "What, a tree house?" She laughed. Then she noticed the crude ladder made of short lengths of timber lashed crossways to one of the tree trunks. "You do not jest."

"Nay." He patted one of the rungs. "Come on then, up with ye. I'll go behind to see ye dinna fall."

"But...what's up there?"

"Oh, 'tis a hunting blind—or it was. I noticed it on the way into the camp. 'Twill be dry at least, and warmer than sleeping on the ground."

She placed her hand on the rung. Dare she hope? "Will you be...are you coming, too?"

Even in the dark she could see his thoughtful expression. "Nay, I shall sleep here, right beneath ye."

"Oh," she said and looked away so he'd not see her disappointment.

"But I'll see ye safely up." Gilchrist helped her onto the crude ladder, and she began to climb. He stayed with her, making certain her feet connected with each rung before she moved to the next.

"Go careful," he said, "and dinna look down."

She wasn't much for heights, and so did as he instructed. "How high is it?"

"Oh, no so high—fifteen or twenty feet."

"Twenty feet?"

He laughed. "Dinna worry, I'll no let ye fall."

'Twas his laugh, more than his words, that comforted her. Her pulse quickened, not from the height, but from his closeness and easy manner.

She could see the platform above her, rough-cut timbers bound together with rope and secured between the small circle of trees. The scent of laurel was thick on the night air. She drew a deep breath then poked her head through the hole that had been cut into the timbers.

"Here it is," she called down to him. "I'm at the top."

Gilchrist steadied her as she pulled herself into the perch. 'Twas surprisingly spacious and more comfortable than she'd expected. The timbers were covered with fragrant, freshly cut leaves topped with a mountain of plaids and furs.

She leaned over the hole in the floor to compliment Gilchrist on his men's handiwork just as his head emerged. Their lips nearly met and she froze in place, sucking in her breath.

"Are ye…all right?" he whispered, not moving.

"Aye," she breathed.

She was aware of his scent—wood smoke and pine—and of his warm breath on her face. Her mouth went dry and her heart beat faster as she hovered there above his upturned face.

The threatening clouds above them parted briefly, and a bright half moon peeked through the treetops and lit on his face. His eyes held a question.

"Mayhap you should come up after all," she whispered.

He swallowed hard. "Mayhap I should."

Chapter Seventeen

He should have never come up there with her.

Gilchrist sat beside Rachel on the pile of soft furs and wondered how to begin. There was much he would say to her. She sat patiently, silent, as if she knew he would speak first.

The moonlight reflected off her pearly skin. God, she was beautiful. Her eyes were wide, vitreous, full of caution and promise—he dared not gaze into them overlong. She wet her lips unconsciously. He stared at her mouth, all too aware of her powerful effect on him.

Before he knew what he was doing, he'd taken her hand in his. "I—I'm sorry," was all he could manage to say.

Rachel remained silent.

"I was a hotheaded idiot to have said those things to ye, called ye—"

"Whore."

The word was a blasphemy on her fair lips, and cut him to the quick. He forced himself to meet her gaze, and saw many things there—anger, pain, hope.

"Can ye forgive me?" He held his breath and squeezed her hand. "Say ye will forgive me."

"Gilchrist," she breathed, and reached for him.

His heart nearly burst from his chest for wanting her. Mustering his resolve, he grasped her by the shoulders and held her at arm's length.

"But—"

"Nay," he whispered. "We canna."

"But why?"

A lock of hair strayed onto her brow. He brushed it off her face and let his hand linger on her dove-soft cheek. He could feel his heart breaking. "Ye know why. Dinna make me speak of it again."

She frowned as he traced the outline of her lips with his thumb. This was far harder than he'd ever imagined. He took her hands in his and kissed each open palm.

She belonged to another—a man she might have loved before the fall stole her memory. He could not allow himself to forget that. Moonlight glinted off her silver ring. He toyed with it, turning it on her finger, and watched her expression change from confusion to understanding.

"Nay." She shook her head. "Gilchrist, you don't understand."

"But I do. More than ye know." Robert Macphearson's braw features burned on the backs of his eyelids. "Ye are betrothed. Ye may no remember it, but 'tis certain."

"'Tis but a ring. If I know not its true meaning, how can you? There is no one else. Why do you not believe me?"

He did believe her. 'Twas plain she remembered nothing. Only he knew the truth of it, and it wrenched his gut.

"Rachel," he breathed. "Sweetling." He cupped her face in his hands and battled the overwhelming urge to kiss her.

Moonlight danced in her eyes and sparked off the midnight fall of her hair. He ran his fingers through her tresses, then lifted them gently away from the nape of her neck.

There it was.

The birthmark.

"What is it?" she asked in response to his frown.

He shook off the roil of emotions welling inside him. "Nothing."

He must leave. Now. Whilst he still had a mind to. He allowed his hands to trail lightly over her shoulders and down her arms. She shivered under his touch. "Are ye cold?"

"Nay, I'm—I'm fine."

He felt the damp hem of her gown and, on impulse, moved his hand to her ankle. "Your skin is like ice." Her slippers were soaked through. "Christ, ye'll catch your death."

"Nay, truly, I—"

He ignored her, stilling her protest with a look, then lifted her feet into his lap. She had to lean back on the furs to support herself.

"What are you doing?" she asked.

He removed her ruined shoes and held her slender feet in his hands. "Ye are as I found ye at the spring—wet and half frozen." He'd have a word with Alex about that in the morning.

"I never did thank you for saving my life that day," she said.

He massaged each foot from ankle to toe, until he felt some warmth return to her. She watched him intently, and finally he met her gaze. "Ye saved mine, as well, ye know."

They sat there like that for a moment, her feet in his hands, until he could no longer bear not to hold her, kiss her, be one with her again.

"I—I must go," he said, and quickly looked away. He pushed her feet aside and slid toward the ladder.

"Gilchrist, do not go."

The longing in her voice nearly broke his will. He mustered his strength and prepared to descend. "Sleep well. I shall be right below ye, if ye need me."

"I do need you." She was at his side in a flash and, before he could stop her, wrapped her arms about his neck. "I need you now, to hold me, love me."

"Nay, dinna." He tried to push her away but she clung to him. Her breath was hot on his neck, her hair redolent with lavender. God help him if she wouldn't relent. "Rachel, ye are bound to another. This canna happen. It isna right."

"It *is* right." She tightened her grip on him and moved her lips to within a hairsbreadth of his. "I am bound to one man—body and soul, heart and mind."

God, this was killing him. "Nay, we canna. I must be certain."

"*I* am certain." Her lips brushed his, and he knew he was lost. Her scent, her warmth, the throaty timbre of her voice. His resolve crumbled like the stone ruin where first he thought to kiss her.

"I love you. Gilchrist, I love you."

He bore her back on the furs in a wild frenzy of need. His arms snaked around her, his body crushed hers flat. He kissed her, long and deep, until she could think no more. All she knew was his heat, the taste of him, his feral scent, his unbridled power.

He was her mate, he and no other. The knowledge coursed through her veins as he thrust his hips against her and cried her name.

"Say that you love me," she whispered. "Say it."

He kissed her again, hard, then drew back to look at

her, his face a bright fusion of passion and pain. She ran her hands through his hair—cascades of quicksilver in the moon's eerie glow—and willed him speak the words.

He did not.

Would that he loved her with half the depth of her feeling for him. She closed her eyes so he would not see her pain, and drew him down for another kiss. Tomorrow she would do what must be done, but tonight she would take what he would give her.

She arched against him and his kisses became more urgent, his caresses less gentle. He cupped her buttocks and forced her legs apart with powerful thighs. She could feel him now, hot steel pulsing against her. She burned for him, brighter than any imaginings she had dared to entertain.

"You're mine, d'ye hear me?" Gilchrist whispered between frantic kisses. His hand moved to her breast and closed over the pink stone resting there.

She'd forgotten it altogether. Their gazes locked in the moonlight. "Yours," she breathed, "and no other's."

He jerked the silver chain from her neck and cast the stone headlong into the woods below them.

Joy surged within her.

Between kisses he wrestled with the laces of her gown. Her hands flew to his belt. In seconds they were naked under the furs, and he was thrusting against her. His mouth was everywhere—teasing, tasting until she thought she'd go mad with desire.

She clung to him and spread her legs. His velvet tip grazed her flesh, sending white-hot sparks to her very core. In one powerful thrust he sheathed himself inside her. She gasped with the shock of it, reveling in his animal ferocity.

He slid one hand under the small of her back and with

the other fisted a handful of her hair. She gave herself up
to his tender assault and met him thrust for thrust as he
set their rhythm.

"No man shall have ye, save me."

"Never," she breathed and ran her hands down the
length of his muscled back. 'Twas slick with perspiration.
She threw back the furs, but the night air did naught to
cool his fire.

Without warning, he lifted her up and rolled onto his
back, dangerously close to the edge of the platform. She
protested, but his questing tongue silenced her.

"Dinna worry, I shall no let ye fall."

She straddled him and marveled at the new sensation.
The darkness, dense foliage and height shielded her from
view, or so she hoped. He thrust upward. She instinctively
moved against him and sucked in her breath so intense
was the pleasure.

"Aye, that's it. That's the way."

The breeze whipped at her hair, and it flew around them
like some witch's mane. Her nipples grew taut in the
frigid air. He drew her down and suckled first one, then
the other, never slowing his deep strokes. Her need surged
tenfold and her emotions with it, as she moved against
him, desperate for release.

He seemed to sense her distress, and through slitted
eyes she watched him smile in the moonlight. When she
could bear no more, his expert fingers were suddenly
there, teasing her over the edge into madness.

"Ah, Gilchrist!"

His thrusts quickened until he, too, found his pleasure.
By then she was spent and floating in some magical dream
state. She was barely aware of him bucking beneath her
and of his own stifled cries of ecstasy. She was his now,

and he hers—forever. He drew her close and after a while she drifted off to sleep in his arms.

Much later they made love again, only this time he was slow and gentle with her. The moon had set; she could not see his face and thus reveled in his touch, his voice, the familiar scent of him.

And though he never said the words, she felt his love burning bright all around her.

Gilchrist woke just before dawn; his first dreamlike thoughts and consummate sensations were of her.

"Sweetling," he breathed and nuzzled against the dark nest of her hair.

Rachel had slept fitfully, but was now at peace curled into the curve of his body. He pulled her tight against his chest and kissed the nape of her neck.

He vowed to keep her warm, safe—for all the days of her life, if she'd have him.

Their lovemaking had been unlike any he'd ever experienced. He'd tried, at first, to hold his feelings in check, but the clarity and depth of her emotions precluded that. And now, he didn't want to hold back. He was a different man because of her faith in him, because of her love.

She made him strong. Without her he'd be lost.

Rachel moaned sleepily and undulated her soft behind against his groin. Desire flamed; he instantly hardened.

"Gilchrist," she whispered, her eyes still closed.

"Mmm." He thrust suggestively against her and cupped a warm breast. Her nipple grew taut between his fingers.

Skylarks warbled in the foliage surrounding their own treetop nest. Dawn's pearly light filtered through the emerald canopy above them, illuminating Rachel's delicate features.

Oh, how he loved her. He hadn't told her last night when she'd asked—he couldn't. He'd been afraid. Afraid of what the past would tell her once she'd discovered it. Afraid of what her future held. But today was different. He was different. He loved her and would keep her, make her his forever.

"Is it day?" she whispered.

"Aye, just."

Rachel sighed dreamily and turned in his arms. Her skin was like hot silk. He drew her close, intending to make love to her again, and her eyes fluttered open.

"Did ye sleep well, my beauty?"

"Mmm." She smiled and brushed her lips against his. "And you, my lord?"

"Like the dead." He kissed her deeply, with the wealth of his newly embraced emotions. She responded, but after a moment pulled away. "What's the matter?" he said. "Are ye weary of my kisses so soon?"

"Nay, 'tis just…" She abruptly sat up, pulling the furs close around her, and peeked over the edge of the platform into the wood below.

"What is it? The men will no be up yet. 'Tis wicked cold, even for spring. They will welcome another hour in their beds."

She met his gaze. "I must go."

"Ah, I'm an idiot. Ye've been up here all the night with me, with no place to…well, ye know." He grabbed his shirt and pulled it over his head. "Come, I shall go with ye."

"Nay, I…that's not what I meant."

"Oh, well…what then?"

"I must go on with my journey to Craigh Mur."

The words did not register in his mind. He shook his head, confused. "I dinna understand."

Rachel gathered up her shift and gown and clutched them to her. "You must understand."

Suddenly it hit him.

"But, ye said ye forgave me. That ye loved me. After last night, all that we shared, how can ye still think to go?"

"I do love you," she said. She pulled her shift over her head and struggled with the gown. He helped her as best he could. "That's why I must go. To find the truth. To remember."

"Ye would leave me?" 'Twas unthinkable.

"Nay, not willingly." She placed a hand on his forearm. "But I would find *myself*."

"'Tis in the past, your old life. Now ye are mine. What more d'ye need know?" His thoughts raced, as he tried to understand her motives.

"I would know who I am, from whence I came, and why. I was on my way to Craigh Mur when some calamity occurred. 'Twas by the grace of God you found me." She squeezed his arm tight. "But I must know the truth before I can be free."

"What difference would it make now to us? I care not."

"Ah, but you do. You said yourself you were certain I am betrothed." She lifted her hand in front of his face and spread her fingers wide. The silver ring shone in the growing light.

"But ye said ye are not, and I believe ye now." Oh, how he wanted to believe it. He grasped her hand and folded it into his. "Rachel, I—"

"'Twould always lie between us. You know it would. You must know for certain. Only then can we be truly free."

His declaration of love stalled on his lips.

She was right.

And he was a coward.

Robert Macphearson's image burned in his mind. He let go her hand and fisted his own in his lap. "And if there is a man to whom ye are bound—" He willed her to hold his gaze. "What then, Rachel?"

He waited for her answer, his gut wrenched into a thousand knots. He was barely aware of the sounds of the waking forest around them.

"I know not," she whispered.

Before he could stop her, she scooted to the edge of the platform and poised her bare feet above the ladder.

"Wait." He grabbed her shoes, which had dried under the furs overnight, and moved to her side. "I will go with ye. When ye find the truth of things, I would be there."

Her face lit up and he knew whatever the cost to him, he'd made the right decision. He would be there when she met Robert Macphearson. And then she would choose. He prayed to God he'd have the strength to let her go, should she wish it.

"And if there is such a man?" she asked suddenly. "What then, Gilchrist?"

He slid the deerskin slippers onto her feet and brushed her lips with his. "I know not." God's truth, he didn't.

He guided her safely onto the ladder and stepped onto it behind her. His body would protect her from a fall should her feet slip on the dew-covered rungs. They climbed down and when they reached the bottom they were both surprised to find Alex leaning against the tree. The warrior looked as if he hadn't slept a wink.

"Good morrow, Laird," Alex said to him, his dark eyes fixed on Rachel. The blackened one seemed worse today, if that were possible. 'Twas not like Alex to go riding into tree limbs. Gilchrist would ask him about it again later.

Rachel nodded in response to Alex's greeting, but did not meet his gaze. Gilchrist wondered at her cautious behavior.

"Good morrow," he said and drew Alex's attention to him.

"I would speak with ye, Laird. Alone." The warrior's voice was as serious as he'd ever heard it.

"Has there been some trouble? I heard naught but forest sounds all night."

Alex knelt suddenly and picked something up from off the damp, leaf-littered ground: the pink stone dangling from its silver chain—his gift to Rachel. Alex's hand closed over it and he leveled his gaze at her. She blushed hotly. "The men heard other sounds last night, and methinks they were no of the forest."

Gilchrist exploded.

He slammed Alex back against the tree. "Shut your mouth! Friend or nay, ye've no right to speak to her so."

"Nay! Nay, I didna mean—" Alex shot him a loaded look then mouthed a word that made Gilchrist's heart stop.

Macphearson.

Rachel had turned her back on them, mistaking Alex's meaning, as had he. She didn't see this last exchange. Gilchrist came up behind her and placed a hand on her shoulder. "Rachel, I would speak with Alex alone. Go back to the camp. We'll be along shortly." He kissed her lightly on the temple.

She nodded and gave him a tiny smile. When she started back toward the camp a half-dozen warriors sprang into view, ready to escort her.

When she was safely out of earshot, he turned his attention back to Alex. "Tell me everything."

"The Macphearsons are up to something."

"Is that why ye veered into the forest instead of making straight for Craigh Mur?"

"Aye."

"I thought as much." Gilchrist nodded, recalling Glenna's hoofprints. "We met up with them ourselves, yesterday."

Alex's eyes widened. "Where? What happened?"

"On the road. They were bringing home two dead warriors." He watched Alex's eyes grow wider. "What d'ye know of it?"

"Nothing, God's truth."

Gilchrist knew he was lying, but decided to let it go for now. 'Twas not the first time one of his clan had been reckless and had killed without their laird's sanction.

He weighed his next words carefully. "They were searching for someone. Did my men no tell ye?"

"Nay," Alex said. "They did not. Who?"

"Rachel."

Alex's face paled. "Ye must no let them have her!"

His sentiments exactly, though 'twas not the reaction he expected from Alex. Rachel was, in fact, a Macphearson—half, at any rate—but he would not have Alex know that just yet. "Ye were taking her to Craigh Mur yourself. Why the change of heart? What have ye seen?"

"It's what I've been trying to tell ye. They think to murder us all. I would have told ye last night, but ye didna give me the chance."

"What nonsense is this? The Macphearsons wish to align, no fight us."

"Ye are wrong. They make ready for war even now. I saw wagons on the forest road last night laden with weapons."

"Bluidy hell, why did ye no wake me?"

Alex shrugged and shot him a patronizing look. "Ye were...busy."

Christ, what if it were true?

Gilchrist recalled Robert Macphearson's bold demeanor on the road yesterday afternoon. Alex's suspicions didn't rightly make sense, but he'd not risk Rachel's life on it. Should it come to a fight, she'd not be safe out here in the wood.

"Gilchrist, Laird." Alex grasped his arm. "Allow me to take her back to Monadhliath where she'll be safe, whilst ye remain here and discover what the Macphearsons mean to do."

'Twas a good plan, Gilchrist had to admit.

"There is movement on the road even now. We must get her safely away before one of them thinks to venture into the forest and we are discovered."

Alex was right. They had only forty men between them, and were within a few miles of the Macphearson stronghold. The Macphearsons boasted nearly a hundred warriors—too many to defend Rachel against, should it come to that.

His mind was made up. "All right," he said and met Alex's expectant gaze. "Do it."

Ten minutes later they were back at camp. Gilchrist lifted Rachel onto Glenna's back.

"But I want to stay with you!" she cried, and fought against his firm grip.

"'Tis no safe, I've told ye."

"But you haven't told me why!" She glared at him from the saddle. "What's happening? Who is it we're running from? Why won't you tell me?"

He was not about to tell her.

He'd kept so much of what he knew from her already.

'Twas wrong—he knew that now—but there was no time to put things right. They must away.

Alex nudged his gelding forward and grabbed Glenna's reins. "Come, we must go now, before we are discovered."

Rachel continued to protest, and Gilchrist hardened his heart.

"Don't let him take me!" she pleaded.

"Dinna worry, Laird," Alex said, and kicked his mount forward. "I'll have her back safe at the castle by nightfall."

"Gilchrist!"

He met her tear-filled eyes briefly, then wrenched his gaze away. He would rather have cut out his heart than send her from him, but he had no choice.

It occurred to him that this parting was nothing as compared to what he'd first intended. He would have taken her to Craigh Mur—to the Macphearsons, to her betrothed. He realized now he'd have never been able to do it, despite his good intentions.

"Godspeed," he said and raised a hand in farewell.

Rachel looked back and a shaft of sunlight lit up her face. Tears glimmered on her cheek. Last night he'd purposefully held back the words he knew she longed to hear.

"I love you," he breathed silently, and gritted his teeth in remorse as she rode out of view.

Chapter Eighteen

She had a bad feeling about this.

As the morning wore on the sky grew dark. A storm was brewing. She could smell it in the air. Each time Rachel quickened Glenna's pace, Alex moved in close and bid her slow the mare to barely a trot.

They should have reached the road hours ago. At this pace, 'twould be days before they arrived back at Monadhliath. Something was not right.

Alex had been unusually quiet since they'd left the camp. On two occasions he'd sent scouts out to the north and west—the opposite direction from where they were heading. At least she'd thought so. Now she wasn't certain.

The forest was dense and the terrain near flat. There were no landmarks at all in any direction. The sun was obscured by rain clouds, and she could not for the life of her tell in which direction they traveled.

"Alex," she called to him.

He nudged his gelding close and arched a brow in response.

"Should we not have reached the road by now?"

"Nay, 'tis too dangerous. I mean to avoid it all together."

His answer made sense to her, but she had the nagging feeling he was not telling her the whole truth.

She was still angry at Gilchrist, as well. There was something he, too, kept from her. She'd felt it last night, and was certain of it this morning. He'd come for her, had begged her forgiveness, yet still he did not trust her.

Would he never believe in their love?

She raised a hand to her lips. His scent was still on her. She closed her eyes and inhaled his musky perfume, and her mind drifted to their heated lovemaking of the night before.

Glenna lurched forward and jarred her from her trance. Now here was something strange... This part of the wood seemed familiar to her. Rachel's gaze was drawn to the tamped-down earth and a few broken oatcakes lying scattered on the ground. She blinked a few times, not believing her eyes.

They were back at the forest camp!

Quickly, she scanned the trees in all directions, but there was no sign of Gilchrist or his men. Alex had led her for hours in what must have been a circle!

She kicked Glenna forward and caught him up. "Alex, why have we returned here?"

"Hmmm?" Alex studied the sky, barely aware of her presence.

"Gilchrist bade you take me back to Monadhliath. Why have we returned to the camp?"

He glanced at her then, and smiled. "Och, well, we have things to take care of before we return home."

Something about his voice seemed different to her. And his eyes, they were huge and glazed. He looked at her,

but 'twas almost as if he did not see her. Her skin prickled.

"What do you mean?" Unconsciously, she nudged
Glenna a few paces backward.

Alex's warriors had already dismounted and were teth-
ering their mounts in the exact same spot they'd rested
the past two nights.

Alex slipped from his saddle and moved to her side in
an almost trancelike walk. "There is something I wish to
show ye in the wood." He extended a gauntleted hand to
her. "Come."

The hairs on her nape stood on end. She gazed at his
proffered hand. The leather of his glove was thin and
worn, the metal rivets dull in the flat light.

A cold fear gripped her. Her head began to throb. She
was on the brink of something, and grasped at the veiled
memory.

"Come," Alex whispered as he gripped her hand. "It's
just a bit farther—over here."

Lightning seared the backs of her eyelids as the terrifying image crashed into her consciousness. A gauntleted
hand reached out in the night. A flash of steel. The
screams of her kinsmen and the sharp stench of blood.
Most of all she remembered the voice—his voice—deep,
ominous, rich as velvet...

Come, it's just a bit farther—over here.

A silent scream rose up in her throat as Alex tried to
pull her from the saddle. She beat him away and kicked
the mare into action. Glenna nearly reared, then lurched
forward, safely out of Alex's grasp.

Suddenly she was flying through the wood. Rachel
clung to Glenna's back and urged the mare to breakneck
speed. The trees were a blur of muted color as they raced
ahead. 'Twas all she could do to dodge the low-hanging

branches which threatened to unseat her and cast her headlong to the ground.

Somewhere on the periphery of her consciousness she was aware of Alex's shouts and the thunder of hoofbeats behind her.

A flood of memories crashed in on her. She narrowed her eyes to mere slits against the wind and opened her mind to the torrent.

Her parents were dead, her home in the Borderlands taken. She'd been on her way to her mother's people when her party was murdered and she was abducted. Her mother's people—

Macphearson!

"Craigh Mur," she breathed.

Thunder rolled overhead. The sky was wicked black. Without warning the edge of the wood came up on them, and Glenna burst from the cover of the trees into a wide, open glen.

"Not so fast, vixen!"

She gasped as Alex came out of nowhere and cut her off, his sorrel gelding nearly toppling both her and Glenna to the ground. He grabbed the mare's bridle as Rachel struggled to get away.

Too late.

A moment later he pulled them back into the cover of the trees, and his warriors surrounded them.

"'Twas you!" she cried.

Alex's eyes burned into her.

"You killed them! My servants!"

He tightened his grip on Glenna's bridle and shrugged. "'Twas necessary. I dinna like killing especially, but ye wouldna cooperate." A thin smile slipped onto his lips. "Don't ye remember?"

Tears stung her eyes. She did remember. "Whoreson," she breathed.

"Aye, many agree with ye. But I canna help what's past. 'Tis the future I look to. Our future."

She bristled at his arrogance. "You'll have no future with me or anyone once Gilchrist hears of this."

"Ha! The *laird* will be halfway to Loch Drurie by now, chasing the Macphearsons 'round the Highlands."

"Bastard!"

"Aye, some call me that, as well." Alex arched a brow. "No matter. Soon they'll call me Laird."

"What are you talking about?"

An arrow whistled past them, and Alex's answer died on his lips.

"Macphearsons!" one of the warriors shouted. "To cover, to cover!"

The warriors scattered, and in the confusion Alex let go Glenna's bridle. 'Twas now or never. Rachel kicked the mare forward and they shot into the open glen.

"Nay!" Alex called after her, but 'twas too late.

Rachel looked up and froze. There it was, looming above her, exactly as she'd seen it in her dream.

Craigh Mur.

The wind was deafening. The sky churned black above her like some unleashed tempest. Her hair whipped at her face. She struggled to keep it out of her eyes so she might look upon the place which had haunted her dreams these past weeks.

The hillock was broad and flat-topped, carpeted in waves of heather and gorse that beat about in the wind. A half circle of standing stones, some broken, stood like sentinels at its crest. Behind them she saw archers, their longbows poised. She felt strangely unafraid.

Alex and his men remained hidden in the wood. She

was the only clear target, yet the archers did not shoot, as she knew they would not. They were Macphearsons, and she was one of them.

A warrior stepped out from behind one of the standing stones. He was huge, a great bear of a man. She was too far away to see him clearly, but knew he was the man from her dream. She could feel his eyes on her, and his scrutiny unnerved her.

Who was he? What was she to him?

Gilchrist's words burned in her mind.... *Ye are betrothed. Ye may no remember it, but 'tis certain.*

Oh, God, where was he when she most needed him? She didn't want to remember—she just wanted to be his. She'd come so far and now, in the end, she was afraid of the truth. Gilchrist had been prepared to stand with her and know it, whatever the outcome. How could she do less?

Rachel returned the warrior's gaze and swallowed hard. She nudged Glenna forward and the mare started up the hillock.

"Nay, they'll kill ye!" Alex shouted over the howling of the wind. He shot from the trees, brandishing his shield.

An arrow whistled past her into the trees. She did not flinch. 'Twas meant for Alex, not her. He promptly dropped back. She held the huge warrior's gaze and continued up the hill.

Lightning flashed above them, illuminating the face of the man waiting above. He was—

Old.

Rachel's head spun. A thousand tiny memories, just wisps of things—faces, names, the sound of her mother's voice—shimmered at the edges of her mind. The wind whipped at her hair and her skirts. Thunder rolled overhead.

Glenna reached the top of the hill, and Rachel reined her to a halt. In a daze she slipped from the saddle and moved slowly into the circle of standing stones.

The Macphearsons studied her through slitted eyes, but did not move. They were far fewer than first she'd thought, barely a half-dozen men, including the old warrior. Their arrows were still nocked, but they lowered their weapons as she approached.

"Rachel Macphearson Hensley," the old warrior called out to her. "Is that ye, lass?"

The name sent a shock wave through her. Her knees buckled and she dropped to the ground, steadying herself with shaking hands. Salt tears stung her eyes as she held the old man's steady gaze.

"Grandfather," she breathed.

In the next instant her awe gave way to terror as Alex and his score of men, broadswords drawn, advanced behind the six Macphearson warriors.

Gilchrist studied the massing thunderheads and frowned. They'd be soaked to the skin by nightfall. He unfurled his plaid and draped it loosely about his shoulders, taking care not to hinder his range of motion or access to his weapons.

The gray stallion fidgeted beneath him, aware of the approaching storm. He quieted the beast with gentle words and a firm hand. From his vantage point on the small ridge, he and his men had a clear view of the road in both directions. There had been no movement for hours.

That morning, after breaking camp, he'd sent two scouts to Craigh Mur. They, too, had reported nothing out of the ordinary. If the Macphearsons were up to something, as Alex had so fervently argued, Gilchrist was hard-pressed to see it. He'd wait for the rest of his scouts to return, then make for home.

His gaze drifted east toward Monadhliath, toward her. If Alex kept to a good pace, he'd have Rachel safely home before the worst of the weather hit. Gilchrist was sorry now he'd not sent more men with them.

A twig snapped behind him.

Gilchrist drew his broadsword and turned his mount in the direction of the sound. His right arm had grown strong over the past weeks—both from Rachel's expert care and his own disciplined labor. While his newly healed skin still itched and pained him on occasion, he felt remarkably good wielding a weapon.

Some of his men were on foot, their mounts tethered nearby, and they moved to flank him, weapons drawn. He narrowed his eyes, straining to see through the thick stand of laurel trees that covered the slope behind them. After a moment, a rider came into view—one of the scouts.

Gilchrist relaxed and sheathed his sword. "Harry," he called out to the man. "What news?" He spurred the gray down the slope and met the scout halfway.

Harry shrugged and wiped his sweaty brow with a square of cloth. "I seen nothin', Laird. Neither man nor beast from here to the northern border o' the wood."

"Damn," Gilchrist breathed.

The two of them rejoined their party on the top of the small ridge. Gilchrist's men grew restless. He knew they waited for some direction from him. Something was amiss; they felt it as surely as did he.

He slid from the saddle and handed the stallion's reins to one of his warriors. He needed to walk a bit, stretch his legs. A small creek cut a ravine off to his left. Gilchrist made for it.

Alex's words nagged at him. Why would the Macphearsons plan some treachery against them? It made no sense. They were small in number—fewer than a hundred warriors he guessed—and their laird was old. The Davidsons outnumbered them twice over, and could call the whole of the Chattan alliance to their back if need arose.

Yet Alex had been so certain.

And Gilchrist, all too ready to believe him. He knelt beside the creek and let the cool water rush over his hands. He splashed some on his face and drew a healthy draught of air. Thunder rumbled in the distance.

He'd had no choice, had he? For the sake of Rachel's safety he'd taken Alex's words at face value and had sent her back to Monadhliath. What else could he have done?

"Coward," he breathed, and chucked a rock into the creek.

He'd wanted to believe Alex. He'd been desperate to believe. He was afraid of losing Rachel—and that fear had clouded his judgment. Afraid that once she knew the truth—about her family, her betrothed—she'd choose Robert Macphearson, the perfect warrior, over him.

"Bluidy fool."

He loved her, and she loved him. What more need she do to prove it? Gilchrist trailed a finger over the angry, twisted scars peppering his right arm. 'Twas his own lack of confidence made him doubt the strength of her love.

She'd never doubted it.

He rose and wiped the water from his face. That last glimpse of her in the morning light, tears glassing her eyes, filled his mind and wrenched his gut.

Don't let him take me!

He'd been afraid of losing her heart and so entrusted her life to Alex's care. Alex. The image of his friend's blackened eye and the lame explanation he'd given for it flashed in Gilchrist's mind. His nape prickled. What if...

"Good God."

His stomach did a slow roll. He dropped the second rock he'd been fingering and raced to the top of the ridge, hailing his kinsmen as he ran. Those warriors who'd been lounging leapt to their feet and instinctively drew their weapons.

"Come on," he cried. "We make for home." Gilchrist's mount grazed nearby. He vaulted onto the saddle and grabbed the reins.

"But, Laird," one of his men called out. "What about the other scouts? They've no returned."

"Leave them!" Gilchrist kicked the gray into action and charged down the hill onto the road. His men followed. They reined their mounts east toward Monadhliath, a thunder of hooves kicking up clods of mud and last year's leaves.

'Twas late afternoon yet the sky was nearly black, roiling with storm clouds. Lightning flashed somewhere behind them—on Craigh Mur, mayhap. That journey would wait for another day. Now he must think of Rachel's safety.

Damn his stupidity!

For weeks now he'd been an idiot, too blinded by his own self-loathing to see Alex's string of lies, the carefully executed grasp for power both Hugh and his brother had warned him of. Alex had played on their lifelong friendship, had compelled Gilchrist to trust him.

He cursed himself and urged the gray faster.

Alex had grown even stranger these last weeks. Gilchrist could see that now, thinking back on the warrior's erratic behavior. A chilling thought struck him. What if Alex already knew Rachel's identity?

Nay, how could he?

A hundred thoughts raced through Gilchrist's mind. He

leaned low over the gray's muscled neck and narrowed his eyes on the road ahead. 'Twas drier today than it had been yesterday, and impossible to tell just where Alex had led his party out of the wood and onto the road home. If he'd led them that way at all.

Gilchrist swore silently under his breath.

An hour later, curbing his panic, he reined his lathered stallion to a walk. The gray's sides heaved with each labored breath. His men pulled up short beside him, their mounts also spent. They'd covered miles and had seen no one—not a trace of Alex and Rachel. They were halfway back to Monadhliath, and Gilchrist had the feeling he'd been led on a wild-goose chase.

"Where in God's name are they?" he roared.

"Laird!" one of his warrior's called. "Look!" The man pointed east on the road ahead.

Gilchrist strained his eyes to see in the twilight brought on by the late hour and the brewing storm.

"There!" another warrior called. "D'ye see them?"

More than twenty riders bore down on them from the east at extraordinary speed. Pray God 'twas Alex and Rachel. Nay, Gilchrist knew in his gut 'twould not be them. The Macphearsons more likely. He drew his sword and waited. His men did the same, fanning out in well-practiced battle formation.

They did not wait long. After a few minutes the riders were close enough so Gilchrist could almost make out their faces and their livery.

"Weel, I'll be…" The first warrior's brows arched in surprise. "Laird, d'ye see who it is?"

Gilchrist's eyes widened. "Hugh!" He kicked the gray forward and sheathed his weapon in one fluid motion.

"Aye, and look who's with him."

A flash of golden hair caught Gilchrist's eye, even in the low light. "Arlys," he breathed. "What the hell?"

Hugh's horse nearly collided with Gilchrist's as the two came together on the road. Hugh's men pulled up short beside him, and Gilchrist's gathered around. The air was thick with the smell of rain and two score sweaty mounts.

"What in Christ's name are ye doing here, Hugh?" Arlys maneuvered her mount through the crowd and waited, breathless, for Gilchrist to recognize her. "And what are ye thinking, carrying a woman with ye?" He shot both Arlys and Hugh stern glances.

"Aye, well ye try keeping her at home." Hugh caught his breath, then nodded to Arlys. "Short o' chaining her in the dungeon we dinna have, I had no choice but to let her come."

"But why the hell are ye here? I told ye to mind the clan."

"Aye, but something's happened ye need know."

Gilchrist's heart skipped a beat. "Rachel, where is she?"

"I know not." Hugh shrugged.

"Alex left with her this morning from our camp in the forest bound for Monadhliath."

Hugh's eyes widened. "Ye let him take her? Christ, are ye—"

"Tell me! What's happened? Where are they?"

"I know not where they are. We havena seen them."

Gilchrist fisted his hands until his nails dug into his palms and battled the urge to strike out at something, anything. He'd not wanted to believe the worst—but there it was.

Hugh unbuckled one of the saddlebags tied across the rump of his mount. "There's something ye must see—and ye willna like it much."

Arlys, who'd been silent until now, nudged her mount closer. "La-laird, b-bodies were found in a shallow grave in the wood above Braedûn Lodge." Her eyes glassed with tears and her lip trembled. "E-Englishmen, dead a month at least. Th-this was found on one of them." Arlys opened her palm to reveal a silver buckle, the letter *H* engraved boldly across it.

H for Hensley.

Rachel's kinsmen.

Gilchrist's mouth went dry.

"Aye, and this was buried with them." Hugh placed a rolled-up garment into his hands.

Gilchrist tried to keep his hands from shaking as he carefully unfurled it. 'Twas silk, of the finest quality he'd e'er seen—but ripped and dirty, with a streak of dried blood across the bodice. On impulse, he closed his eyes for a moment and inhaled of the rich fabric.

Lavender.

"Rachel," he breathed.

"Aye," Hugh said. "'Tis what we thought, as well."

Gilchrist's chest tightened. "Where exactly did ye find them—the bodies and the gown?" He met Hugh's steady gaze and his stomach did another slow roll. For he already knew the answer.

"Alex's favorite hunting spot."

Chapter Nineteen

She remembered!

Rachel's eyes flew open. "Nay!" She bolted upright and beat at the warrior who gripped her shoulders.

"Steady, steady, lass." He pushed her firmly back onto the straw mattress.

Her eyes focused and as she met his gaze her hammering heart quieted. "You—you are—"

"Ranald Macphearson, your grandfather." He smiled and squeezed her shoulders.

"Of—of course you are." She studied his craggy face in wonder. He was indeed old—sixty or seventy, she judged. His hair had once been dark, like hers, but now 'twas streaked with silver, as was his beard. Yet his eyes were young—clear and sparkling gray as a dove's wing.

He was exactly as her mother had described him, though she'd not seen him again after she'd quit his house some twenty years before.

Rachel scanned the small chamber. 'Twas spare, but a good-size wood fire blazed in the hearth. "Where are we?" she asked.

"My hunting lodge—no far from Craigh Mur."

She put a hand to her brow. "I—I must have

swooned.'' From the shock of seeing him, of remembering.

''Aye, ye fainted dead away.'' He laughed. ''God's truth, I didna expect such a reaction.''

'''Twas just…well, all at once, I knew 'twas you.''

''Aye, and I would have known ye anywhere, lass. Ye are the image of your mother.''

She smiled, remembering this. Everyone used to comment on their likeness.

''D'ye have her skill as well?'' he asked.

''You mean the healing arts?''

He nodded.

''Aye, she taught me all she knew, and arranged for others to teach me more.''

''She had the touch, and knew the way of such things sure enough, God rest her soul.''

Her heart swelled with emotion. ''You received my letter, then?''

''I did, nigh on three month ago. Both of them dead.'' He drew his hands away and fisted them in his lap.

''Aye, Mother and Father. Methinks 'twas no accident. There were many who coveted our land. And now…''

'''Twas taken from ye?''

She nodded. ''There was naught I could do about it. I had no other kin. Had I stayed, I would have been forced to wed, likely to a man I had never met.''

''Such is the way of things in England—and here they are no much different.''

''Aye,'' she breathed, and toyed with the silver ring on her finger. There was much she now remembered that she would have Gilchrist know, but 'twould have to wait.

''With Mother and Father gone,'' she continued, ''there was nothing left for me there, no reason to stay.''

"So ye thought to come to me. But, lass, how did ye know of us?"

She sat up in the bed and took his hands in hers. "Why, mother told me. I grew up on stories of the Highlands and the mighty Clan Macphearson."

"Weel, 'tis no so mighty these days."

"Mother made it all sound so wonderful, you and the clan."

His eyes glassed and he squeezed her hands as if 'twould stop the tears. "I cast her out, ye know. Her and her English lover."

"I know," she whispered.

"They wished to marry, and I'd have none of it. I was a fool." He focused his gaze on the hearth fire. "She must have hated me all these years."

"Oh, nay! She loved you."

His tears broke then, and he brushed them away with the back of his hand. "All those years wasted. Years I might have known her—and ye. She was my only child, ye know."

"Aye." She squeezed his hands again. "And I hers. But I am here now. There will be time aplenty for us to know one another."

A half smile graced his lined face. "There is something I wish to see," he said.

She arched her brows in question.

"Just here." He moved a hand to cup her nape. She leaned forward in response to his gentle pressure, and he lifted her hair away from her neck. "Ah, 'tis as I'd suspected."

"Oh, the birthmark!"

"Aye, 'tis a Macphearson mark. Your mother's was the same, as is mine."

She looked up, surprised, and he let her hair fall back into place. "You have it, too?"

"Oh, aye." He turned his head and lifted his hair so she might see. "I'm an old man, and most of my hair's gone silver now, but ye might see it yet."

She did see it. A streak of snow-white hair nestled amongst a field of black and silver. "Aye, 'tis there!" They both laughed. She felt suddenly warm inside. Tiny sparks of joy tickled her belly.

It dawned on her that others had seen the mark on her and had known its meaning.

Moira. And Alex!

She'd been so preoccupied with her grandfather and her newfound memory, she'd forgotten Alex entirely. She gripped her grandfather's hands. "Where is Alex? What's happened? The last thing I remember before fainting, he and his men—"

"Aye, the whoreson. Alex Davidson, is he no?"

"He is, but do not judge their clan on his actions. He acts alone, and in direct defiance of their laird's wishes.

"He herded us—me and my men—here like chattel. He holds them in the cellar, methinks, while we are locked up here, prisoners in me own house."

Rachel wondered that Alex hadn't killed them all, but dared not say it. "He's dangerous, Grandfather. Half mad, likely."

"Aye, and he'll wish himself dead long before I'm through with him."

She didn't want to encourage him. 'Twas plain he was no match for Alex's youth and strength.

"He would ne'er have taken us had all my men been close."

She recalled he'd only had a half-dozen warriors protecting him on Craigh Mur. "Where are your kinsmen?"

"Most o' them are out looking for *ye*."

Her brows shot up.

"Aye, when ye didna arrive last month, we started the search."

"I had no idea. I—"

"Ye were with the Davidsons all this time?"

She nodded.

"And they kept ye from me? Whoresons, I'll have their—"

"Nay! They didn't know who I was. God's truth!"

He scowled and his brows collided. "What d'ye mean they didna know? Did ye no tell them?"

How would she ever explain? "'Tis a long story, and one I would tell you in detail—but later." She let go his hands and rose from the bed.

A small window overlooked the courtyard entrance to the lodge. She looked out into the night. It had rained since that afternoon, and the ground was wet and muddy. The sky was starless, choked with thunderheads threatening yet another downpour.

"We must find a way out of here," she said. "We must get help. Gilchrist cannot be far."

A low laugh made the hairs on her nape prickle. She whirled, then gasped. "Alex," she breathed.

He stood in the doorway, smirking, his dark eyes shining in the firelight. Her grandfather immediately stepped between them, but neither he nor she had any weapon with which to defend themselves.

"Gilchrist is miles away by now," Alex said. "The fool."

Rachel's heart sunk. Alex was right. Gilchrist would assume Alex had taken her back to their demesne. He'd likely be on his way there himself.

Her grandfather glowered at Alex. "He speaks of the Davidson laird?"

"He does," she said, moving to her grandfather's side. "Gilchrist Davidson Mackintosh—the laird and warrior who saved my life."

Her grandfather arched a brow and studied her face for a moment. "I can see there is much I've yet to hear. Ye think much of him, this laird and warrior."

"Aye," she breathed. "Gilchrist has protected me these last weeks from those who thought to harm me—and you—for their own gain." She glared at Alex.

"Ha!" Alex cried. "Ye call rolling around in a hunting blind all night *protection?*"

Rachel's cheeks blazed.

"What d'ye want with us?" her grandfather demanded. "Why are ye here?"

Alex smiled, then kicked the door closed behind him, and barred it from the inside. He sauntered to the bed and lounged casually across the straw mattress. "Why am I here?"

Rachel judged the distance from her to the door at ten paces. She could be there in a flash, long before Alex—but could she get the bloody thing unbarred and opened before he was on her? Nay. Besides, he was armed to the teeth, and she would not put her grandfather at risk.

The Macphearson stood silently, and Rachel could see the rage building inside him. She must temper him, somehow, or Alex would surely kill him.

"Aye," she said, and approached the bed. "Why do you hold us? What gain could we possibly bring you?"

Alex laughed softly, and looked her up and down. "What gain, ye ask? Ye value yourself too little, Rachel Macphearson."

She tipped her chin high and waited for him to continue.

"'Tis no secret your clan is in a shambles," Alex said to her grandfather. "And that ye wish to align with the Chattan."

Her grandfather narrowed his eyes. "What of it?"

Alex smiled. "The Davidsons are of the Chattan clans—the strongest of them—and I am a Davidson."

Rachel had an uneasy feeling about where this was leading.

"Aye," her grandfather said. "So?"

Alex nodded at her. "She is a Macphearson."

Truth dawned.

"What, you're not thinking to— Are you mad?"

"Ye wish to wed her," her grandfather said flatly, "to forge the alliance."

Alex merely smiled.

"You *are* mad, if you think I'd consider such a thing."

Her grandfather arched a silvery brow, then sat heavily in a chair by the hearth. "The man who could seal such an alliance would curry much favor with his clan—and with the Chattan."

"Your grandfather is a clever man," Alex said.

"Oh, so you think to use me—and my family—to buy affection from yours?" Rachel crossed her arms in front of her.

"And power, no doubt," her grandfather added.

"I shall be laird," Alex whispered, "and ye shall be my lady."

Her stomach roiled. It all made sense to her now. Every last detail. Alex's wooing, and Moira's attempt to keep Gilchrist from trusting her, loving her. She suspected Moira had fed her son's lust for power, driven by her own bitterness.

"That night in the wood," she said, "when you slaughtered my kinsmen, and thought to take me by force—even then you planned this." Her blood began to boil.

"Aye. The idea struck me the moment ye told me your name—and your situation. 'Twould have been far easier, Rachel, had ye submitted to me then."

"And what makes you think I'll submit to you now? You cannot force me to wed you—no priest in the land would marry us without my consent."

Alex rose slowly from the bed and towered over her. "Ah, but I'll have your consent, won't I?" His eyes had a wildness about them that frightened her.

Her grandfather shot to his feet. Alex pushed past her and shoved him roughly back onto the chair. In a flash he was at the hearth, his dirk poised at her grandfather's throat.

Rachel stood as if paralyzed, pulse racing, eyes wide. "Don't. Alex, please!"

Alex knelt and grabbed a brand from the fire, whilst his dirk held her grandfather at bay. "Please, what?" he whispered, then lowered the dirk and pointed the fiery end of the brand at her grandfather's eye.

She willed her legs to move toward them, one step at a time. "Even if...if I agreed to this marriage, when all discover your treachery—against your own kinsmen and mine—you will likely be hanged, not made laird."

Didn't he see that? Nay, he did not, for he *was* mad—she could see it in his eyes.

"Ye shall love me instead of him."

"Instead of Gilchrist?" she breathed.

"Aye. Ye shall both love me again." Alex's eyes grew wide and glazed, and seemed to look right through her grandfather. "Gilchrist is no even one of us, is he, Father?"

"Father?" Her grandfather frowned in confusion and shot her a questioning look.

Alex held the firebrand not an inch from the old man's eye, his hand shaking badly. "Och, I know ye dinna like me to call ye that. Very well—Alistair, then."

She must do something, and quickly. Alex was out of his head. He didn't even know them.

"Alex," she whispered. "I'll do it. I'll wed you—tonight if you like." Very slowly, she placed her hand on his forearm. "Come, let us go find a priest."

Alex's expression clouded, as if he didn't understand her words. "But Margaret," he said. "Ye are already wed—to mine father here." Alex glanced at her, then nodded at her grandfather. "I shall be your son—and laird one day—and everyone shall love me."

His hand shook more, and Rachel gripped his forearm to steady it, lest he put out her grandfather's eye. "Of course we love you, Alex," she said, playing along with his delusion.

"More than Gilchrist?"

"Oh, much more," she breathed, and slowly tried to move his arm away.

Alex's gaze met hers and he snapped back to reality. "Liar!" he roared and swung the brand. "Whore!"

Her grandfather's hand shot up and grabbed Alex's fiery weapon. He catapulted from the chair, knocking them all to the floor. Alex's dirk flew from his hand and clattered across the hearth stones.

Rachel screamed, terrified Alex would kill him. The two men wrestled on the floor for possession of the brand. Its tip flamed anew as it cut the air.

Shouts went up among Alex's men who stood guard outside the door. They beat against the timbers, but 'twas barred now from the inside.

She must do something! But what? She scrambled to the hearth, retrieved Alex's dirk, then leapt to her feet.

The two men rolled toward the bed, swearing and grunting. Her grandfather held his own. He was more formidable than she'd first suspected. The elderly laird had a good two or three stone on Alex, and used his weight well to his advantage.

Rachel moved in with the dirk and the two men rolled again. Alex was on top. She saw her chance and took it. She lunged, brandishing the blade.

Alex caught her movement out of the corner of his eye and, at the last minute, twisted out of the way. She fell on him, knocking the breath out of her, and drove the dirk deep into the timber floor.

The two men grabbed for it, and in the struggle the flaming brand was thrown clear. It landed atop the straw mattress which ignited with a crackle. Flames leapt into the air.

Her eyes went wide.

"Get out, lassie, get out!" her grandfather shouted as he struggled with Alex who now wielded the dirk.

Rachel rolled off them and glanced at the barred door, a dozen paces away. Alex's men shouted in vain on the other side. She began to crawl toward it, when her grandfather let out a strangled cry.

She turned and her heart skipped a beat. Alex held the blade against the old laird's throat. Without another thought she lunged toward them, but tripped and landed hard, hitting her head on the edge of the pallet.

The room spun.

She drew a deep breath and coughed from the acrid smoke that belched from the straw mattress. Then the whole of the bed went up, and the timber wall behind it.

A crackling and roaring filled her ears. She coughed again and tried to move, but could not manage it. A sheen of sweat broke upon her brow. Her last coherent thought was of the heat, the terrible, terrible heat.

Chapter Twenty

He'd never forgive himself if anything had happened to her.

Gilchrist leaned low over the gray's lathered neck and whispered encouragement. "I know ye're spent, laddy, but ye mustna fail me now." The stallion picked up speed.

"Where are we headed?" Hugh shouted over the clamor of their hoofbeats.

Where *were* they headed? Where in God's name had Alex taken her? 'Twas full on night, and the road black as midnight. Gilchrist glanced skyward but could see no stars. A light rain began to fall.

"Damn it!" he swore and strained to see ahead into the blackness.

"We're nearly to Craigh Mur, if memory serves," Hugh shouted. "It canna be much farther."

Gilchrist knew Hugh was right. He'd traveled this same stretch of road twice now in as many days. Clods of mud flew from their mounts' hooves as the rain picked up. 'Twould slow their progress for certain.

All he could hope was that he'd guessed right, and that Alex had taken Rachel back through the wood to Craigh Mur. Alex would have dealings with the Macphearsons—

of that Gilchrist was now certain. Perhaps he thought to ransom her? Christ, let it be that. At least he'd need keep her safe in the doing. She'd be no good to him dead.

"Laird!" Hugh cried. "Look! On the ridge."

Gilchrist snapped to attention. "Aye, I see it." He pulled his mount up short and called for his men to do the same.

"Torches!" Arlys called out. He'd nearly forgotten her. She nudged her mount in between his and Hugh's. Her flaxen hair reflected what little light there was—and 'twould likely get her killed.

"Stay behind us, d'ye hear?" Gilchrist motioned for two of his warriors to flank her. "And cover up that head of yours." He cursed Hugh silently for allowing her to come.

He counted near a dozen torches, held by riders on an open hillock north of the road.

Craigh Mur.

"Is it Alex, d'ye think?" Hugh asked.

"Nay, he'd likely conceal his whereabouts, no announce them." Gilchrist wiped a light sheen of moisture from his face. "'Tis Macphearson."

"The laird himself?" Hugh asked.

"Nay. Robert Macphearson."

"D'ye know him?"

"Aye." Gilchrist gritted his teeth. "Come on."

They approached the hillock cautiously, weapons sheathed. The road passed Craigh Mur on its southern slope and 'twas here Gilchrist stopped. His men fanned out behind him. The Macphearsons could not see them for the darkness and the rain—but knew they were there all the same.

Gilchrist started up the slope. "Robert Macphearson!" he shouted to the torch-bearing riders huddled between the standing stones on top. The wind was fierce and, for a moment, he was not certain the Macphearsons had heard him.

He thought to call out again, then held his tongue. A lone rider approached the edge of the slope, his torch held high. As Gilchrist drew closer he recognized the warrior.

"Who's there?" Macphearson called down to him.

"Gilchrist Davidson Mackintosh!" he shouted back. "I would speak with ye."

Macphearson did not respond. He was counting them—or those he could make out—Gilchrist was certain. He'd have done the same in the warrior's position. Macphearson waved them up.

There were more warriors now than when Gilchrist had met them on the road yesterday. He counted a dozen, then nodded to Hugh who cut a like dozen from their ranks and bid them ride escort up the hill. Moments later Gilchrist rode into their circle of torchlight.

"We meet again, Davidson," Robert Macphearson said. The wind whipped at the warrior's damp hair. The pink stone hanging from the leather thong around his neck glimmered in the torchlight. "What is your business here? Hunting again, are ye?" He arched a brow.

"Nay."

"I didna think so."

The rain had stopped again, but thunder rumbled low in the distance. Sheet lightning flashed in the north, briefly illuminating the standing stones behind them. 'Twas an eerie place, and now that Gilchrist was convinced Rachel was not here, he was anxious to move on.

"The woman ye sought yesterday," he said.

Macphearson narrowed his eyes. "What about her?"

"Did ye find her?"

"No yet. What concern is it of yours?"

Gilchrist knew not these lands, and needed Macphearson's help if he was to find her. He held the warrior's penetrating gaze. ''She's here somewhere—and likely in grave danger.''

Robert Macphearson kicked his mount, and the stallion sprang forward nearly colliding with Gilchrist's gray. The warrior's hand moved to the hilt of his sword. Gilchrist held his ground, resisting the urge to draw his weapon. He cautioned Hugh with his eyes.

''Ye were lying yesterday!'' Macphearson bellowed. ''Ye know where she is.''

''Nay, I seek her as well.''

''For what purpose?''

Gilchrist weighed his words carefully. He must be level-headed now—for Rachel's sake. ''To restore her to her clan, and to safeguard her from those who would harm her.''

''Ye've seen her! Ye've—''

''Aye. She was with us some weeks, and—''

Like lightning, Macphearson unsheathed his sword. Gilchrist did the same. The sounds of metal scraping metal carried over the wind as two dozen warriors followed suit.

''Hold!'' Gilchrist shouted. ''There is more ye need know.''

Macphearson eyed him, gauging the odds. Gilchrist knew that he knew more Davidson warriors waited below on the road. Just how many, Macphearson couldn't be certain. Gilchrist had the advantage, and he'd use it to gain the man's help.

''What more?'' Macphearson asked. ''Tell me.''

''We didna know who she was until yesterday when we met ye on the road.''

''Liar.''

"Nay, I speak the truth—but 'tis a long story. One I shall tell ye as we ride."

Macphearson's lip curled into a snarl. "Och, and now we ride together, eh? Just like that?"

The warrior's arrogance wore thin. "Ye wish to find her, don't ye?" Time was running out and a feeling of desperation grew in Gilchrist's gut. He'd take the chance. "She's with my kinsman, Alex Davidson."

"What?"

"Aye. He's taken her—against her will and mine."

Macphearson brandished his blade. The metal glinted silver in the torchlight. Gilchrist raised his own weapon almost imperceptibly.

"Where are they?" Macphearson demanded.

"I know not, but I suspect Alex would have dealings with your laird."

Thunder boomed and they all glanced skyward. Dark clouds roiled overhead, full to bursting. The wind picked up, whipping at their hair and garments.

"And ye would stop him, this…Alex?" Macphearson asked.

"We must!" Hugh piped in from behind and nudged his mount forward.

Gilchrist stilled him with a look, then turned his attention back to Macphearson. "Aye, I'll do more than stop him when I find him."

The warrior studied him, sizing him up it seemed, allowing his gaze to drift over Gilchrist's burned arm and hand. "There is more here than meets the eye."

Gilchrist willed him to his gaze. "Aye, and ye shall know it soon enough. But now, let us find her."

Macphearson considered his options. In truth, he had none. They both knew it. The warrior turned his weapon over and over in his hand, then paused before sheathing it. "When this is done, Davidson, ye and I shall yet have business together."

Gilchrist's eye was drawn to the hammered silver work decorating the hilt of Macphearson's sword. It reminded him of another such decoration—Rachel's betrothal ring.

"Aye," he said, nodding. "I look forward to it."

They sheathed their weapons in unison, and their men did the same.

"Now," Gilchrist said. "We've already scoured the forest and the road east, all the way back to Monadhliath."

"The road to our village is clear," Macphearson said. "We've covered it twice in two days."

"Then—then where are they?" a feminine voice asked.

Arlys's caped silhouette moved into the torchlight as she wedged her mount between the riders at Gilchrist's back.

"What are ye doin' up here?" Hugh demanded.

Gilchrist snorted. "I thought I told ye to keep her well back."

Arlys threw off the hood of her cape and tipped her chin at them. Her fire-gold hair shimmered in the torchlight. "I've as much right to be here as ye."

"Hmmm...pretty," Macphearson noted.

But Gilchrist wasn't listening. He'd caught a whiff of something on the air. He turned his mount east and sucked in another breath. Then another. A sick feeling washed over him.

"What is it?" Hugh asked, his eyes widening. "Ye look pale, man."

He turned his mount again, this time west, and strained to see out into the dark. On impulse, he closed his eyes and drew another deep draught. Rain, heather—and something else.

Something unmistakable.

Smoke.

"Look!" one of Macphearson's warriors cried.

Gilchrist's eyes shot open. The man pointed west. All of them followed his gaze. Tiny flames danced on the horizon, a half league away. "What is that place?" Gilchrist demanded. "Your village?"

"Nay," Macphearson said. "'Tis too close. 'Tis—'tis the laird's hunting lodge!"

A cold fear gripped him. Sweat broke out on his palms. "My God," he breathed. "Rachel."

Without a word, they kicked their mounts into action and charged down the hill. The rest of Gilchrist's men waited at the bottom, weapons drawn.

"Come on!" he shouted over the thunder of hoofbeats and the clatter of weapons and livery.

They reined their mounts west and raced along the muddy road toward the lodge. Terrifying images flashed in Gilchrist's mind. The smell of burning timber flooded his senses. He urged his stallion faster and prayed silently.

God, let it no be too late.

"This way!" Robert Macphearson cried and led them off the road onto a narrow spur.

The trees were dense and the trail rocky. There was barely the space to ride two abreast. Gilchrist shot forward and passed Macphearson on the right, causing both their mounts to nearly lose their footing. The warrior barked a string of curses. Gilchrist ignored him and pressed on.

Christ, how much farther could it be?

They topped a short rise and the trees thinned. There! He could see it now, barely a furlong away. A good-size hunting lodge, two stories built of timber and stone, topped by a thatched roof. Flames leapt into the air, shooting ash and sparks into the night.

'Twas nearly all ablaze.

Gilchrist leapt from his mount before the stallion was even stopped. "Holy God," he breathed and wavered on shaky legs before the inferno.

A wall of heat hit him and he dropped to his knees, eyes riveted to the entrance, sweat breaking across his brow. Smoke stung his eyes and filled his lungs, the stench of it nearly choking him.

Then there was the sound—oh God, the crackling and roaring, intensified by the force of the wind. It filled his ears, consumed him. If he closed his eyes he'd swear he was there again...

Braedûn Lodge.

"Where are they?" Macphearson shouted and pulled him roughly to his feet.

Gilchrist snapped back.

Hugh was suddenly by his side, and Arlys with him. The rest of the Davidsons remained in their saddles, struggling to keep their mounts from bolting.

"Alex is in there!" Arlys screamed and lunged toward the entrance.

Robert Macphearson grabbed her and pulled her back. "Nay, lass, 'tis too late." She struggled against him, but the warrior held her fast against his chest.

Too late.

"God, no," Gilchrist breathed. He willed his leaden feet forward, one step at a time, his eyes fixed on the open door.

"Nay!" Hugh shouted and grabbed his arm.

A half-dozen Davidson warriors—Alex's men—burst from the entrance and fell to the ground before them, choking and sputtering, their hands and faces streaked with soot.

Gilchrist grabbed one of them by the collar and hauled

him to his feet. "Where is she?" he demanded, and shook him hard. "Where?"

"Who's in there, man?" Hugh slapped the warrior on the back as the man tried to clear his lungs of smoke.

"They, she…" he choked out.

"Rachel!" Gilchrist shouted. "Is she in there?"

Arlys screamed and struggled. 'Twas all Macphearson could do to hold her.

"So-some o' the Macphearsons was in the cellar. We—we got them out. They's around the back wi' the rest of our men."

"Rachel, ye dolt!" Gilchrist jerked the man roughly. "Where is she?"

"She—she—" He hacked and coughed again. "Alex has her, wi-with the Macphearson laird."

"Where, man?" Hugh demanded. "Where?"

The warrior's gaze drifted to a window on the second floor. Flames shot from the opening. Smoke belched thick into the night. "U-up there," he said and pointed with a shaking finger.

Gilchrist stood, transfixed and tongue-tied, his body bathed in a cold sweat. He fought the urge to wretch.

"Nay!" Macphearson shouted.

"Would ye let them burn?" Arlys shrieked.

Gilchrist was barely aware of Hugh's firm hand on his shoulder.

"Would ye?" she screamed.

Gilchrist swallowed hard, tears stinging his eyes.
Would he?

Chapter Twenty-One

She understood him now.

Gilchrist's horror, his guilt, that paralyzing fear.

Rachel rolled onto her stomach and coughed convulsively, her lungs rebelling against the acrid smoke. The chamber blazed around her—timber walls, fur window coverings, the straw mattress and every stick of furniture.

With a roar the thatched roof ignited and a shower of fiery sparks rained down on her. Terror gave rise to panic as she brushed the burning bits of straw from her hair and clothing.

"Gr-Grandfather," she choked out, and blinked back stinging tears, desperate to see him through the wall of smoke.

She inched her way across the floor to where he lay, still as death. Alex flailed and moaned nearby, the hilt of his own dirk protruding from his belly.

Her grandfather's face was streaked with soot and sweat. Instinctively she put a finger to his leathery neck and checked for a pulse. He was alive!

"Oh, thank God," she breathed. She shook him, but he didn't respond. "Grandfather! Grandfather, please! We must get out—you must wake up!"

He muttered something unintelligible and turned his head toward the sound of her voice. She shook him again, pleading. His eyelids fluttered briefly.

"Grandfather!"

She reached blindly for his hand and grasped it. The old man squeezed it once, then his fingers went slack in her hand. His head lolled to the side and he slipped into unconsciousness.

Rachel let out a strangled cry. Scrambling to her knees, she beat away the cinders that lit on both her and him. The heat was so intense her body was bathed in sweat. She wiped her hands on her gown, grasped his shoulders, and pulled with a grunt. His bearlike body didn't budge.

"Oh, God, how will I get him out?"

Her terror spiraled to new heights as the flames licked at them, singeing the hem of her gown and the edges of her grandfather's plaid. Alex screamed as a fiery timber fell from the roof and grazed his bare leg.

She must get help—she must, or they'd all burn!

Oh, where was Gilchrist?

Rachel coughed violently as she tried in vain to fan the smoke away and see a path clear to the door. Small fires had broken out all over the floor from the blazing thatch which fell from the rafters.

She inched her way, crawling on hands and knees in the direction of the barred door. What lay on the other side, she knew not—likely another hellish inferno. What she did know, was they'd die a fiery death for certain if she did not try.

Halfway there. Keep moving. Just a few more—

Without warning, a blazing rafter cracked loudly overhead. Rachel glanced up in horror and screamed. She rolled as it came crashing down.

"Rachel!" a voice on the other side of the door

shouted. The wood split as a blow was struck from the outside. "Rachel, are ye in there?"

"Gilchrist!"

She scrambled to the door and fumbled with the bar. Flames lashed out at her from behind. She jumped sideways and the door crashed open.

Gilchrist threw his sword aside and swept her into his arms. "Oh, God, Rachel," he whispered against her hair, choking back a shuddering sob which she, too, shared.

"Oh, Gilchrist! I knew you'd come." Relief washed over her, tempering her fear.

He started to drag her from the chamber. "Come on. We must get ye out."

"Nay!" She pulled away from him and choked back another sob. "My grandfather is in there…and…and Alex." She stepped back into the inferno.

"Nay!" He pulled her back roughly and lifted her off her feet. "I'll come back for them, but now I must get ye out."

She struggled in vain against his grip.

Alex screamed hideously somewhere across the room. Rachel envisioned the flames lapping at his legs. "Laird!" he cried. "Dinna leave me!"

Gilchrist choked back another sob, tightened his grip on her, and backed into the corridor. He turned and they immediately collided with a huge warrior.

"Macphearson!" Gilchrist shouted over the roar of the blaze.

"My laird is in there?" the warrior demanded, blue eyes wide and wild.

"Aye," she breathed.

"I'll get him out. Go on, the both o' ye!" Macphearson pushed past them and leapt through the now burning doorway.

Gilchrist shifted her weight in his arms and raced down the blazing hallway. The air was less smoky here, and Rachel sucked in a breath.

They reached the staircase and, in horror, she saw that most of the steps leading to the first floor had already caught fire. Gilchrist did not hesitate. He skipped down them, stumbled across the threshold, and out into the night.

Rachel coughed up the fetid smoke and filled her lungs with air.

"Ye're safe," Gilchrist rasped. "Ye're safe now, love."

Rachel's eyes widened as her gaze lit on Hugh. He stood close to the lodge's entrance, struggling with a shrieking fury of limbs and blond tresses.

Arlys!

Gilchrist collapsed at their feet, shaking. Rachel gripped him tightly, and he her. They knelt together, hearts pounding chest to chest, and breath coming in short gasps.

She was barely aware of the confusion all around them—shouting men, terror-struck horses, the heat and the roaring, the stench of burning timber.

Moments later the Macphearson warrior burst from the flaming doorway, her grandfather hanging limp from his shoulder like a sack of grain.

"Is he alive?" she cried.

The warrior set him carefully into the arms of two waiting clansmen. "I know not."

Rachel scrambled to the old man's side. "Grandfather, can you hear me?" No response. "Oh, sweet Mary, don't take him from me now."

Gilchrist's hand lit on her shoulder. She choked back

salty tears and traced the line of her grandfather's cheek with a trembling finger. His eyes blinked open.

"Ah, God, he lives!" the young Macphearson cried, jubilation shining on his soot-streaked face.

"You saved my grandfather's life," she said. "Oh, thank you."

The warrior met her gaze and his smile broadened. "Ye must be her—Rachel."

"Aye."

"I am Robert Macphearson."

She smiled at him, then turned to Gilchrist. She needed to hold him, to know that he was truly here, and that everything would be all right.

To her surprise, his eyes were glassed with tears and his expression bittersweet. His strong, comforting hand slipped from her shoulder.

"Gilchrist, what is—"

A hideous scream cut short her question.

"Alex!" Arlys wailed and fought violently against Hugh's grip on her.

Gilchrist shot to his feet and started toward the lodge. Rachel bolted after him and threw her arms around his waist. "Nay, do not!"

He turned and grasped her shoulders. He spoke not a word, but in his eyes she read his intent.

"'Tis too late, Gilchrist. You cannot save him." She tightened her grip on him.

"Laird, she's right," Hugh shouted. "Ye'll perish! Dinna think to do it."

Arlys wailed again.

"Friend or enemy, I willna leave a man to burn," Gilchrist said. "I canna." He looked past her to Robert Macphearson. The warrior rose and the two locked gazes.

Rachel began to tremble. Her tears broke as she

watched some silent understanding pass between the two men.

"Take her," Gilchrist breathed. He peeled her hands from his waist and thrust her toward the warrior.

"Nay!" she cried and reached for him again. "'Tis suicide!"

Robert Macphearson yanked her backward, his gaze fixed fast on Gilchrist.

"Take her," Gilchrist said to him, then turned and sprinted back into the blazing lodge.

There was no time for fear or hate, regret, or any emotion.

Gilchrist raced up the steps and along the corridor, dodging flaming timbers and burning bits of thatched roofing which rained down on him from above.

Smoke belched from the chamber where they'd left Alex. Gilchrist ripped the plaid from his shoulder, covered his mouth with it, then burst through the doorway.

"Alex! Where are ye?"

The smoke was so thick he couldn't see. He heard a faint whimpering near where he guessed the window to be, and moved quickly toward the sound. His booted foot came down on a burning timber. "Ah, Christ!" he swore, and leapt awkwardly over the obstruction.

The crying was nearer now. Gilchrist's lungs burned from the smoke. He dropped to the floor where there was more air and crawled forward on hands and knees.

There! Alex lay sprawled on the floor near the window, as he'd suspected. Gilchrist reached him and grabbed his chin. "Can ye move? Try to get up."

Alex's eyes met his. "Gilchrist," he rasped.

"Get up! Come on, friend. I shall help ye." Gilchrist tried to get his arms under him.

Alex grabbed his hand and moved it downward over his chest to— God, what's this? Gilchrist's hand closed over the hilt of a dagger stuck blade-deep in Alex's belly.

"No matter," he whispered. "Rachel will mend ye." 'Twas a mortal wound for certain, but he had no intention of leaving Alex there to burn.

"Go on," Alex murmured. "Take your bride and leave. Leave me. I deserve no less."

Gilchrist ignored him. He put his arms through Alex's and tried to lift him. "Christ, you're heavy." He labored again, grunting with the effort. Alex's body almost flew off the floor. "What the hell?"

"I thought ye might need some help."

Gilchrist's watery eyes widened as he made Hugh out through the smoke. Relief surged through him. "What are ye doing here? Are ye mad?"

"Aye, as mad as you. Now come, let's get the hell out of here."

Together they carried Alex from the blazing chamber, snaking around fiery rafters that had fallen from the roof and ignited the floor. Not a minute too soon. As they hefted him through the doorway, the wooden planking gave way.

"Hurry!" Hugh cried.

They raced along the corridor and down the steps. Flames licked at their legs. Gilchrist gritted his teeth and moved like lightning.

When they burst outside, the first face he saw was Rachel's. God, how he loved her. She and Arlys stood clutching each other, terrified eyes fixed on the doorway. Hugh fell to his knees, coughing and sputtering, and a half-dozen clansmen rushed to take Alex from their arms.

Then she was there, clasping him to her, peppering his

face with small, violent kisses. "Oh, Gilchrist!" Her arms went around his neck. "I thought I'd lost you."

"Nay," he whispered, holding her tight. "Never." Robert Macphearson knelt by his laird and helped him to drink from a water skin, though his eyes were on Rachel. Gilchrist hugged her tighter as she wept in his arms. He leveled his gaze at the warrior and sent a silent message.

Later.

Arlys's hysterical screams distracted them all. She hovered over Alex, shaking hands poised over the hilt of the dagger. The weapon heaved up and down in his belly with each labored breath he drew.

Rachel rushed to his side and grabbed Arlys's hands. "Nay! Don't touch it."

"Take it out!" Arlys shrieked. "Take it out!"

Gilchrist held her back while Rachel examined Alex's injuries. His burns were minimal, nothing that wouldn't heal in time. But Alex had no time, and they all knew it. Blood seeped black from the lethal wound, soaking his shirt and plaid.

Rachel's eyes glassed as she met Gilchrist's gaze. "There's naught I can do for him."

He should have felt satisfaction, given Alex's betrayal, but he did not. Only pity, and a hollow ache he recognized as love. Love for a man who had been more brother than friend to him—once.

Arlys began to sob in long, heartrending gasps. Gently, she lifted Alex's head and cradled it in her lap. His hand flailed a moment, then she clasped it to her breast.

"Dinna weep," Alex rasped.

"I—I love you," Arlys whispered, tears glistening in the fire's bright glow.

"And I ye," he breathed.

Rachel reached absently for Gilchrist's hand, her gaze

fixed on the lovers. He took it in his and squeezed it hard. Robert Macphearson looked on, stone-faced.

Soon, Gilchrist said to him with his eyes.

"Laird," Alex choked out as he tried to rise.

Gilchrist turned his attention to Alex, moved closer and pressed him gently back down onto Arlys's lap. "Dinna try to move. Rest now, friend."

"There is much I—I would say to ye…Gilchrist." His breathing grew more labored.

"Not now."

"Aye, hear me." He grunted in pain. "Come…come closer."

Gilchrist leaned over him, his face inches from Alex's. "I'm here, friend. What is it?"

"I—I've been no friend to ye."

Gilchrist swallowed hard and met Alex's glazed eyes.

"My sins are so—so abominable, ne-never can ye…" Alex moaned again, and Arlys let out a strangled cry.

"Dinna fash about it now," Gilchrist whispered. "'Tis over, done with."

Alex shook his head. "Nay, I—I would have ye know the truth of things."

Gilchrist already knew the truth. Alex would have used Rachel to forge an alliance with the Macphearsons—either that, or destroy them. The first plan would have gained him no small recognition amongst the Chattan, and the second…well, notoriety if not approval.

In the beginning Gilchrist had been so blinded by his own self-indulgent misery, he'd not recognized Alex's treachery for what it was. And later—too late—bombarded with dozens of tiny clues, he'd not wanted to believe it, for fear of losing Rachel to Macphearson.

"'Twas an accident," Alex whispered. "I—I never meant it to happen."

"The fire, ye mean?" Gilchrist said.

Alex nodded.

Rachel's hand lit on Gilchrist's shoulder. "He doesn't mean this fire. He means…"

She paused and, in the heavy silence that followed, a thought so unthinkable he recoiled, flashed across his mind.

"What?" Gilchrist said, looking to Rachel. "What does he mean?" Cold horror welled inside him.

"Braedûn Lodge," Alex rasped.

The words seared his gut. "Nay, it canna be." His eyes widened as he searched Alex's face for the truth. "Ye—ye were off hunting. Ye werena there."

Alex closed his eyes and nodded. "I—I was there." He swallowed hard and fought for breath. "In Alistair and Margaret's chamber. I—I got out before ye came."

"Nay!" Gilchrist gripped the front of Alex's bloody plaid and jerked him up.

Arlys protested as Alex cried out in pain.

"Don't," Rachel said. "Gilchrist, don't."

"Tell me!" he commanded, fighting the urge to slam his fist into Alex's face.

"A-Alistair," Alex breathed. "He loved me once, l-like a son. Before ye came." He shook his head and tears leaked from his closed eyes. "'Twas an accident. I—I just wanted him to love me."

Rage and pity melded together until all Gilchrist felt was a bright and wrenching emptiness. He eased Alex down onto Arlys's lap. The lass wept silently now, her tears spilling onto Alex's dark, tousled hair, gone red in the fire's light.

Thunder cracked overhead and the sky opened. Rain soaked them in seconds and turned the soft ground to mud. Its fresh scent cut the thick, smoky air. Gilchrist looked skyward and breathed deep, trying to get a grip on his emotions. Water streamed down his face, cooling his hot skin.

"Forgive me," Alex breathed, and reached blindly for Gilchrist's hand.

Not hesitating, Gilchrist grasped it. He gazed at the fallen warrior, but saw only the tortured boy he once knew. Alex had wanted so badly to believe he was Alistair's son. They would never know the truth.

"Forgive me," Alex mouthed again and opened his eyes against the driving rain.

Their gazes locked. Hot tears glassed Gilchrist's eyes and melted into the cool rivulets of rain streaming down his face. He squeezed Alex's hand. "I forgive ye, friend."

The edge of Alex's mouth curled into a bittersweet smile. His hand went slack and his eyes widened in death. 'Twas over. Arlys covered his face with her body and wept.

"Come now," Rachel whispered and drew Gilchrist gently away. "Let her have a moment with him."

Kneeling in the mud, Gilchrist turned toward her and cupped her face in his hands. "Are—are ye all right?"

Rachel nodded.

"He didna hurt ye?"

"Nay, I am well. Truly."

Relief mixed with a kind of heaviness washed over him. Steam sizzled off the burning timbers of the hunting lodge as the rain continued to pummel down in sharp, stinging sheets. "Ye're soaked. We must get ye to cover before ye catch your death." He rose and pulled her up with him.

Robert Macphearson knelt beside Arlys. She was still now, clutching Alex's limp body to her breast. "Come on, lass. Come with me.'' He offered her his hand, but she made no move to take it.

Hugh and two of Alex's men knelt beside them. ''Let us take him, now,'' Hugh said to her, ''and prepare him as befits a warrior of our clan.''

Arlys nodded shakily to Hugh, then took Robert Macphearson's proffered hand. The warrior led her away to a crude shelter made of oiled skins which his men had hastily constructed at the edge of the clearing.

''Moira was behind much of what Alex has done,'' Rachel said, surprising him.

''Aye, I suspected as much.'' His gaze followed Macphearson.

''What will you do with her?''

Turning his attention back to Rachel, he grazed a finger across her cheek. ''Her son is dead. 'Tis punishment enough.''

Rachel nodded.

After a moment, he allowed her to pull him toward a nearby tree where the old laird sat surrounded by his kinsmen. ''This is my grandfather,'' she said. ''Ranald Macphearson.''

''Aye.'' Gilchrist nodded. ''I know.''

Rachel's eyes widened. ''You do?''

There was much he needed to tell her, but now was not the time.

''So, ye are The Davidson now,'' Ranald Macphearson said.

''Aye.'' He looked the old man in the eyes. ''Gilchrist Davidson Mackintosh.''

The old laird nodded. ''I knew your uncle well, once upon a time. Alistair Davidson was a fine man.''

Gilchrist nodded, his gut twisting with emotion. ''Aye, I loved mine uncle well.''

"As I do mine," Robert Macphearson's voice boomed behind them.

Gilchrist turned, caught off guard by the warrior's quick reappearance. Macphearson knelt beside Rachel's grandfather, taking his hand.

"The laird is your uncle?" Gilchrist asked.

"My great-uncle, by marriage. I...owe ye much, Davidson. Ye dinna know what the old man means to me."

Gilchrist held the warrior's steady gaze and swallowed hard. An image of his own uncle—in his prime—flashed in Gilchrist's mind. "Ah, but I do."

"I would ne'er have braved the fire had ye no gone in afore me," Robert said. "My thanks, Davidson."

"Aye, and I must thank ye, too," Ranald said and nodded at him. "For saving my granddaughter."

Gilchrist did not expect such civility from them, at least not from the young warrior. "'Twas mine own fault caused this." He nodded toward the smoking ruins of the lodge. The heavy rain pummeled the fire into submission.

"Nay, 'twas not." Rachel gripped his arm. Her hair was plastered wet to her face. Her gown was soaking and she shivered beside him.

The time had come to settle things. He must get her out of here, and quickly. "Go with Arlys," he said, his mind made up. "There is business I have yet to discuss with your cousin." He shot Robert Macphearson a loaded look.

"But—but I would stay and hear this business," she said.

"Nay." He signaled to Hugh. "On the morrow I must leave and there is much to be decided before then."

Her eyes widened. "You would leave?"

"Aye, I would bury him at Monadhliath." He nodded to the place in the trees where his kinsmen were carefully wrapping Alex's body. "Come." Grasping her arm, he pulled her toward the shelter where Arlys rested.

Hugh jogged up beside them.

"Hugh, stay with her." He shot his friend a grim look.

Hugh glanced back at Robert Macphearson, then nodded, understanding Gilchrist's intention.

"Wait!" Rachel struggled against his grip. "There are things you must know. The ring—I remember now. 'Tis not what—"

"In my horse's saddlebag ye'll find a dry plaid. Have Hugh retrieve it for ye."

"Nay, you must hear me!" She dug her heels into the soft mud, but her strength was no match for his.

He didn't care about the bloody ring. This would be settled, and now. Macphearson's gaze burned a hole into his back. Gilchrist pulled Rachel forward. "I know all I need to know. Now go," he said and pointed her toward the shelter. "Get some rest. I shall speak to ye later."

Tears glassed her eyes. In the fire's dying glow he thought he'd never seen her look more beautiful.

"Gilchrist, I—"

"Go," he whispered, then hardened his heart and turned away from her.

Chapter Twenty-Two

No man would take her from him. Not now, not ever.

Gilchrist slogged through the mud into the stable yard at the side of the charred house where Robert Macphearson waited alone. "We must speak," Gilchrist said, and met the warrior's gaze.

"Aye."

"Where is your laird? I would have him hear this, too."

Macphearson stepped closer, and Gilchrist sized him up. "He's gone—borne safely back to our village where he can recover in his own bed."

"'Tis unfortunate." He flexed his burned hand and waited, ready for the fight he knew was inevitable. "There is just the one thing I've come to discuss and methinks ye know well what it is."

"I do." Macphearson's face hardened. "The alliance."

The alliance?

Gilchrist frowned. "Aye, that, too, I suppose. But first I would speak of Rachel."

"Ah, my cousin." Macphearson's eyes lit up. "What about her?"

The warrior had the bloody nerve to act surprised. It only fueled Gilchrist's resolve. He flexed his disfigured hand again and squared his shoulders, comforted by the weight of the broadsword strapped across his back. "So, ye wish to do this the hard way. That suits me fine."

Macphearson screwed up his face, as if Gilchrist had said something daft. "Methinks there's naught hard about it. Ye wish to wed her, and she you. 'Tis plain. And my clan seeks an alli—"

"I'll see ye dead, Macphearson, before I see ye wed her. D'ye understand?"

The warrior cocked his head like a dog hearing a high-pitched whistle. "*Me* wed her?"

A branch snapped in the dark wood behind the stable yard. They both went for their weapons.

"Gilchrist!" Rachel cried out. The two of them froze. "You must hear me—*now!*" She burst breathless from the wood into the stable yard. Hugh slammed into her from behind.

"Get her out of here," Gilchrist called to him, ignoring her, though it tore out his heart to do so.

Her eyes widened as she took in the two of them, weapons half-drawn. "But—"

"I hadna thought of it," Macphearson said, cutting her off, "but now that ye mention it, Davidson, 'tis no a bad idea."

"What?" Gilchrist said, not really listening. A warmth spread over him as he watched Rachel bathed in the amber glow of the dying fire. Out of the corner of his eye he caught Macphearson looking her up and down. He snapped to attention.

"Marriage," the warrior said, matter-of-factly. "Aye, 'tis no a bad idea at all."

Gilchrist shot Hugh a murderous look, his meaning clear.

Hugh shrugged ineffectually then half dragged, half

carried Rachel back to the shelter. Her protests carried over the noisy confusion of clansmen extinguishing the fire. A moment later they heard Hugh cry out, and a string of feminine curses echoed from the trees.

Macphearson arched a brow.

"She probably kicked him," Gilchrist said in answer to the warrior's silent question.

"She does seem a headstrong lass." Macphearson grinned. "Now, about what I was say—"

"Wait!" What *had* he just said? All at once, the truth struck him like a thunderbolt. He grabbed Macphearson's arm. "You're no her betrothed, are ye?"

"Take yer bluidy hands off—"

"There's no arrangement between ye, no understanding—with her or your laird." He squeezed the warrior's sinewy forearm, his pulse quickening with each second. "Is there?"

Macphearson wrenched himself free, his face twisted in anger mixed with no small amount of confusion.

Gilchrist's heart swelled to bursting. Rachel was right! She was right all along, and he'd been the biggest of fools.

"Nay." Macphearson rubbed his arm. "There is no betrothal. No with me or with any of my kinsmen. But as I said, the ide—"

Gilchrist didn't wait for the warrior to finish. Seconds later he was sprinting through the mud toward his mount.

She was a healer, but this pain had no remedy.

Rachel stared at the smoking pile of charred rubble and the trampled, muddy ground. She pulled Gilchrist's plaid tighter around her damp gown and swallowed hard.

He was gone.

The remains of some makeshift shelters amidst the trees

and a muddle of hoof and boot prints were the only evidence the Davidsons had been there at all.

Gilchrist had promised to speak with her. He'd promised! Oh why had she let Hugh drag her from him? Something had happened last night between Gilchrist and her cousin, Robert Macphearson. Something important, but what?

Hugh had threatened to bind her did she not stay put in the shelter until Gilchrist came for her. She'd been exhausted and had closed her eyes—just for a minute. And now 'twas day and Gilchrist was gone!

The storm had passed and the sky was clear. Water dripped from the trees. Rachel stepped out into the sunlight and let its warm radiance bathe her face. "Where *are* you?" she whispered.

Closing her eyes, she drew a breath. Spring had come, and with it a new life for her. A life she couldn't imagine without Gilchrist Davidson Mackintosh.

Something tugged at the back of her gown, startling her.

"Lady," a soft voice whispered. A child's voice.

Rachel whirled. Two dirty faces looked up at her, with eyes as wide as their smiles. The older girl was about seven, Rachel guessed, and dressed in boys' clothes. The younger girl was just a sprite, and clung to her companion's waist.

"That's my sister," the older one said.

The sprite giggled.

The older one thrust a bundle of garments into Rachel's hands. "Me da said to give these to ye." She inspected Rachel's wet and ruined gown, and frowned. "Ye'd best put them on straightaway. Me da will be angry if ye take sick."

Rachel could not help but smile. Before she could thank

them, they sprinted off into the wood, laughing. They looked vaguely familiar to her. Curious. She'd never met the girls before in her life.

Ah, well. She'd best take their instruction. She stepped behind a tree and peeled off her wet gown. 'Twas filthy and ripped in a dozen places. She would have judged it past saving in her old life, in her parents' house in England. But now she thought to keep it. Who knew what lay ahead for her.

She struggled with the gown, half on, half off, as it caught on something—a tree, no doubt. "Bloody hell!" Her head was trapped in the bodice.

"Ha!" a voice called out.

Rachel froze as she heard footsteps approach. They made a sucking sound in the mud. She whirled blind and struggled against the fabric which trapped her. "Bloody nuisance!"

"Ye dinna oft' hear such language from an English lady's fair lips."

His voice made her skin prickle and her pulse quicken. With one swift tug he freed the gown, and it slid easily over her head.

"I expect ye learnt such talk from me." He smiled the most brilliant smile she'd ever seen. Her heart swelled to bursting.

"Gilchrist!"

"Who else?" He reached into his sporran and produced an apple. "Here, I've brought ye something to eat. Ye must be fair starved."

She shook her head, astonishment and relief washing over her in a torrent that set her head spinning. "Nay, I— I thought you'd gone."

Gilchrist's fair brows collided in a frown. "Aye, well, we're about to leave, but first I—"

She grabbed his forearms and he dropped the apple. "There are things you must know. Gilchrist, I remember now." She took a breath and fought to control her shaking voice. "The ring, it's not mine. I'm not betrothed!"

He smiled again, apparently neither flustered nor surprised by her declaration. "Och, that. Aye, I know."

Her eyes widened. "You know?" She shook him. "You know?"

"Oh, aye. I learnt it last night."

"But—" She scanned the forest and the clearing. "Where are they all?"

"At the village. 'Tis only another two furlong from here. Most went last night, late, after the fire died. I stayed here with ye and—"

"You were here? All night?"

"Aye, most of it." He grasped her hands and pulled her to him. "Ye didna think I'd leave ye?"

"Nay...aye, but—" She was so confused.

"Ye were dead asleep when I returned, and I didna wish to wake ye. I had ridden into the village to finish my business with your grandfather. He told me all about the ring."

"'Twas my mother's," she said. "I am...named for her." Rachel's voice caught as she remembered her mother's gentle face.

"Aye, and to hear it told, ye are the image of her, as well." He lifted her hair from off her nape and nodded. "Aye, there it is."

"The birthmark—she had it, too!"

"Aye, and half the bloody clan, by the look of it." Gilchrist laughed.

Rachel suddenly remembered her dream. "Why, the man and the woman in the garden were my parents!"

Gilchrist frowned. "What garden?"

"I used to hide and watch them when I was a child."
She laughed to herself.

"What are ye talking about?"

"Oh, nothing." She'd been afraid to tell him about the
dream, but now that she remembered the truth, there was
much she would share with him. "I'll tell you all about
it later." She pulled him close and kissed him. "I knew
I was not betrothed. I knew it deep inside, all along."

Gilchrist's face clouded. "Aye, and I didna believe
ye."

She drew him down for another kiss, but he pulled
away.

"Rachel, there is something ye must know." His eyes
grew serious and it made her afraid.

"What is it? Tell me."

He gripped her shoulders, drew a deep breath, and studied her face.

"Tell me."

"I—I knew who ye were—that night in the forest
camp. I knew and I kept it from ye."

"Oh." 'Twas the last thing she expected him to say.
"But why?"

He looked away and didn't answer.

"Why didn't you tell me? You sent me back to Monadhliath with Alex. Why on earth didn't—"

"Ah, Rachel, I was an idiot. I was—" She willed him
meet her gaze, and finally he did. "I was afraid."

His words stunned her. "Of what?"

He shook his head. "I met Macphearson in the wood
that day—the young one, your cousin."

"Robert."

Gilchrist nodded. "Aye, the same. I thought—I thought
he was— Bluidy hell, what a dolt I am!"

Her brows shot up as truth dawned. She fought the

smile tugging at her mouth. "You thought Robert Mac-phearson was my betrothed. Oh, Gilchrist!" His strange behavior the night before made perfect sense to her now.

"I was wrong not to tell ye what I knew. If I had, none of this would have happened." He gestured to the smoking ruins of the hunting lodge.

"Nay, how could you have known?" She slipped her arms around his waist and pulled him closer. "You weren't wrong. The truth was neither yours to hide nor to reveal. 'Twas mine to discover on my own. I had to face my fears, heal myself."

"As you have healed me," he breathed, and grazed a finger along her cheek. "I was a fool."

She smiled. "Aye, but one I love." As he tilted his head to kiss her, another thought struck her. "Wait," she said and pulled back.

His brows arched in question.

"Last night when you left me...you—you thought I was betrothed to Robert Macphearson?"

"I did."

"You would have given me up to him?" She pushed at his chest, not wanting to believe it.

Gilchrist grabbed her around the waist and pulled her close. "Nay, never." He smiled, blue eyes flashing mirth. "But I would have had a hell of a time explaining to my brother and the other Chattan lairds how I turned an alliance into a war—and over a bride."

Her heart skipped a beat. "Bride?"

"Aye," he breathed. "If ye'll have me."

Heat flushed her face as the warmth of his eyes, his embrace, coursed through her.

"I love ye, Rachel." He grazed her lips with his.

"Oh, Gilchrist." She hadn't dared let herself believe it until now. "When did you know?"

He laughed and squeezed her. "From the moment ye swung that firebrand at me in the cave, though I tried for all the world to deny it." He laughed again. "A wildcat ye were...ye still are."

He kissed her and her heart soared.

"So," he whispered against her lips. "Will ye wed me?"

"Aye, but—"

He kissed her again.

"My grandfather. What if—"

"Shhh..." He stilled her lips with his. "'Tis been all arranged—last night."

"What?" She struggled in his embrace, but he wouldn't let her go.

"Aye." He kissed her again. "The alliance is made."

Her eyes widened and she drew her head back. "You would use me in your bargain? Why 'tis—"

"Nay, love. Alliance or no, you're mine, and I would have kept ye no matter what The Macphearson had decided on."

She relaxed in his arms and they kissed again. His lips were warm, his tongue like hot glass. She tore her mouth away to ask one final question. "And now that I am finally returned to my grandfather, he would allow you to take me away so soon?"

"He would not," a deep voice boomed.

Startled, they both looked up to see Ranald Macphearson mounted on a snow-white gelding. He looked remarkably fit, despite the ordeal of the night before.

"Aye," Gilchrist said. "And I wouldna let ye stay."

She looked from one to the other, waiting for some explanation.

"I'm comin' with ye, lass," her grandfather said.

"You are?"

"Aye. The clan is safe enough in your cousin's capable hands." The old laird nodded back over his shoulder.

Gilchrist's men sat mounted and ready, waiting near the path that led down into the wood toward home. Rachel was surprised to see Arlys standing in the soft mud, one hand on Alex's mount. The warrior's body lay tied across the gelding's back, bound in dark hunting plaids.

Robert Macphearson watched her from the wood. The children who'd given Rachel the clean clothes played in a small copse behind him. She understood, now, why they'd seemed familiar to her.

"Robert is married," she said, and shot Gilchrist an amused look.

"A widower," Gilchrist said. The barest hint of a blush warmed his features. "With two bairns."

Rachel's eyes widened. "Ahh."

Robert Macphearson plucked a sprig from a nearby bush and approached Arlys. He cautiously offered her the token.

"'Tis whortleberry," Gilchrist said. "Plant badge of Clan Davidson."

Arlys accepted the small gift and the beginnings of a demure smile blossomed on her lips. They exchanged a few words, then Robert led her away from the mounted warriors.

"She stays?" Rachel asked. This was a surprise.

"For a while." The voice was Hugh's. He rode up behind them leading Glenna and Gilchrist's stallion. "We all thought it best."

Gilchrist nodded and squeezed her waist.

Rachel looked to her grandfather. "And you would come with us?"

"I would." A bittersweet smile graced his wrinkled

face. "I missed my daughter's wedding, but willna miss my granddaughter's."

She smiled at him.

"Besides, there is one among ye I would see again."

"Murdoch," Gilchrist said.

The old laird nodded. "Aye. 'Tis been long years since he and I shared a pipe together by the hearth."

"He knew about me!" Rachel said. "The whole time. Didn't he?"

Gilchrist shrugged. "I canna say. 'Tis possible."

"Yet he said naught."

"'Tis his way," Gilchrist said and sighed. "I fear there is much I need atone for in his eyes."

Hugh snorted. "Och, he's no angry with ye... Well, no more than usual. When I rode from Monadhliath he bade me tell ye ye're a thickheaded dolt." He cracked a sheepish smile. "Beggin' yer pardon, Laird."

Gilchrist laughed. "Aye, and he's right." He drew Rachel closer and grazed her hair with his lips.

Glenna nickered and tossed her head back, then stomped the ground with an impatient hoof.

"I think she's trying to tell you something," Rachel said, and beamed a smile at him.

"Aye." Gilchrist kissed her, then lifted her onto the mare's back. He mounted his own steed and reined him east toward Monadhliath. "Let's go home."

"Home," Rachel said, and met his confident gaze. "I know where that is now."

* * * * *

Mother's Day is Around the Corner...
Give the gift that celebrates Life and Love!

Show Mom you care by presenting her with a one-year subscription to:

HARLEQUIN
WORLD'S BEST
Romances

For only $4.96—
That's 75% off the cover price.

This easy-to-carry, compact magazine delivers 4 exciting romance stories by some of the very best romance authors in the world.

Plus each issue features personal moments with the authors, author biographies, a crossword puzzle and more...

A one-year subscription includes 6 issues full of love, romance and excitement to warm the heart.

To send a gift subscription, write the recipient's name and address on the coupon below, enclose a check for $4.96 and mail it today. In a few weeks, we will send you an acknowledgment letter and a special postcard so you can notify this lucky person that a fabulous gift is on the way!

Yes! I would like to purchase a one-year gift subscription (that's 6 issues) of WORLD'S BEST ROMANCES, for only $4.96.
I save over 75% off the cover price of $21.00.   MDGIFT00

This is a special gift for:

Name

Address   Apt#

City   State   Zip

From

Address   Apt#

City   State   Zip

Mail to: HARLEQUIN WORLD'S BEST ROMANCES
P.O. Box 37254, Boone, Iowa, 50037-0254 Offer valid in the U.S. only.

This spring, make your
destination The British Isles
with four exciting stories from

Available March 2000

A WARRIOR'S KISS by **Margaret Moore**
(Wales)

and

THE VIRGIN SPRING by **Debra Lee Brown**
(Scottish Highlands)

Available April 2000

THE CONQUEROR by **Shari Anton**
Third book of
KNIGHTS OF THE **BLACK ROSE**
(England)

and

LADY OF THE KEEP by **Sharon Schulze**
(Ireland)

Harlequin Historicals
Where reading is truly a vacation!

Available at your favorite retail outlet.

She's stolen his heart, but should she be trusted?

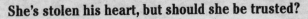

CANDACE CAMP

Lord Thorpe's new American business partner, Alexandra Ward, is beautiful, outspoken *and* the perfect image of a woman long thought dead. Her appearance on Thorpe's arm sends shock rippling through society, arouses hushed whispers in the night. Is she a schemer in search of a dead woman's fortune, or an innocent caught up in circumstances she doesn't understand?

Someone knows the truth, someone who doesn't want Alexandra to learn too much. Only Lord Thorpe can help her—if he can overcome his own suspicions. But even if he does, at what price?

A STOLEN HEART

"Oddball characters and misadventures are plentiful in this delightful romp, making it one of Camp's best."
—*Publishers Weekly* on *Indiscreet*

Return to the charm of the Regency era with

GEORGETTE HEYER,

creator of the modern Regency genre.

Enjoy six romantic collector's editions with forewords by some of today's bestselling romance authors,

Nora Roberts, Mary Jo Putney, Jo Beverley, Mary Balogh, Theresa Medeiros and Kasey Michaels.

Frederica
On sale February 2000

The Nonesuch
On sale March 2000

The Convenient Marriage
On sale April 2000

Cousin Kate
On sale May 2000

The Talisman Ring
On sale June 2000

The Corinthian
On sale July 2000

Available at your favorite retail outlet.

HARLEQUIN®
Makes any time special ™

Visit us at www.romance.net

PHGHGEN